TAMSIN WINTER

BAD INFLUENCE

PRAISE FOR
TAMSIN WINTER

*"FAST BECOMING A FAVOURITE
FOR YOUNGER TEENAGERS"*
THE OBSERVER

"A TOTAL TREAT TO READ"
BETH GARROD

*"SO MUCH HEART AND
WARMTH"*
SARA BARNARD

"AUTHENTIC AND SENSITIVE"
THE METRO

*"UPLIFTING AND
HEARTENING"*
SUNDAY EXPRESS

*"CLEAR-SIGHTED...
DRILY FUNNY"*
THE GUARDIAN

*"BEAUTIFULLY CRAFTED
AND VERY IMPORTANT"*
LUCY STRANGE

*"FUNNY, SMART,
MISCHIEVOUS"*
THE I

*"BOLD, BIG-HEARTED AND
VERY NECESSARY"*
THE BOOKSELLER

*"FUNNY BUT
THOUGHT-PROVOKING"*
THE IRISH TIMES

"A POWERFUL ANTIDOTE TO CASTING SHADE"
THE SUNDAY TIMES

For my brilliant big sister

Content note: This book contains mild swearing and teenage themes

First published in the UK in 2023 by Usborne Publishing Limited, Usborne House, 83-85 Saffron Hill, London EC1N 8RT, England. usborne.com

Usborne Verlag, Usborne Publishing Limited, Prüfeninger Str. 20, 93049 Regensburg, Deutschland, VK Nr. 17560

Text copyright © Tamsin Winter, 2023

Author photo © Andrew Winter, 2017

Cover illustration by Amy Blackwell © Usborne Publishing Limited, 2023

A CIP catalogue record for this book is available from the British Library.

JFM MJJASOND/23   ISBN 9781474979078 05792/1

Printed and bound using 100% renewable energy at CPI Group (UK) Ltd, Croydon, CR0 4YY.

MIX
Paper | Supporting responsible forestry
FSC® C171272
www.fsc.org

1

It started on the way to school. My entire life unravelling, that is. Like one of those itchy, pastel-coloured jumpers Nana used to knit us for Christmas that always fell to bits by New Year. A few people were giving me funny looks as I walked up the hill, so I already knew something was up. But my sister Hannah told me to stop dawdling. It was spitting and neither of us had brought an umbrella.

It's uphill all the way to school from our cottage and the muscles in my thighs were aching. It was only the second week back after the summer holidays and my legs weren't used to it again yet. I stopped for a second and someone on a bike yelled, "Get out of the way!" instead of ringing their bell like a civilized human being. There aren't too many civilized human beings at my school.

I have Orchestra practice Monday lunchtimes, so I had my cello strapped to my back and leaned forward as

I walked. When you get about halfway up the hill you can see the North Sea behind the row of houses. A flock of kittiwakes was floating on the surface of the water, bobbing with the choppy waves. It was really windy, and I was slightly worried about over-balancing and getting swept over the cliffs out to sea. I'm pretty sure my cello case would float, but I'm not particularly confident in my open-sea survival skills. I can get into difficulty rock pooling. I was just imagining using my cello as a makeshift raft when I noticed a group of girls on the other side of the road laughing at me. The tallest one, Madison Hart, gave me the kind of look you might give your shoe if you'd just stepped in a dog turd.

It's not like I hadn't seen that look before. Last year, I overheard Madison and her friends talking about Venus flytraps. It was during our library lesson so we were supposed to be reading but they weren't. I'm a Library Ambassador and I'd seen a book about Venus flytraps so I thought, *This is my chance. A legitimate reason to talk to the popular girls!* I turned my chair around to join their table and said, "There's a book about Venus flytraps in the non-fiction section. I can get it for you if you like?"

Only they all burst out laughing. Madison looked at me as though I'd just crawled out of the bin, and said,

"Don't talk to us, Maggot, like, ever."

Gracie Chapman added, "You are such a freak."

Then Mrs Gordon shushed us, so I turned my chair back around and carried on reading *I Capture the Castle*, blinking tears of humiliation back into my eyes. I found out later they were talking about a new song called "Venus Flytrap", and I felt even more like an idiot.

I can't exactly blame Madison. It was DJ who started it all. He's the one responsible for my "Maggot" nickname and subsequent major unpopularity. It was right at the beginning of Year Seven when he blurted out, "Oi, how come you're so pale? You look like a maggot." The name stuck like he'd tattooed it to my face. I'm in Year Nine now and I still hear it on a regular basis. I try not to let it bother me. There are more important matters, after all. Like marine ecosystem deterioration and reading the entire Classic Books List Mrs Gordon pinned up in the library and my dad being constantly disappointed in me. But still, DJ and his friends enjoy reminding me how low I'm placed in the social hierarchy at school. I'm pretty much rock bottom. Once DJ put his hand up in science and asked if my freckles were a form of facial disease. Everyone except my best friend Nisha laughed.

But there was something in Madison's sneer that morning on the way to school that put me on edge. Like she knew something I didn't. And I got a really bad feeling in my stomach.

"Hannah, do I have breakfast on my face or something?" I asked the back of my sister's head.

Hannah briefly glanced over her shoulder at me, her shiny red hair whipping about in the wind. "Nope," she said, matter-of-factly. "But you do have a massive spot on your forehead."

"Yes, thanks, I know about that." I ran a finger over the volcano-sized lump above my left eyebrow. Maybe I should have squeezed it. Just then, a boy a little way ahead of us turned around and shouted something. It was Arran Parsons. I recognized him immediately because he's the only boy in my year with a moustache. He's in one of the popular crowds so he usually ignores me. I didn't catch what he said, but the eruption of laughter that followed from his friends told me it wasn't very nice. My stomach flipped over. *Why is Arran shouting at me? Maybe my humungous spot is visible from all the way up the hill.*

I put my hand over my forehead, but Arran shouted again, even louder. Then there was no mistaking it. Obviously, I'd heard that repulsive word before. I'd just never heard it directed at *me*. Hannah must have heard him that time too, because she stopped walking and I almost crashed into her. My cheeks burned crimson and a sick feeling pooled like salt water in my stomach.

"What did you just say?" Hannah shouted back at him. Hannah's always been more daring than me. It's like she doesn't care what anyone thinks of her, not even Dad. I'm the exact opposite. I hardly think about anything else.

I tugged on the edge of Hannah's coat. "Leave it, Hannah. Please."

"Ask your sister! She's the one sharing!" Arran shouted back, holding up his phone. His blond hair was shaved at the sides, but dyed black and gelled into spikes at the top. I don't know what that style is called, but it reminded me of a great crested grebe. Then he said it. "Nice bangers by the way." And I felt as though I'd plunged feet first into the freezing depths of the North Sea.

"What does he mean by that?" Hannah asked, turning to me. My cheeks were probably deep scarlet by now. "Amelia, what's going on?"

I stared at the ground. Tiny dots of rain were spattering the concrete and the tops of my shoes, and the wind was swirling autumn leaves about like sparks from a bonfire. *Now, wind,* I thought. *Now would be a really good time to pick me up and carry me out to sea.*

"Amelia?" Hannah said again. "Why did he say *that*?" My sister repeated the horrible word Arran had shouted at me. It felt like an arrow had struck me in the chest. I couldn't catch my breath.

"How am I supposed to know?" I said, trying to hide my scarlet cheeks with my hair. "I don't even know him."

Then my phone started going. My phone never goes on the way to school. Nisha gets a lift early with her dad on his way to work and goes straight to the library where you're not allowed to use your phone. And let's face it – who else was going to message me?

"Why is your phone going off like that?" Hannah asked, stepping towards me. For a moment I thought she was going to frisk me like security guards do at the airport. Inside my pocket, I held on tight to my phone.

"It's not my phone," I said weakly.

"Right," Hannah replied. "Like someone else has the opening bars to Fauré's Élégie as their message tone." I immediately regretted letting Ju-Long show me how to download that message tone after Orchestra practice last week. We were almost at the school gates, and crowds of people were starting to appear from different directions. Most of them seemed to be looking at me.

Hannah took my arm and gently pulled me to one side of the pavement, out of the surge of people heading up the hill. "What's going on, Amelia? Why is everyone staring at you?"

I stood there for a few seconds, summoning up the courage to lie to my sister. I knew from experience it wasn't a good idea. But I couldn't bear for her to know what I'd done. "Arran's just joking around," I said, feeling my heart sink low enough to meet the tide. "I'd better go. I don't want to be late." But I couldn't disguise the tears collecting in my eyes.

"Amelia!" Hannah shook my shoulders to try and make me look at her, but I kept my eyes fixed on a flattened piece of chewing gum stuck to the ground, wishing I could somehow trade places with it. "Tell me what's going on."

"Nothing," I said quickly, my voice quivering slightly. I couldn't meet Hannah's eyes. Because the truth was, I knew exactly why people were staring. And that knowledge was almost drowning me. I had to find somewhere to hide. "I'll see you later."

I brushed past Hannah, accidentally knocking her with my cello case, and carried on into school. One of my socks had slid down and gathered under my heel, but I didn't stop to pull it up even though I'd probably get a blister.

Once I was a few metres away from the music block, out of the crowds, I allowed myself to glance at my phone. It wasn't some stupid meme or so-called "joke" DJ had created about me this time. It was the thing I'd feared the most since hearing Arran Parsons shouting "*Slag!*" at me: The Photo.

Hot tears blew across my face into my hair, the ones I'd been holding in so Hannah wouldn't find out. I didn't bother wiping them away, even though the salt stung my skin in the wind. Now I knew for certain why people were staring at me. And why my phone was going off as though I was a member of the popular crowd instead of the maggoty-nobody I actually was.

I still don't know why I was striding *towards* school instead of running in the opposite direction – to one of the docked boats on the shore and setting sail for a desert island or something. Maybe because right then, I didn't have the faintest idea just how bad it was all going to get.

2

Three days later, I was sitting outside Mrs Weaver's office. The blinds were closed so I couldn't see what was happening inside. I could imagine my dad's face though, his forehead creased in frustration and silent fury, like when the New York Yankees have gone a point down. Or when I only came second in the Year Eight Spelling Bee last year. Despite always trying my best, I'd seen that look more times than I cared to remember. A look that makes you feel like a total and utter failure.

The dull roar of lunchtime noise came drifting down the corridor like a bad smell. All the fields were out of bounds because they were waterlogged, even though it was only September, so everyone was hanging out in classrooms and corridors. My stomach was doing backflips, terrified someone would spot me.

Selina, my dad's girlfriend, was sitting in the chair next

to mine. She had a sympathetic look on her face that made me feel a hundred times worse for some reason. She tilted her head to one side, gazing sadly at me through extended eyelashes. Her lipstick shade was called Velvet Allure. I know because she'd spent the last ten minutes telling me all about the contents of her make-up bag. As though I was sitting outside the principal's office wondering which shade of bronzer sculpted and defined Selina's contours. I guess she could tell I wasn't interested, because she put her make-up away, then put her wrist under my nose.

"Your dad just bought me this perfume. It's called Purple Nightshade." She indicated for me to inhale. "Mike's so romantic."

I know she was trying to take my mind off what was happening. But my brain automatically went to the first thing I knew so what came out of my mouth was, "The purple nightshade plant is highly toxic."

Selina would have probably looked concerned if her face wasn't full of those chemicals that paralyse your facial muscles. It would be hard to tell how old she was if I didn't know already. She's twenty-nine. Only fourteen years older than Hannah. Twenty years younger than my dad! It's one of the reasons Hannah says we're not allowed to like her.

"Toxic?" Selina asked.

I didn't mean to say the rest of it. But my stomach was doing somersaults and I was terrified about having to talk to Mrs Weaver about The Photo, so my mouth went into overdrive. "Yeah," I said, my eyes flicking from the office door to Selina's face. "I read this murder mystery novel where a character uses purple nightshade to kill people. It was set in the nineteenth century, but I'm pretty sure it was accurate. First, it paralyses your vocal cords, then it restricts your breathing, and finally you get these violent convulsions." I mimed the final stages of purple nightshade poisoning in case Selina didn't know what the word "convulsions" meant. Then I straightened my uniform and checked for the hundredth time that my top button was done up. "It's a pretty flower, but ultimately fatal. My dad sure has a weird idea of romance. It can literally kill you."

In my defence, it was impossible to tell if Selina was horrified because her face didn't move. But I guess she must have been, because she spent the next few minutes reading about purple nightshade on her phone. I wasn't lying or anything so I didn't mind. But when she pulled a packet of wipes out of her bag and started removing the perfume from her wrists and neck, I did feel kind of bad.

Don't get me wrong, I don't hate Selina. It's just that I'm not supposed to *like* the person our dad started dating three weeks after leaving Mum. But Selina is one of those people who is impossible to dislike. Mostly I just pretended I didn't like her in front of Hannah. Still, I had no idea what she was doing here. She'd been with my dad for about a year, but Selina wasn't *family*. If I was going to get excluded or suspended or executed by firing squad, or whatever punishment Mrs Weaver had in store for me, I didn't want Selina there to see it. Maybe she thought me getting in trouble at school for the first time was a spectator sport, like when she came to watch me play baseball. More likely, Dad was taking her out to somewhere fancy for lunch afterwards and she didn't want to wait in the car. But mainly, I didn't want her there because I felt so ashamed.

I shuffled my feet around and my left foot accidentally swung into her leg. "Sorry," I said quietly.

"Hey." Selina smiled and squeezed my arm. "You've got nothing to be sorry for." I'm not sure if she meant accidentally kicking her leg or The Photo. But then she said, "Listen, none of this is your fault, okay. Whatever they say to you in there, whatever your dad says, you never asked for any of this. You've got nothing to feel ashamed about."

I nodded, but it was like her words were as empty as the air. I couldn't imagine what Mum was saying about me in the office. Not without feeling as though my heart was in one of those steel clamps we use in Design, getting tightened by the second. She'd had to close the shop, so she was probably thinking this was all a giant inconvenience. That the retail world shouldn't have to stop because I sent a romantic photograph. Only Mum wouldn't use the word *romantic*. She'd probably use one of the words she'd said the night she first found out. *Indecent. Stupid. Senseless. Disgusting. Utterly foolish, Amelia!* Words that had stuck in my ears like leeches and wouldn't come out. I could still hear them even now.

The faint sound of Dad's distinctive American accent drifted through the wall. I hunched a little lower in my chair and prayed for it all to be over. I wished I could erase what I'd done. Go back and delete everything. Only, I didn't know how far back I'd have to go. Because all this actually started way before that dumb photograph. The photograph was just the bit everybody saw.

I took off my glasses and rubbed the bridge of my nose. Mrs Weaver's office window looked blurry, and the pattern on the carpet tiles disappeared. Life would be easier if everything could stay like this. Completely out of focus. A blurred world where nobody sees anything clearly. Then no one would know it was even me in the photo.

I hadn't opened the heavy book on my lap. Mum had said they'd probably be a while talking without me, so I'd brought it with me. Taking along *Crime and Punishment* seemed appropriate considering the circumstances. I thought it would help Mum and Dad to forgive me. Only now all I felt like doing was face-planting it. I jumped as the office door suddenly opened. Mrs Weaver's face appeared, blurred. I smiled and quickly put my glasses back on. She did not smile back.

"You can come in now, Amelia," she said in her gravelly voice that always sounds like she needs to cough. "We'd like to hear what you have to say."

I swallowed the planet-sized lump in my throat and stood up. *Crime and Punishment* dropped to the floor with a hard smack. Selina picked it up and put it on my chair. Then she squeezed my hand. Her long nails tickled my palm. It felt sort of nice. I smiled to let her know I appreciated it. Hannah and I had made a pact out of loyalty to Mum to freeze out Selina at every opportunity. Like Hannah says, blood is thicker than Botox. But even if Selina's face did remind me of my old Bratz doll, I couldn't freeze her out completely. Over the past few months she'd been nothing but nice to me. Way nicer than Dad. And she has this sunshiny quality. Like a bearded dragon. They look kind of weird but they are gentle and friendly and you can train them to sit on your shoulder. Besides, it's not like I could afford to be that picky. I could count the people supporting me on one hand and still have fingers left over.

I tried to walk towards the office door, but for a moment I couldn't move. None of the books I'd read had prepared me for facing the high court judgement of my parents, Mrs Weaver and Mr Harding. *Oh God*, I thought, *please don't let Mr Harding have seen the photo.*

I'd had to see Mr Harding at the start of Year Eight, exactly a year ago now. It was a few weeks after Mum and Dad had split up and they'd thought it would be a good idea if I spoke to somebody about how I was feeling. Only the person the school picked was Mr Harding, vice-principal in charge of student welfare. Also my religious studies teacher. It was one of the most embarrassing moments of my life. I had to miss PE and go to his office for a meeting instead. He had a box of tissues out on the table and I remember thinking that whatever happened I should make sure I didn't cry. It felt like a test that I badly wanted to pass. So I spent the whole session telling Mr Harding how much I was looking forward to studying Judaism that term. And that maybe I could write a blog about it for the school website. Also I had an Orchestra performance at the town hall coming up that I was excited about. It must have worked because my heart was still in jumbled-up pieces about Dad leaving, but I never had to go to Mr Harding's office and talk about it again.

"Come along, Amelia," Mrs Weaver croaked, signalling for me to follow her. "Let's try and get this sorted out, shall we?"

As I walked in, Dad's eyes were fixed on the floor, as though he couldn't bear to look at me. It felt like being hit in the heart by one of baseball legend Aroldis Chapman's fast pitches. He can throw the ball at over one hundred miles per hour. I sneaked a look at Mum as I sat down on the chair between them. I could tell straight away she'd been crying. The crumpled-up tissue in her hand was a dead giveaway. *Aroldis Chapman fast pitch to the heart number two.* Three strikes and you're out.

"Amelia," Mrs Weaver began, resting her hands on her desk. She must have been married for a really long time because her finger had expanded around her wedding ring so much it looked like a tight gold belt. I wondered how she'd remove it if she ever got divorced. They would have to cut it off. The ring I mean, not her finger.

Mrs Weaver is one of those people who strongly believes in eye contact. She noticed me looking at her hands, so I quickly moved my eyes to hers. Then I gulped involuntarily.

"As you know," she said, "I've spoken to your parents. But before the school board makes a final decision about any action we're going to take, we'd like to hear what you have to say on the matter. We'll get to the, erm, photograph in a moment." She said "photograph" like it was a dirty word. I felt like crying all over again. "But perhaps you'd like to start by telling us about this list business."

The List? I thought. *How does Mrs Weaver know about The List?* The giant lump returned to my throat and for a moment I couldn't say anything at all.

Mrs Weaver smiled stiffly at my parents, and Mr Harding looked at me expectantly. It made me think about the Ancient Greeks looking to Aletheia, Goddess of Truth, waiting for her to reveal the secrets of the Oracle. Only nothing I could tell them was exactly a secret any more.

"You'd better tell the truth in here, Amelia," Dad said, in full baseball coach mode. His American accent always got stronger when he was mad. He still hadn't looked at me. I nodded and he added, "I hope you know you've let us all down."

Strike three. I was out. Tears began to flood my eyes.

"Mike," Mum said. "Amelia feels bad enough already, without you making it worse." Dad scoffed and Mum rubbed my arm. I wanted to crawl onto her lap and sob into her chest like I used to when I was little. For her to tell me all of this would go away. But I stayed in my chair and tried to focus on Mrs Weaver's sympathetic eyes.

"In your own time, Amelia. We know this is a sensitive matter," Mr Harding said. He was a really loud breather, which made the seconds before I said anything stretch out even longer.

I ignored the bile collecting in my stomach, and tried to remember the exact moment I first heard about The List.

3

SIX MONTHS EARLIER

The List happened towards the end of Year Eight. No one's ever officially admitted to starting it, but we all suspect it was DJ. His real name is Daniel-James Gillingham, but everyone calls him DJ. Except for Mr Fitzgerald, our history teacher, who never calls anyone by a nickname, unless Richard the Lionheart counts. And except me. Because ever since DJ coined my "Maggot" nickname at the start of Year Seven, I'd decided not to speak even one word to him if I could help it. He's the most annoying person out of everyone in our class. Like pins and needles in human form.

I remember it happened just after the first May bank holiday. There had been this extreme heatwave and my skin was peeling. I'd stayed at Dad's that weekend and used some of Selina's tanning oil. I figured it would give me the "fast, natural-looking shimmering glow" it promised on the bottle. The same kind of bronzed skin Selina has. Only the company ought to put some kind of warning on the label. Because when it's thirty-five degrees and you've got skin the same colour as Olaf's, it does not give you a natural-looking tan; it gives you second degree burns. Hannah kept joking about my red skin now matching my hair. Hannah's hair is this beautiful, rich auburn. It's wavy and bouncy and her skin has a kind of peachy glow, like the inside of a cockle shell. My hair is a fiery copper colour and extremely frizzy, like bright orange candyfloss. I'm paler than a ghost and covered in ten million freckles. My sister looks as though she's been kissed by Alectrona, the Goddess of the Sun. I look like I got into a fight with her.

Selina said she felt awful for lending the tanning oil to me, even though technically I'd found it next to her handbag in the kitchen and used it without asking. She didn't tell my dad I'd taken it though. I begged him not to make me go to school the next day. But he said I had to "ride it out and see this as a learning curve". Thankfully Selina went out and bought this special aloe vera gel that took the redness down a bit. As she was rubbing it in, she told me I should protect my skin in the summer. She talked about UV radiation damaging the DNA in our skin cells and causing premature ageing. I was quite surprised she knew stuff like that because Hannah was always going on about how stupid Selina was. Anyway, the next day my skin felt a bit better, but I still looked as though you could use my face as a barbecue.

I FaceTimed Mum hoping she'd agree to let me stay home. But she said I couldn't miss school and besides, she had to open the shop. *The retail world can't come to a halt because you're sunburnt, Amelia!* Mum thinks the world economy will collapse if people can't buy lavender oil and wind chimes for one day. Gramps took the phone and said, "Not to worry, sweetheart. Red suits you." Which wasn't exactly the reassurance I needed.

Gramps has lived with us ever since Mum and Dad split up last summer. It happened when we got back from visiting Gramps in hospital after his stroke. Mum said she didn't want him living on his own any more and that he should come live with us. Only Dad said he'd rather nail his ears to the side of a moving train than listen to Gramps's sarcasm every day. So Mum tipped a box of rose petal bath flakes over Dad's head. That was the final nail in the coffin of their marriage. Dad packed up his stuff and moved out. He took the little baseball player ornament from the mantlepiece and the big picture of the New York subway map from the kitchen. The nail's still in the wall but Mum never replaced the picture. She didn't open the shop that weekend, even though Ravens Bay gets flooded with tourists every summer. Instead, she kept finding bits of dried rose petals in the living room rug and crying about it for ages. I'm still not sure if she was crying about Gramps's stroke, or Dad leaving, or the state of the living room rug. Maybe it was all three.

Anyway, the morning after the tanning-oil disaster, my skin was cracked and peeling, so I wasn't exactly looking my best. No matter how much aloe vera gel I used, my face still resembled the Arizona desert during drought season. Of course, this had to be the day Mrs King assigned us partners in science to dissect flowers. And naturally, she put me, the person with the highest test scores, with DJ, the person with the lowest. I tried to look at it the same way Theseus must have looked at facing the Minotaur. Or when the New York Yankees had to come back after losing the 1960 World Series. Only nothing could make me feel better about working with someone famous around school for low-key bullying, letting off a stink bomb during the Christmas concert, and drawing pictures of genitalia on textbooks.

As I took the stool next to his, DJ gawped at my face and said, "Yuk! Maggot's shedding her skin!"

His friend Lachlan on the next bench paused from probing a gas tap with the end of his pencil and smirked.

"It's further proof she's reptilian."

DJ laughed. "Maybe you'll get lucky, Maggot, and your freckles will come off." Then he asked Mrs King if he could wear a lab coat and protective goggles because I was moulting.

I know I should have said something back. But I've never exactly been good at sticking up for myself and Nisha was on the other side of the room. Anyway, Mrs King had made her work with Leo McKillan, who never wears deodorant, so she had her own problem to deal with. Besides, they'd only have made worse jokes about me if I reacted. So, I ignored DJ's remarks about using my face as a Bunsen burner and made sure I thoroughly wiped the microscope after he'd used it so I didn't get any of his eye bacteria on me. I didn't want to touch even one atom of his being. Afterwards I heard him tell his friends I was "even grosser than a maggot up close". Which is ironic coming from somebody who spent most of the lesson firing spitballs at the ceiling.

Anyway, that was the day they must have made The List. I went to Nisha's house after school so we could work on our science homework. Her mum was making vegetable fritters with bhakri – these round flatbreads that puff up like little clouds. The smells floated up the stairs and made my tummy rumble. I was flicking through the

27

pages of my textbook on plant anatomy and waiting for another layer of Selina's rescue moisturizer to soak in, when Nisha's phone pinged.

"Oh no," she said. "I've been tagged in something… by DJ."

"Just ignore it," I said as I watched Nisha tap her screen. "It's bound to be something gross." DJ did not tag people like me and Nisha in posts unless it was something vile. The last time I got tagged by DJ, he was comparing me to a parasitic fungus.

Before I started secondary school, I imagined being invited to birthday parties and forming secret clubs and having sleepovers all the time and being *liked*. Giving inspiring speeches in assembly and everybody cheering at the end. (I don't know where I got this idea from. Maybe from binge-reading the entire *Malory Towers* collection when I was eight.) I guess school is like that for some people. Like Madison Hart and her friends, for example. And my sister. School is so easy when people like you. The reality for me is that I am intensely unpopular. And so is Nisha, by virtue of association. Luckily she doesn't seem to mind. Besides, she has all her friends from Dance Club and the dance school she goes to on Saturday mornings. Plus, she knows a bunch of people from the temple she visits sometimes in Middlesbrough.

28

My "friends" from Debate Club barely acknowledge me in the corridor. And let's just say Orchestra and the Library Committee aren't exactly renowned for improving your social life.

"I'm not sure what it is," Nisha said, her eyes scanning her phone as she scrolled. "It's some kind of list."

"A list of all the idiotic things DJ has done this year? Because that will be a long read." But Nisha didn't reply so I went back to reading about the cell structure of plant organs. I was certain it was more riveting than anything DJ had to say. But after a while, I looked up. "Nisha, you've been quiet for over a minute. It must be something interesting."

Nisha studied her screen for a while in silence, her eyes not giving anything away. Then she said, "Urgh!" through gritted teeth.

"What is it?" I asked.

"You don't even want to know."

"I do," I said, sitting up. "If it's something mean about you then—"

"It's not just me. It's about half of the girls in our year! Look." Nisha handed me her phone and went over to her dressing table, peering at herself in the mirror.

"*Fit or Fug*," I read. "What does that even mean?"

"You're going to hate it." Nisha glanced at me then

went back to her reflection. "It's a list. See those rankings at the side? I'm fifty-fifth." The textbook I'd been reading slid to the floor and I lost my page.

"But that's ridiculous," I said. "You scored ninety-two per cent in the maths test last week."

Nisha sighed the same way she does when she mentions a famous person I've never heard of. "Amelia, it's not that kind of list. *Fit or Fug?*" I looked blankly at the phone then back at Nisha. I had no idea what she was talking about. "Fit means attractive and fug means ugly. And I'm fug," she stated matter-of-factly. "It means they think I'm *ugly*, Amelia. They've ranked the girls in our year on how pretty they are, and I have come out almost bottom."

"That's ridiculous!" I said.

But Nisha wasn't listening. She took her phone back from me and read aloud. "Fifty-five: Nisha Desai. Giant ugly mole thing on her arm. Bigger sideburns than Mr Cole." She put down her phone then swept her shiny black hair over her shoulders. Nisha has the longest hair in our year. Not that we've officially measured it or anything, I can just tell. She usually wears it in a plait that goes all the way down her back for school. She could sit on it if she wanted to. She's the best person I've ever met and the exact opposite of ugly.

"Nisha, you are amazing. DJ is the biggest idiot in the entire school."

"Thanks." Nisha half-smiled then leaned towards the mirror, studying her hairline. "Maybe I could wax these bits."

"You do not need to wax anything. DJ needs to wax his mouth permanently shut," I said, watching her examine the sides of her face in the mirror. "Hang on a minute, am I on there?"

Nisha tapped her phone and scanned her screen. "I can't see your name."

"I suppose I should feel grateful I'm too unpopular to even be considered." Nisha went back to looking in the mirror. The corners of her eyes were glistening with the beginning of tears. "Hey," I said. "Don't get upset. DJ isn't exactly the most pulchritudinous boy at St Clement's Academy." Nisha gave me the same pained look she always does when I use one of the words from my New Word Every Day poster. My prize for coming second in the Spelling Bee at the start of Year Eight. Sarika Dhar got the first-place trophy. Mum complains about the poster all the time because the gold scratched-off bits end up getting trodden into my bedroom carpet. She doesn't appreciate the effort that went into getting that thing. I'd practised hard-to-spell words all summer. I was certain this would be my moment of glory. Then Miss Chabra asked me to spell *curmudgeon* and I knew it was all over. Dad would have been impressed if I'd won the trophy. The New Words poster just made him say, "You gotta up your game, Amelia. Second place is the first loser." And he's right, you know. Everybody in the top five got the same poster. I did get my photo on the school's Instagram though. Standing next to Sarika with my eyes on the trophy I didn't win. And the unusual words do come in handy, if you don't mind the whole class groaning at you for using them. I know one thing for certain though: I'll never misspell *curmudgeon* again as long as I live. Missing out on first place is one of the worst things that can happen to you, if you ask me.

"Pulchritudinous means beautiful," I said, smiling. "Anyway, I would not trust DJ's judgement on anything. He couldn't even recognize a daffodil in science today! And he called the microscope *binoculars*." I pulled Nisha into a hug. "Plus, he's seriously deficient in oral hygiene. I accidentally smelled those spitballs he was making and honestly, I gagged."

Nisha laughed, but then her face went back to looking sad. She pulled up her cardigan sleeve and traced her fingers over her birthmark. Nisha calls it Splash because it looks like a delicate splash of brown paint. When we were younger, her mum told us it was the mark from being touched by a goddess. I still kind of believe that.

"You're beautiful, Nisha," I said. "And that's not even the best thing about you. You're clever and kind and smart and an amazing dancer. And – need I remind you – the reigning hula-hoop champion of Ravens Bay Primary School. You're going to get into the best dance college in India and be in films and tour the world and DJ will eat his stupid words." Nisha sniffed. "You're literally the best person in our whole school. Mrs Weaver put that painting you did of the harbour up in reception. You are so talented. Who cares what that idiot thinks?"

Nisha nodded then sighed. "I know. But it's not just him, Amelia. Look – loads of boys have commented. And some of the girls."

"Really? Because I actually feel like commenting on it." I grabbed my bag and fished about for my phone.

"Hey, Amelia, wait!" Nisha's eyes flicked from her phone to me. "You know what, let's just forget the whole stupid thing. Don't even look at it."

Just then, my phone beeped in my hand. It was a notification.

djgilly_999 mentioned you in their story.

"Am I on the list?" A feeling of panic rose in my throat. "You said my name wasn't on it."

33

"Amelia…" Nisha started to say as I tapped my phone. "There's another page. Sorry, I didn't see it. But seriously, don't look."

Ignoring her warning, I tapped my phone, waiting for the page to load. Then what I read made my stomach drop. "I'm *bottom*?"

4

Nisha put her hand on my shoulder as we both peered at my glowing screen. "Like you said, it's just a stupid list."

I gave Nisha a look then went back to staring at my phone. "I'm bottom out of everyone. It says *Extreme Fug Zone*. Meaning *extremely ugly*, right?"

"It doesn't mean that," Nisha said, resting her head against mine. "It means DJ and the other people who wrote this list are the ugly ones."

I knew she was right. Like, in my brain I knew she was right. But I felt shame spread over my body like an ink stain. Tears hovered in my eyes, not spilling over, just suspended there, like they were too sad to even leave my eyeballs. I already knew I was considered a total loser at school. And that nobody fancied me. But the ugliest out of everyone? We both watched my screen as I scrolled down again.

Extreme Fug Zone!!!

61. Ears – Kristen Sandringham

62. Ella Walker

63. Hattie Lawson

64. Maggot – Amelia Bright

"So," I said, trying to stop the tears from spilling over. "Not only am I a maggot, I'm the ugliest girl in our year too."

"Amelia," Nisha said, putting her arm around me. "You are not ugly in the slightest."

But it was impossible to get through to me. I was barely even listening to her. "*Sixty-fourth*," I said, still staring at the screen. "I'm literally last."

"It's the first time I've scored higher than you in anything." Nisha grinned at me, but I looked away. "Amelia, come on. I'm joking! Like you were just telling me, it's a dumb list some of the boys made. It doesn't mean anything. We should just forget about it. Rating girls like this is gross."

"It's not just gross it's completely *wrong*!" I blinked and tears spilled down my face. "And it's not just some of the boys – look!" I zoomed in on a comment from Madison: **lol, this is so accurate**. There must have been hundreds of others. "Everyone is commenting!"

I knew I shouldn't have taken it so seriously. But being

at the bottom of that list summed up everything that was wrong with my life. No matter how hard I tried, no matter how many competitions I entered, hard words I learned, books I read, and music exams I passed, I was always judged on what the popular people thought. And they thought I was nothing. They didn't care about my accomplishments. In fact, all that stuff counted against me. The only categories they considered worthwhile were *fit* or *fug*. And the results were in – I was an Extreme Fug. How could I just forget about that?

"Mrs Gordon said your new glasses were really pretty today!" Nisha said.

I sighed. "Mrs Gordon is a librarian. She doesn't know anything! She has a collection of tiny llamas on top of her computer." I actually liked Mrs Gordon's tiny llama collection. But at this exact moment I didn't want to think about the fact that the only person to compliment my looks was the school librarian. "This is about the *popular people* at school, Nisha. And all of them think I am repulsive."

"Well, you're definitely not repulsive," Nisha said. "Why do you even care? You said it yourself – DJ has a brain the size of a pea."

I took off my glasses and wiped my eyes. "That is factually true. But that makes it worse. I'm *supposed* to be clever, right? It should be easy for me to figure out a way to get accepted by them." I dropped onto Nisha's beanbag and sighed. "I may as well just give up. I'm never going to succeed at school."

"Duh, you *are* succeeding." Nisha gently shook my shoulders. "You do well in everything!"

"I do well *academically*." I rolled my eyes. "But what's the point in that if no one actually likes me? The only thing people are likely to remember about Amelia Bright is this list! That's if they can even remember my real name. They'll probably put *Maggot Bright: Extreme Fug Zone* under my photo in the Yearbook."

"Amelia, people do like you! Don't I count for anything?" Nisha looked at me like I was out of my mind.

"Okay, you and a few people from Orchestra like me. But literally no one else. I mean, can you think of another person who genuinely likes me?" I sat up and folded my arms. I knew Nisha wouldn't be able to think of anyone else. I was the opposite of my sister. Hannah does well academically *and* hundreds of people like her. No doubt she'll get Head Girl next year. She's always elected Class Representative. I'd put my name forward twice and both times I'd got the least number of votes. When I'd told Dad, he didn't even try to hide the look of disappointment on his face. "You gotta get people to like you, Amelia!

Like your sister!" he'd said. As if it was that easy. Like if I just tried a bit harder, I could magically morph into Hannah before everybody's eyes.

The stupid thing is, that's exactly what I wanted to happen. I love my sister. I love her so much sometimes I wish I could be her instead of me. I know one thing for certain: Hannah would have been at the top of this list. She got *nine* Valentine cards this year. Nine! The only Valentine card I've ever had is one from Gramps. And that was only because he felt sorry for me.

It was probably around this moment – waiting for Nisha to come up with someone other than the school librarian who didn't hate me – that I realized succeeding at school had nothing to do with grades whatsoever. If you wanted to be somebody, the important thing was getting people to like you. And this list made it crystal clear – unless I did something drastic, I would spend all my teenage years being the social equivalent of a sea slug. I had to somehow win over the popular crowd. Even if it meant making friends with DJ "Spitballs" Gillingham. And possibly giving up quoting classic literature in lessons.

It's not like I hadn't tried to be popular before. I'd even baked chocolate chip cookies for my class on my birthday. But this is the thing about people at my school. They will still call you a maggot, even when their mouths are half-full of your home-made cookies.

"I have to do something, Nisha," I said eventually. "I'm sick of being bottom of the popular pile at school." I stood up and looked at my reflection in the mirror. "I need to somehow shake off this maggot image and emerge as a…"

"Fly?" Nisha waited for me to laugh. I didn't. "Sorry," she said. "I just don't think you should be taking this list so seriously."

"Well, I am taking it seriously! I know I don't get along with DJ and his" – I paused to think of the right word – "*swarm*. But I've been so stupid! They have far more influence than I realized. This list is proof of that. Look how many times it's been shared! Everyone is commenting on it. I need to completely re-evaluate my strategy when it comes to school. And fast."

"Strategy?" Nisha said. "What are you talking about, Amelia? School isn't a competition you need to win."

"Yes, it is, Nisha," I said, keeping my eyes on my reflection. "That's exactly what it is. And right now I'm not even a runner-up. I'm last."

"Okay," Nisha said. "You're scaring me now. Who even wants to be liked by people who make lists like this anyway?" She began re-plaiting her hair so quickly I could barely see her fingers move. "You remember that quote from *The Chronicles of Narnia*, right? 'Don't run from who you are'."

"Yeah, well," I replied. "That was Aslan, he's a lion. I'm a maggot. I do need to run from who I am. Besides, he also said, 'One of the most cowardly things people can do is shut their eyes to facts'. Well, my eyes are wide open and the facts are..." I tapped my phone and read out the *Reason for Ranking* comments next to my name. "*Ginger. Part reptile, part fungus, part ghost. Skin-shedding mega nerd. Seen more attractive things in Gossland Bog.*"

Tears prickled my eyes again. But I also felt this mighty thump of injustice in my chest. It was so strong my bottom lip trembled and I couldn't catch my breath. Were these really the facts about me? The truth of everything I was? I tried my best in everything at St Clement's Academy, every single thing I did. Yet to these people, I was barely even human.

"Hey," Nisha said gently. She leaned her head against mine just as I gulped back my tears; some of her hair accidentally went into my mouth. "Forget about the stupid list, Amelia. It is not fact. You don't think those things about me, do you?" I sniffed and shook my head. "Exactly. Nothing on it is true. It's just a bunch of people being mean." Her dark eyes glittered in sympathy with mine.

"You'll always be top of my list."

"Thanks. You're top of mine too." I sniffed and took the tissue she offered me. "Well, tied with Mrs Gordon."

Nisha laughed and we heard her mum's voice calling from downstairs, "Khavanu teyghayu che chokriyo. Aa Kadi chakwa ma khub khub saras che."

"Ha mam'mi," Nisha called back, then she turned to me. "Dinner's ready. My mum's kadhi has got to make you feel better." She nudged my arm when she saw I was still glued to my phone. "Seriously, Amelia. Forget the dumb list." Nisha prised my phone from my hands and dropped it into my bag. "There! Let's not look at it again. And we'll wreak our revenge on DJ tomorrow in dodgeball, okay?"

I'm not going to lie, the idea of slamming a dodgeball into DJ's face cheered me up dramatically. I smiled and followed Nisha downstairs.

But no matter how hard I tried, I couldn't forget The List. The logical part of my brain knew it was stupid and unfair and wrong and gross to rate us all like that. But part of my heart, quite a big part of it actually, desperately wanted to not be at the bottom.

5

A couple of weeks later people had finally stopped talking about The List. So I thought maybe I'd be able to forget about it. Until one morning in form time, when DJ frisbeed a picture over to me. He said it was my prize for coming last on The List. "A mask to cover your fugly face, Maggot. Even Frankenstein's better looking than you." I wanted to point out that Frankenstein was the scientist who *created* the monster. But I felt too ashamed. So I left the monster's face on my desk, waiting for the right moment to quietly crumple the stupid thing up.

To make it even worse, it was the week our class got a new form tutor: Mr Malcolmson. Our real tutor, Ms Budnitz, had left temporarily to have a baby. Only, she hadn't told us when she was coming back. It was annoying, because I liked her a lot more than Mr Malcolmson. Ms Budnitz loved books and she didn't mind if we ate in her classroom at lunchtime. Mr Malcolmson was sarcastic and he let Lachlan header his football into class.

That morning Mum had forced me to bring in a Boston fern for Mr Malcolmson as a welcome present. I told her taking in a potted plant for your teacher is like holding up a gigantic sign saying *Bullies! Begin your reign of terror here!*

But Mum had laughed and said, "It's a proven fact that plants improve psychological wellbeing. So if anything, this will reduce your chances of being bullied." My mum knows literally nothing about school.

Gramps chuckled behind her like the whole thing was some kind of joke. But he whispered, "Stick it in the skip at the end of the road," as I was leaving. And believe me, I considered it. But I couldn't do that to an innocent plant.

Anyway, Mr Malcolmson walked in and immediately spotted the Frankenstein's monster mask on my desk. "Ah ha! I see we have a fan of Mary Shelley!" he declared extra loudly so everyone went quiet. I actually was a fan of Mary Shelley until that exact moment, but I didn't say anything. Mr Malcolmson held the mask in front of his face and said, *"Beware, for I am fearless and therefore powerful!"* in a Frankenstein's monster type of voice. Everybody laughed except me. DJ and Lachlan were cracking up behind me and I felt my stomach boil with rage. But I smiled and handed Mr Malcolmson the stupid fern.

It was a Monday, so we were supposed to be doing private reading. I'd planned to start *Pride and Prejudice*. Mrs Gordon had told me I'd enjoy it, which is Librarian code for *Read this book or die*. I'd only just taken it out of my bag when Mr Malcolmson told us to put our books away. He gave us a questionnaire to fill out instead and told us to call him "Mr M". He said, "I want you all to see me more as a buddy than a teacher." I thought about taking back the Boston fern. I put down my book and read the paper in front of me. The first question was *Describe your personality?* Technically an imperative not a question, but I decided not to say anything. I picked up my favourite pen and wrote:

I play cello for the school orchestra (Grade 5). I'm on the debate team and we came second in the regional finals last year. I strongly believe we would have won had our team captain not been recovering from a bout of laryngitis and refused the throat lozenges I offered him. I'm pretty confident we'll win this year. I have read sixteen books since January. I'm about to start the Saturday baseball season again. It runs May to July and my team is called the Redcliffe Rockets. I've been playing baseball ever since I was big enough to hold a bat. (My dad is American.) He says I'm not what you would call a natural player but I'm not that easy to strikeout either. It's not my favourite thing in the world, but I adhere to the personal motto of Amelia Earhart: Adventure is worthwhile in itself. Besides, my dad won't let me quit. I have a crested gecko called Morph, which is short for metamorphosis since he can change colour. I also have a Sphynx cat with one eye called Barnacles. He already had that name when we got him. And the missing eye. Some people consider Sphynx cats ugly since they have no fur. But I think Barnacles looks just fine. It's his personality that is the real problem. I believe animals give us a greater perspective on the world and teach us...

I paused as Mr Malcolmson read over my shoulder.

"Amelia Bright," he said, "this doesn't sound like a personality, it sounds like a Nobel Prize application!" He laughed and almost everybody else in our class joined in. I stared at my paper for a moment, waiting for the feeling of total and utter humiliation to fade. I screwed my eyes shut, wishing I'd written in my special ink that you can rub out so I could start again.

DJ shouted, "Just write *Ginger Maggot*, that should cover everything!" He's not particularly inventive in his bullying, which is something I should be grateful for, I suppose. Mr Malcolmson walked over and whispered something serious-looking to him. Perhaps he was telling him that he was a gigantic disgusting grub with nothing but mucus for brains. But DJ was nodding along. So I guess he wasn't saying that.

For the entire morning, I thought about what Mr Malcolmson had said. If all that stuff I wrote down wasn't my personality, then what was? Maybe I didn't have a personality. Maybe there was a gigantic gaping void inside me instead, like the Flint Caves of Shipton we'd visited in Year Seven. A giant void I'd accidentally filled with extra-curricular activities. Maybe that was why I was so unpopular. That, and physically resembling something that had slithered out of Gossland Bog. I opened my pencil case and looked at my reflection in its metal lid. It was kind of bent out of shape from the time DJ stamped on it last term, but I could still make out my face. Freckles blurring into each other and a nose that was still peeling. Glasses that almost doubled the size of my eyes. As much as I hated to admit it, The List was right. Mine was a fugly face. I was impossible to like. Inside and out.

It was a bad start to the day, and a really bad start to the week. If I couldn't even get Mr Malcolmson's stupid questionnaire right, then what hope did I have in maths doing a test on algebraic manipulation? Okay, that was a bad example. I'd spent the entire weekend studying algebraic manipulation and the test was easy. Maybe I'd just never got anything simple so badly wrong before. But that feeling of Mr Malcolmson laughing at my questionnaire stuck in my mind like a splinter. I was used to coming top in almost everything at school, and suddenly I was losing. Not just with my classmates, but now with the teachers too.

At lunchtime, I was supposed to go straight to Orchestra, but I ran all the way to the English block and knocked on the office door. Miss Chabra answered.

"Hello! Our resident spelling champ!" she said. "How are you, Amelia?"

I gave her a brief smile. Like I said, I was in a hurry because I had Orchestra. "I only came second in the Spelling Bee, Miss Chabra. Sarika is the champion."

Miss Chabra smiled. "Don't do yourself down, Amelia. You did brilliantly."

I looked at her and felt extremely awkward. I knew she was wrong – Dad had reminded me second place is the first loser – but I didn't want to contradict her. "Okay, well, I'm sorry to bother you, but could I please speak with Mr Malcolmson?" She looked indecisive. I knew from experience that teachers hated you bugging them at lunchtime, so I exaggerated how out of breath I was and added, "It's kind of urgent."

Mr Malcolmson finally appeared at the door holding a travel mug that smelled strongly of leek and potato soup. "Amelia Bright! What a pleasure!" he said cheerfully, or maybe sarcastically, it was hard to tell with him. "What can I do for you?"

"I'd like another copy of the questionnaire, please," I said. "I messed mine up, so I'd like to redo."

Mr Malcolmson bit his lip, and I could see tiny dents formed in his chin, like he was stifling a laugh. I really did prefer Ms Budnitz.

"Amelia, it was just a bit of fun. You don't need to redo it."

"But I filled it out wrong, sir. The question about my personality. I'll do it at home tonight and bring it back tomorrow. Please."

Mr Malcolmson put his mug down on the shelf by the door, so I thought I was getting through to him. But he said, "I was just teasing you, Amelia." I blinked a few times, not quite understanding what he meant. "Your answers were perfect. And they definitely showed me your personality." I watched his face for a few seconds, trying to figure out whether he was making fun of me or lying or what. "Besides, I'm afraid I don't have any spares. Now, I'm sure you'd rather be outside enjoying the sunshine." I just knew that was a dig at my peeling nose.

I forced out a "Thank you, sir," and I heard him chuckle into his travel mug as he closed the door. Despite my best efforts to learn from George Eliot's words that hatred is deadly as fire, while I sprinted to the music room it became clear to me that I hated Mr Malcolmson with an intense and unwavering passion. I hoped that Ms Budnitz's baby would hurry up. Then she could come back to school and Mr Malcolmson would have to crawl back to wherever they keep spare form tutors. I wondered if I was allowed to send Ms Budnitz an email.

I was nearing the end of Year Eight and my life was pretty much the opposite of how I'd planned. I was supposed to be popular, well-liked, admired even. I was supposed to be finding secondary school a breeze, like Hannah. But the majority of my year group thought I was physically repulsive. (The nose peeling probably didn't help.) And now Mr Malcolmson had made me question whether I even had a proper personality.

My intelligence was supposed to be the one thing I had going for me, but I could not figure out how to get people to like me. It was harder than Mrs Hayles's Monthly Maths Challenge. I tried to keep a winning attitude. Like Dad always said, "Brights don't quit". But the sad fact was, I was losing at school. On an epic scale. It's not like I aspired to be as popular as Madison Hart or anything.

Although for her to acknowledge my existence just once, considering my locker is next to hers, would be something.

I felt flames of unfairness burn inside me. I wanted people to see me as an actual person, not some sub-human, bog-dwelling maggot. Someone they liked enough to vote for as Class Representative, just once. Someone they listened to, respected. Someone who might have a shot at being Head Girl one day. Someone who couldn't count her friends on the fingers of one hand. Someone my dad could be proud of. And more than that, someone *I* could be proud of. Instead of feeling like I had this gigantic grey cloud over my head, telling me nothing I did was ever good enough.

6

Trying to sneak into Orchestra with a cello is not exactly easy, especially when you're as clumsy as me. I managed to open the door silently, but as I was sneaking through, I bumped into a box of cymbals. Every pair of eyes turned to stare at me. Only Ju-Long's face was smiling.

"Miss Bright, how delightful of you to improve upon Vivaldi!"

I swallowed. "Sorry, Mr Giuliani." He gestured for me to take my place behind the violins. Benedict Smith, the only other person in our school who plays cello, rolled his eyes at me. "Sorry!" I whispered as he moved seats to let me take his. A sad *wah-wah-wah* came from the wind section. I glanced over at Ju-Long on the trumpet and smiled. I'm first cello, Benedict is second, even though he's in the year above. A fact Benedict has held against me ever since I joined the orchestra in Year Seven. Like it's my fault I have to do a minimum of six hours' practice a week. My mum used to play in the Royal Philharmonic Orchestra; what does he expect?

"Now finally our First Cello has arrived," said Mr Giuliani, "let's start with 'Poor Unfortunate Souls'."

I balanced my cello between my knees and took out the music. Not that I needed it. We'd been practising for weeks and I knew it by heart. It was for the production of *The Little Mermaid* at the start of July. Ms Romero's version was a lot scarier than the Disney one though. In our version, Ariel's sisters try to get her to murder the prince, then she dissolves into sea foam at the end. I knew Ms Romero was staying true to the original tale, I just hoped the families of St Clement's Academy wouldn't be disappointed there wasn't a happy ending. Some of them probably hadn't recovered from our production of *The Nightmare Before Christmas* in December. I straightened my back and allowed my cello to lean against me. I'd had it for just under a year, but already it felt like a best friend. I breathed in its woody perfume, adjusted my position and readied my bow for the opening bars.

"If you're quite ready, First Cello?" Mr Giuliani gave me a look that could dissolve steel. He hated it when people came in late. I'm not sure how he felt about people crashing into the cymbal box, but my guess is not great.

Mr Giuliani gave a nod and the entire room straightened their backs. I couldn't prevent my lips stretching into a smile. Apart from the library, this was the one place in school I loved. In here, I wasn't Maggot. I was First Cello. Respected by everybody in the orchestra (mostly) including Mr Giuliani (usually). I'd even been given two solos in the show. And the best thing was, one of them was during "Poor Unfortunate Souls", the song Nisha was dancing to and choreographing. Zadie Ali in Year Ten was playing Ursula and Nisha was one of the imprisoned souls. Nisha wouldn't be able to look at me during the performance, but I'd be able to watch her screaming in agony and being fed props of dead fish now I'd learned my solo off by heart. No one in Orchestra was supposed to actually watch the performance. Mr Giuliani told us to keep our eyes on him at all times. But with the stage lights dimmed, I was pretty sure he wouldn't notice.

Finley Morris played the opening bars of "Poor Unfortunate Souls" on the piano, and I came in perfectly on cue with an E. As the rest of the strings joined in, it was like we were no longer in the practice room but had been transported beneath the ocean to Ursula's underwater cave. I became Ariel. I could feel the tones of dark currents dragging me towards Ursula's ghastly lair, hypnotizing me, as my bow stroked the strings. Through the low vibrations, the sea witch taunted me with her Faustian pact to transform my tail, steal my voice, take possession of my soul and—

"Open. Your. Eyes. First. Cello!" I was jarred out of my daydream by Mr Giuliani tapping his baton on the rostrum in time with the music.

Next to me, Benedict sniggered. "Every single time!" he whispered.

I ignored him but he was technically correct. I always got lost in the music. My cello tutor, Angela, says this is not a bad thing. It's important to connect with the music you're playing. She says that's what makes the difference between a good musician and a great musician. And I aspired to be a great musician. One day I'll be better at cello than Hannah is at singing. But I am supposed to keep my eyes open.

"Okay, you're sounding fabulous, everybody!" Mr Giuliani said as we relaxed our instruments. "Violins, don't come in too early. And, First Cello, that was perfect! Perfect! But do try to stay in the building." A murmur of laughter went around the room, but I didn't mind. Mr Giuliani saying I was perfect (twice!) made me so happy I had to press my lips together to stop myself from smiling too widely.

At the end of lunchtime, Mr Giuliani asked me to stay

behind. I thought he was going to tell me off about being late, but he said, "Amelia, what can I say? You sounded beautiful! *Magnifica!* How would you feel about playing a solo outside the reception lobby before each performance?"

"Outside?" I asked.

"Yes, Mrs Weaver wants to create a certain ambience as the audience arrives." He waved his hands around like he was conducting again. My stomach performed a 360. Playing alone was completely different from being in the orchestra, tucked away next to the wind section, hidden by the violins, with Finley on piano at the front. There I was kind of protected, shielded by the orchestra, all of us playing as one body. A solo outside reception meant being properly alone. In the open air. It meant people noticing me.

If he'd asked me two weeks ago, I would have been over the moon. But since The List happened, I really did not want to be in the spotlight. It might only illuminate what a gigantic maggoty loser I was.

"It's up to you," Mr Giuliani said, handing me a folder stuffed full of sheet music. "I can make it a violin quartet if you don't feel up to it. But I think you're ready. Take these, have a look and let me know as soon as possible. You already know some appropriate pieces, I'm sure."

A solo performance. Outside reception. Meaning every single person who came to watch the school production would see *me* performing first. I thought about the things the boys wrote about me in The List: *Part reptile, part fungus, part ghost. Skin-shedding mega nerd. Seen more attractive things in Gossland Bog.*

Then I thought about sitting outside the school's grand reception lobby, with its domed roof and wide curved steps leading up to the entrance filled with trophy cabinets. Wearing formal dress. With the beauty of the music enveloping me. If I could get Hannah to do my hair and make-up…and play the best cello I've ever played in my life, I wouldn't look less attractive than the creatures in Gossland Bog. I wouldn't look like I belonged in the Extreme Fug Zone at all. The words Amy says towards the end of *Little Women* drifted into my mind: *I am not afraid of storms, for I am learning how to sail my ship.*

I flicked through the folder of music, stood up straight and finally freed my smile. "I'll do it."

7

I was still on a high from Mr Giuliani asking me to play outside reception, so when Mum woke me up at seven a.m. on Saturday for baseball, I didn't mind so much. Baseball is not really my thing. It's my dad's thing. He says it's the greatest sport in the world, that there is no better feeling than your team scoring a home run. He says playing baseball makes you part of a great American legacy. He says it's iconic, exciting, legendary. Only I kind of suck at it. And even though today's game was just a practice, Dad never saw it that way.

"Come on, honey," Mum said as she knocked on my bedroom door for the third time. "You know your dad will be here early. First practice of the season! *Let's knock it out of the park!*" she said in a voice that was supposed to mimic my dad's.

"I'm up!" I called, even though I wasn't. It always stalls

her for a few minutes. I lay in bed and tried to remember which cupboard I'd put my baseball stuff in.

By the time I'd finished putting my room back together after searching everywhere for my glove, Dad was at the door. I heard him say, "Hey, Penny, how's it going?" to my mum.

"Oh, you know, Mike!" Mum replied, in the exact voice she uses when me and Hannah haven't put our clothes in the laundry basket. "Two teenagers to raise; an ageing father to look after; a shop to run single-handedly. Not to mention a reptile! And Hannah's diabolical cat. So, yes, never better!" I knew the word "diabolical" from my New Word Every Day poster. It means "having characteristics of the devil". It was the perfect adjective for Barnacles. Hannah would disagree, but that's because she's the only one he hasn't attacked.

Anyone with half an ear could tell Mum was being sarcastic, but Dad didn't seem to notice. "Great! Great!" he said, and I could tell from upstairs he was smiling. "You catch the game on Wednesday?"

I ran downstairs before Mum said something unpleasant.

"Amelia!" Dad said. "Ready to knock a few out of the park, huh?" Dad swung an invisible baseball bat and clicked his tongue to signify the impact of the ball. He was wearing his Yankees T-shirt and had his baseball cap on backwards, a thing he'd started doing since dating Selina. I peered out of the front door as he gave me a hug and spotted Selina in the car. She leaned forward and waved at me. I half-waved back.

"What's Selina doing here?" I asked. The whole reason I carried on with baseball was so I could spend more time with Dad. Not Selina. Also, now Hannah had quit I'd thought I would get the front seat.

"She's come to support the Rockets, dummy!" Dad said, putting me in a gentle headlock and rubbing his knuckles over my hair, making it even frizzier than usual. He always gets like this in baseball season. I was already nervous about the practice game and him going into "coach mode" made the knot in my stomach even tighter. It was hard to impress my dad with my almost-faultless academic record. It was virtually impossible on a baseball field. I wrenched myself free and hauled my bag onto my shoulder. Mum handed me a bottle of water and winked.

"It's just a practice," she whispered. "Don't let him tell you otherwise."

"Hannah, are you coming?" Dad shouted up the stairs, the same way he did when he lived with us. We all waited for a reply that never came. Dad called again then turned to Mum. "Isn't she up yet?"

Mum smiled but her jaw was clenched with annoyance.

"She doesn't want to play any more, Mike. Didn't she already tell you? Maybe you could take her out later instead, after the game."

"I can't later. I figured Hannah would change her mind." Dad called again up the stairs. "Hannah! The Rockets are relying on you this season! You're our only decent player!" he added, which felt like a slap round the face. Mum tutted and rubbed my back. There was still no reply from Hannah, but Barnacles appeared on the top step, snarled and gave Dad a one-eyed glare. I'm pretty sure he shuddered. "Hannah! Aren't you at least coming to watch your sister?"

Hannah's voice sailed down the stairs. "No, thanks. I hate baseball!"

A pained look appeared on Dad's face, but only for a split second. Barnacles padded down the stairs and stretched out on the hall floor, digging his claws into the carpet. Dad moved his feet out of the way.

"That's not true," he said as he lightly punched my arm. "No one hates baseball, right?" I nodded. "Okay, come on then, Amelia! The Bright baseball reputation is riding on you!" It was like he'd just dumped the entire world onto my shoulders. I tried my best to look pleased.

Just then, the annexe door opened and Gramps padded down the hall in Mum's floral dressing gown. "Oh, he's back, is he?" he said, side-eyeing my dad. "Thought you'd got rid of him." It was kind of hard not to laugh.

"Morning, Dad," my mum said. She kissed Gramps on the temple and whispered, "Be nice." But Gramps never does what anyone tells him. Even the doctors. I kind of loved that about him, just like I loved having him live with us – even if he did wear Mum's dressing gown the whole time.

"Hey! How are you doing, Walter?" Dad asked and he kept smiling even when Gramps walked straight past him into the living room.

Mum kissed me goodbye. "Do not take any risks with these hands, okay!" she said and kissed my fingers. She always does that before a match. Ever since Billy Chapman fractured his thumb. I've told her a million times that he was doing a cartwheel over third base at the time, but it makes no difference.

In the car, Selina kept trying to make friendly conversation. "How's school going? Mike hardly tells me anything!" and "How's Morph? Mike says he was a rescue lizard," and "How are your cello lessons going? Mike's been getting me into classical music, haven't you?" I gave the shortest answers I could without getting into trouble with Dad. I knew it wasn't technically Selina's fault they got together just after Dad and Mum split up, but even riding in the car with her felt disloyal. I wished I could be like Hannah and point-blank refuse to go. But there was this gigantic part of me that was desperate to impress my dad. No matter how impossible that might be playing baseball. I was just always hoping that one day, the universe might malfunction and I would outshine my sister. Mum would tell me again and again that it's not a competition between Hannah and me. But for some reason, Dad always made it kind of feel like it was. And I always wound up in last place.

Dad put on Classic FM and Selina loosened her seat belt so she could turn and face me. Her cheeks shimmered bronze in the sunlight. "Do you get nervous before games, Amelia?"

I squirmed a little in my seat, not wanting to be honest and admit nerves in front of Dad. "Not really," I said. "Like Hank Aaron said, 'Never let fear get in your way'!"

Dad glanced at me in the rear-view mirror and tutted. "That was Babe Ruth. And he said, 'Never let *the fear of striking out* get in your way'. Hannah would have known that."

I bit my lip and wished I'd thought for longer before saying anything. I should have known it was Babe Ruth.

"And you'd better not get struck out today, Amelia," Dad added, not taking his eyes off the road. "I know it's a practice game but I do not want to see you fail out there."

I swallowed the lump in my throat and forced out, "I won't."

Selina reached over and squeezed the hand I had resting on my knee. "Don't worry," she said. "I don't have a clue about baseball. I doubt I could even hold the bat the right way round!" I looked at her hand on mine and she immediately took it off. I think that was the first time she'd actually touched me. It wasn't bad or anything, just unexpected. "Hey," she said, turning the music up and changing the subject, "this music is lovely. Maybe we'll hear you play cello on the radio one day!"

"I doubt it," Dad said, eyeing me in the rear-view mirror. "Unless Amelia starts taking her practice more seriously. You know Nicola Kennedy who I work with? Her son practises violin for four hours a day! Your mum says you barely do that in a week."

I sighed. I'd never met Nicola Kennedy's son but I hated him. He was home-schooled, so no wonder he could practise so much. And the truth was, I practised for much longer than four hours a week. Mum wouldn't know since she's at the shop most of the time. I felt like telling Dad that, but instead I bit my tongue and stayed silent. There was no point trying to disagree with him. I watched Selina rest her hand on Dad's thigh as he drove. It kind of made my stomach turn. Hannah had told me that Selina was just a temporary glitch. Only, so far it was a pretty long temporary glitch. I hoped Dad wasn't planning on bringing her to the school production. But, at least if he was coming, I'd be able to show him how good I am at cello. Maybe then he'd stop comparing me to the Kennedy boy.

I tapped Dad's shoulder. "Are you definitely coming to watch *The Little Mermaid*? Mr Giuliani's asked me to perform solo outside reception to greet everybody and I'd really like you to see."

Dad took his eyes off the road for a second to look at me and smile. It wasn't a bad feeling. "Yes, Amelia! You bet! That's great! I hope you're gonna put in the practice." I bit my lip again and gazed out of the window, trying not to let my heart sink too low. "And it means a lot to me that you've invited us both." Dad squeezed Selina's knee and she beamed at me so brightly it was impossible to explain that's not what I meant. Hannah would kill me for accidentally inviting Selina. "Put us down for a couple of tickets on the Saturday night, okay?"

I nodded and sank back in my seat, wondering how I would explain this to Hannah. She'd said on numerous occasions she wouldn't even set foot in the same building as Selina. Maybe she would make an exception for the school hall. I hoped so, considering she was playing Ariel.

We stopped at Dad's favourite American diner on

the way. It's called Breakfast at Tiffany's. It's this gigantic metal static caravan with bright red booths that creak when you sit down. There are posters of Elvis Presley and Marilyn Monroe and Frank Sinatra on the wall and an old-fashioned jukebox in the corner that only takes dimes. You can buy them at the counter. Selina was in some kind of delirium about the place. She must have said "Wow!" over a hundred times. It felt weird being there without Hannah.

Dad flicked me a dime across the table and I went over to the jukebox. The coin jangled and the front of the jukebox lit up. I pressed the Select button and watched it load the first record. "Come Fly With Me". Dad loved Sinatra. He'd been singing that song to me ever since I was little. It was his idea to name me after Amelia Earhart, the first woman to fly solo over the Atlantic.

Dad gave me a smile, like he knew why I'd chosen that song, but he didn't say anything. He nodded, agreeing with something Selina was saying about the retro decor, but I could tell his mind was elsewhere. *Maybe Hannah's right*, I thought. *Maybe Selina is just a temporary glitch*. But after we'd ordered, they kissed on the lips for ages. I spent the rest of breakfast looking out of the window. But I could still hear the slurpy sounds of them kissing and it completely put me off my waffles.

When we arrived at the baseball ground, Dad helped me carry my kit to the clubhouse. My bat felt heavier than it did last season. I should have done some practice with Dad last month like he told me. But he takes baseball so seriously, I have to limit playing in front of him to just the league matches. I decided this last summer, after he got so frustrated with me missing his pitches that he threw my bat into the sea. Luckily it floated. Because of course I was the one who had to wade in to get it. Now I tell him I practise with Sam Henderson from school. I don't even know a Sam Henderson. I know it's not okay to lie, but when it comes to my dad, sometimes I don't have any choice. Hannah says I should just quit playing baseball like she did. But I have this rule ingrained into my DNA: Do Not Fail. At anything. And especially do not fail in front of Dad. Which ironically was exactly what happened whenever I played baseball.

I laced up my boots, grabbed my glove and bat, and ran to practise pitches and hits with the other kids out on the field. Hoping more than anything that I didn't mess up too badly.

I had no idea whatsoever that this game would change the trajectory of my entire life for ever. It had nothing to do with baseball. And everything to do with meeting Evan Palmer.

8

I'd been out on the field practising my catches for about ten seconds before Dad started shouting at me. "Raise your batting arm!" and "Lift your head up!" and "How do you expect to catch anything with your glove at that angle?" It was kind of humiliating. Everyone on the team was used to my dad's coaching style – he was shouting the same things at them, so at least I wasn't singled out. But the way Dad carries on, you'd think we were playing for America's Major League Baseball.

I looked up from practising my swing as Dad yelled, "NUMBER EIGHT! What are you – a Rocket or a snail?" at Freddie Matthews, who'd just missed an easy catch. I hoped the game would get started soon before my dad annihilated the entire team.

Just then a car pulled up in the car park playing Ravel's "Boléro", a piece I'd learned for my last cello exam. I stopped focusing on my ball and instead watched as the car parked and a boy got out. His baseball cap barely contained his dark curls and although he was wearing the Rockets' kit, I'd never seen him before. He grabbed a rucksack out of the boot and turned to face the field.

"NUMBER THREE!" Dad's booming voice sailed over like a slap round the head. "STOP GAWPING AT THE NEW KID AND GET OVER HERE!"

The curly-haired boy smiled at my no-doubt bright red face and the ball I was supposed to catch landed by my feet. As I bent to pick it up, Dad shouted again. "NUMBER THREE!" I wasn't Amelia or Bright on the field, I was Number Three. And Dad wasn't Dad, but Coach. I still sometimes called him Dad by accident though. "Get over here!"

"I'm coming!" I shouted and ran over to the dugout.

"Sorry, Coach," I said, out of breath. "I didn't know we had any new players this season."

"Well, once everyone's here, I'll introduce you all. But first, I want to see you actually catch some of those balls. Haven't you been practising the alligator snap technique?" I was about to lie and say yes, definitely, but Dad yelled, "So, let me see it!"

"Yes, sir," I muttered and caught the ball enough times for Dad to take his eyes off me and focus instead on Poppy

Pemberley's swing. I felt relieved, but also a little sorry for Poppy. She was still getting her confidence back after taking a ball to the face last season.

Twenty minutes later, I was in the changing block taking a break. My arms were already aching from the warm-up and I was dreading messing up my catches. I wondered if I'd be able to fake stomach ache when I heard Dad blow the whistle three times. The game was about to start. I leaped up, grabbed my glove and sprinted out to the field.

"Where have you been, Number Three?" Dad sounded exasperated with me already. "I just allocated teams!"

"Sorry," I said, feeling like I'd lost the game already.

"You're on B Team, with me," said Harry, shooting me a smile. He'd been playing as long as I had and thankfully didn't seem to mind my dad's coaching style. I mean, it can't have felt good being called "a useless sack of feral swine" last season. But Harry kept smiling anyway. I ran over to the dugout bench and listened as Dad read out our fielding positions. "Number Three, you're on centre field." My heart sank. There are two crucial abilities when it comes to centre fielding in baseball: quick reactions and accurate passing. I have neither of these abilities.

"But, Dad—" I began. "I mean, Coach. Surely I'd be better on base?"

Dad looked at me like I'd been sick on his boots. "Get your head in the game, Number Three, and keep those arms up." He slapped my shoulder in a way that I guess was meant to be encouraging, but it really stung. And that's when I noticed the curly-haired boy looking at me. I straightened my cap and smiled, feeling a weird glow in my cheeks. We were still looking at each other when I realized Dad had blown the whistle already.

"Now, listen up!" Dad was saying. "Our first game next week is against the Durham Dolphins. And knowing the Dolphins, they'll put their best hitter out first. So that's exactly what I'm going to do. This is a practice, but I want to see your best out there." Dad moved us into a huddle as Poppy's dad, who was umpire, sounded the klaxon. "ROCKETS...ROCK!" we all chanted and Harry accidentally knocked me in the face with his glove.

I took my position centre-field and slapped my fist into my glove a few times. I had to catch well to impress Dad. Just catch a few balls and throw them to base. I shook out my shoulders and hopped from one foot to the other, trying to look like I was a first-class centre fielder, even though I knew I was the opposite. Last season the only legend I created for the Redcliffe Rockets was World's Most Disappointing Daughter. I needed this season to be better.

"PLAY BALL!" Poppy's dad shouted and I readied myself for our star hitter, Preston James. I tried to get my glove into a comfortable position. But as I looked up, the curly-haired boy I'd seen earlier was taking his position in the batter's box. How come he was starting the game? I watched him raise his bat and could tell even from way over here that he was good.

I took a deep breath and nodded at Dad's signal to raise my arms. But the new boy's first hit sailed right over my left shoulder. I ran as fast as I could to collect, then messed up the pass, meaning the new boy scored a home run on his first hit. I kicked the grass as the score changed – *Rockets A: 1. Rockets B: 0*. I made the mistake of glancing at Dad. He made his *What the hell was that?!* face that I tried to shake off with a shoulder roll. But it followed me for the rest of the game.

For my dad, nothing is more important than baseball. He played in college and dreamed of scoring a position in the big league. He could have made it too, he says. But he got a knee injury in his third year and his dreams went up in smoke. Then he met my mum while she was on tour in New York with the orchestra and it was love at first sight. For my dad anyway. When Mum's playing harp she always closes her eyes like me. Dad waited after the show to meet her, then followed her all over the world. Now he works as an accountant in Middlesbrough, which I don't think quite matches up.

The rest of the game went slightly better for my team than the opening, but by the fifth innings we still needed eight points to win. For my dad, you'd have thought the world was on the brink of destruction.

"ROCK. ETS. B!" he shouted, clapping his hands on each syllable. "Get. Your. Selves. To. Ge. Ther! You have ONE chance. ONE chance to win this game." I gulped as he locked eyes with me. "Squeeze six points from the rest of this innings and you get to go home the winning team." During practice games, Dad seemed to forget we were all technically on the same side. A bead of sweat ran down his forehead as he looked at me again. He was going to put me into bat next, I just knew it. And he probably expected me to score all six of those points. "Number Three, you're up." Dad tossed me a bat before I was ready and it landed on the grass. I clenched my teeth, waiting for his reprimand. But he looked out at the pitch. The curly-haired boy was on the pitcher's mound, practising his underhand pitch. Harry and Poppy looked at me expectantly from their bases. Dad kneeled in front of me. "This new kid is left-handed. He's good. And he throws fast. Expect a curveball."

I nodded, trying to figure out what I was supposed to

do with that nugget of information. *Just hit the ball, Number Three,* I told myself. *Just hit the stupid ball as hard as you can.* I picked up the bat and began walking towards the home plate.

"Amelia," Dad called, temporarily forgetting I was Number Three out here, which felt kind of nice. "You're a low hitter. Only swing on the low balls."

I nodded and adjusted my glasses. "Got it."

"And remember," he added. "If you're gonna hit…?"

I smiled. "Hit big." The phrase he'd drummed into me my whole life. Somehow it always made me hold my head a little higher. I took my place on the home plate and swung my bat into the empty air a few times. I nodded to the curly-haired pitcher that I was ready, despite the icy feeling of terror in my gut. I tried to forget Dad's critical eyes would be watching my every move and focused instead on the pitcher fifteen metres in front of me.

I blew out a short breath and prayed. *Hit the low ones,* was all that was going through my mind. And when a low ball finally came, I smashed it with all my might, which admittedly wasn't exactly a rocket thrust, but it was a decent slog. It sailed perfectly between their mid-fielders. I dropped the bat and ran for my life, hardly even hearing the cheering from the dugout. Only the thump of my heart and the wind in my ears and Dad yelling, "ALL

THE WAY! ALL THE WAY!" until I finally slid into home base. I watched the scorer add three points to our score and heard my dad shout, "YES, AMELIA!" My heart exploded with pure sunlit joy. Only then did I let myself breathe.

9

"Nice triple!" the new boy called after I'd slogged another of his pitches and reached third base.

"Thanks," I called back. My right hand was stinging and I could feel a blister coming. I glanced up at the scoreboard. We needed two more points to draw level, three to win. I waited as Harry let some of the low balls go. Then suddenly he slogged the bat and ran to first without noticing the ball was right at his feet. I had no choice but to sprint to home base. Luckily, the catcher fumbled the ball and I was able to slide to safety before his foot hit the home plate. I was still in. Just.

Dad shouted, "YES, NUMBER THREE!" and that was enough to lift my heart out of the dirt. I got up, dusted off my hands and picked up the bat.

"How are you with curveballs, Number Three?" the new boy asked as I came in to bat again.

Curveballs. I recited Dad's advice in my head. *Thrown slower to knock the batter off balance. It moves down and to the left. The most common mistake is to hit too early. Wait a beat.* I looked the pitcher directly in the eyes. I swear he winked at me. Maybe he was squinting at the sun, but I found it kind of patronizing. Some boys could be like that in baseball.

"Just throw the ball," I said. "You're not Aroldis Chapman." Chapman was a pitching legend. In 2011 he threw the fastest ball ever recorded in baseball history. If I could do that, Dad would never stop celebrating. And if I could win the game with this hit, it would be the best start to the season ever.

The curly-haired boy laughed. "A Yankees fan too?"

I nodded, then almost jumped out of my skin as Dad shouted, "PITCH THE BALL!"

I only just managed to position the bat before the ball came at me. I was expecting a curveball. He'd practically *told* me that's what he'd be pitching. So when a fastball came at me, I'll admit for a second I was thrown off. But my dad's a fastball pitcher, and if there's anything I've practised my entire life besides cello, it's how to hit a fastball. I barely had time to think. I let my bottom hand take over and slogged it as hard as I could. The ball went long and high, and for a second my heart sank. High balls are easier for fielders to catch. But already I could hear the Rockets cheering as the ball sailed over the fences marking the boundary line. An automatic home run. *We'd won!* I didn't even have time to cheer before my team piled on me.

"Nice hit!" the curly-haired boy called as his team headed to their dugout. "It's Amelia, right?"

"Amelia *Bright*." Harry smiled at me. "The living legend."

"I'm Evan." He pulled off his cap and walked over to shake my hand. I hoped he wouldn't notice the blister on it. "Evan *Palmer*. Proud to lose to a hit like that."

"Thanks." I didn't mention it was the first time I'd ever hit it out of the park in my entire life. "I was expecting a curveball."

"Anyone who busts out Aroldis Chapman's name ought to expect a fastball." I laughed as he jogged backwards towards the changing block, keeping his eyes on me. "And nice freckles by the way."

I didn't reply because it felt like my face had been set on fire. I hid my cheeks with my hands and headed to the dugout, and to Dad's arms enveloping me.

"Knocked it out of the park!" he said, and waves of pride flowed through my heart. "And, Palmer," he called to Evan. "You're our new star pitcher!" Dad lifted me onto his shoulder as the whole team shouted, "ROCKETS... ROCK!" I wish I could tell you it was embarrassing, but actually, it felt incredible. I'd hit *two* home runs! I'd won us the game! Dad was impressed. And Evan Palmer, our new ace pitcher, had said my freckles were *nice*!

Okay, it's not an adjective that would make it onto the New Word Every Day poster. But it was the best thing a boy had ever said about how I looked. Not part reptile, part fungus. Not weird or abnormal. Not that he'd seen more attractive things in Gossland Bog. *Nice freckles*. I'd been teased about my freckles my entire life. I have so many you could play dot-to-dot on my face for three days. My eyes are green with tiny brown speckles, so it looks like I even have freckles on my eyeballs. But Evan said they were nice. And that little word meant everything. It meant someone looked at me and didn't see a ginger maggot. It meant there was at least one boy on the planet who didn't think I belonged in the Extreme Fug Zone. And if he could see that from the pitcher's mound, maybe there was hope for the people at my school.

It sounds stupid now, after everything that's happened. But winning that game really was a big deal for me. And Evan Palmer liking my freckles was like scoring another home run. I'd stepped out from under the maggot cloud for a day, into the sunshine of getting noticed for being good. Someone worthwhile. Even someone popular. And I could not stop smiling.

10

We always eat together after the first practice game of the season. Poppy's parents bring their vegan hot dog van and everyone gathers around on picnic blankets, inhaling fried onions and seeing who can handle the biggest squirt of spicy sauce. Selina busied herself handing out napkins and cans of soda. She kept saying congratulations to everyone, even the players on the losing team. But nobody seemed to mind.

I finished my hot dog and put my napkin in the bin by the van. I didn't feel like sitting on the blankets listening to Harry's seventeenth replay of my winning home run, which got more elaborate each time. So I went to sit on the bench by the floodlights, away from everybody's gaze, and read my book. I was at the bit where Elizabeth rejects Mr Collins's proposal on account of him being a major idiot, and I guess I was kind of absorbed. Because suddenly

I heard someone cough and say, "Hey."

I looked up and there was Nice Freckles By The Way. I mean, Evan. I don't know how long he'd been standing there. But all of a sudden, I felt like I wasn't sitting on the bench, but plummeting down a tunnel slide with no end. It was a new feeling for me. In relation to a boy, I mean. It wasn't bad exactly, just kind of scary. And really embarrassing.

"Hey," I said, trying to act as cool as physically possibly when I could feel my face turning the colour of spicy hot-dog sauce.

"What time does everyone usually head back?" he asked. "My mum said to message when I need picking up."

"Oh, she didn't stay?" I glanced over at the small crowd of parents standing by the van drinking coffees. Dad was in the centre and even from all the way over here I could hear him talking.

"She's not that into baseball," Evan said, typing into his phone. "But my dad said he'll try and watch the game next weekend."

"So, did you move to the Rockets from a different team?" I asked. "I take it that wasn't your first game of baseball."

Evan nodded. His eyes were the colour of swimming pools. I looked away, hoping I hadn't stared at him for too long. "My family just moved here from Wales," he said. "I used to play for the Cardiff Coyotes." I raised my eyebrows like I was impressed, even though I'd never heard of them. That explained his accent then, which was like audible caramel. "It's cool being by the sea!"

I nodded, desperately trying to think of something interesting to say. What came out of my mouth next was the result of sheer panic. That's the only way I can explain it. "I've got a gecko," I said. And immediately wanted to die.

Evan smiled. "Yeah? Like, a real one?"

I smiled back, relieved he didn't seem to think it was a stupid thing to say. "He's a crested gecko. Bright yellow. See?" I put down my book and pulled my phone out of my pocket to show him some pictures. "He's called Morph, short for—"

"Metamorphosis?" I couldn't help gawping at him. No one had ever guessed that before. "Because he changes colour, right?" he added, like it was the most normal thing in the world to figure out in two seconds.

"Yes!" I tried unsuccessfully to suppress the biggest smile that burst onto my face. Evan sat down next to me and his arm brushed against mine. My stomach felt weird. Like when you slam into the end of the zip wire at the country park and almost get knocked off the seat.

"I found an octopus washed up on the beach when I

was on holiday once." He scrolled through his photos and stopped on a pinky-white octopus carcass, its tentacles just reaching into the water. It was one of the saddest and coolest things I have ever seen. He told me he'd got into octopuses since he saw it and was reading a book about them. "What's that you're reading?"

I held up *Pride and Prejudice* and said, "Jane Austen. It's probably not your kind of thing."

But Evan said, "My mum likes her. I'll see if she has it!" And for some reason the idea of us reading the same book made me go bright red. "We never had girls on our team in Cardiff," he said, looking right into my eyes. I felt for a second I might fall into them. "It's pretty cool."

"Well," I replied, "when your dad's the coach you don't exactly have much choice."

"Coach is your dad?" Evan said, wide-eyed. "Wow, he's like, proper American." And for some reason that made us both start laughing and we didn't stop for ages.

Soon, the chugging sound of car engines drifted over. Evan stood up and stretched. "Looks like everyone's going," he said. "It was a pleasure to lose to you, Amelia Bright. I'm glad we'll be on the same side next week."

"Me too," I said, standing up. "We can flatten the Falcons!"

Then, before I could feel like an absolute dope for

saying something my dad would say, Evan said, "You're really pretty, you know." I bit the insides of my cheeks to stop my smile from going too massive. I could already feel I was blushing badly. Evan's hand brushed against my arm and I felt a kind of tingling where it touched me, like the brush of a feather. I wasn't sure if he'd done it deliberately but I didn't move away. Then he leaned forward and did something no one had even contemplated doing before in my entire life.

He kissed me on the lips.

I wasn't sure what to do because it had never happened to me before. But I probably wasn't supposed to jolt backwards like I'd been electrocuted, then stand there looking gormless with my heart racing as if it was about to detonate. And I definitely did not mean to say what I said afterwards, which was, "Thanks."

I felt my cheeks turn beetroot so I did a kind of half wave, turned one hundred and eighty degrees and ran towards the car park, feeling completely intoxicated by Evan's kiss, but mortified I had been so completely unprepared for it.

All the way home, I replayed that first kiss in my mind. Mainly regretting how badly I'd messed it up. It was the kissing equivalent of a foul ball. It would not surprise me if I woke up tomorrow morning with whiplash. And I hadn't put on any ChapStick since the start of the game, so my lips were dry as sand. Evan must have felt like he was kissing the pitcher's mound. It only lasted about three seconds, so did it definitely qualify as a kiss at all? Because if I could wipe it from my record and start again, I would. I mean, I'd still want Evan to kiss me. He was the most interesting boy I'd ever met in my life. I just wish I hadn't messed it up so badly. They should really cover this kind of thing in Relationships Education. Although the idea of Mr Malcolmson teaching us about kissing made me feel ill.

I stared out of the window at the traffic going in the opposite direction, only half-listening to Selina's monologue about how much she'd enjoyed her first baseball game. I mean, how was I supposed to know kisses happened like that? Mum and Dad never kissed that much when they were together. Not on the lips anyway. And whenever Dad and Selina did it, I made sure to look in the opposite direction. In films there's this sort of build up so you know it's going to happen. A soppy gaze. A *slow* lean in. *Asking* if you can kiss someone so they might actually be ready! People should tell you that boys don't stick to the rules. They really ought to write books about this stuff. Then maybe I'd have known what to do.

I'd never seen any books about kissing in the library. I wondered if I dared ask Mrs Gordon if she had any.

I sent Nisha the longest message in the world telling her what had happened, finishing with, **So, what do you think????**

She replied: **OMGGGGGGGG AMELIA!!! You had your first kiss?!!**

Neither of us had kissed anyone before, unless you counted this one time we practised on our hands after watching *High School Musical*. But that only happened once and we promised to never tell anyone.

Amelia: Like I said, it was a disaster. I think I did it wrong 🙈

Nisha: I don't think you can do a kiss wrong!!!

Amelia: I almost fell over backwards.

Nisha: LOL. In a good way? Do you like him?

Amelia: He likes octopuses. And reading!!

Nisha: So you like him??

I thought about Evan's dark curls in the sunlight. How he'd told me my freckles were nice. That I was pretty. How he'd looked at me like I was someone good, someone impressive. He even said he was going to read Jane Austen.

Amelia: He's really nice. I just wish I did the kiss better.

Nisha: Maybe you'll get another chance
😧 😧 😧

Amelia: Maybe.

Dad was singing along with the radio, which meant he was in a good mood. But I couldn't join in. I opened the window and looked out at the approaching cliffs. I mean, as far as first kisses go, mine wasn't exactly an acclaimed performance. But this wasn't any regular first kiss. This kiss actually meant something. Something huge in fact. It meant that not everybody thought I belonged in the Extreme Fug Zone. It meant that someone who didn't know I was Maggot saw me totally differently. It meant The List couldn't be one hundred per cent correct. But more than that…it meant there was hope.

11

On Sunday, I was supposed to be writing a blog for Mrs
Gordon to put on the school website about the new books
available in the library. But all I could think about was
Evan Palmer. And the three seconds his lips were touching
mine. For those three seconds everything was perfect.
Evan *liked* me. He wasn't put off by my freckles. Or my
frizzy hair the colour of cheese Doritos. Or the fact I had
a gecko. Or that I love reading. Or even my dad acting
like baseball's a matter of life and death. Evan just seemed
to get me. I replayed the kiss again in my mind, obviously
changing my involuntary neck-jerk reaction to something
more normal.

I glanced up at the New Word Every Day poster above
my desk, fished a coin out of my savings jar, scratched off
the gold square covering today's new word and blew off
the excess bits. (Mum was right, it does get stuck in the

carpet.) I was hoping for a romantic, spiritual or poetic word to suit how I was feeling. But what I got was this:

Unprepossessing: not attractive, unappealing to the eye, creating an unfavourable impression.

The New Word Every Day poster could be irritating sometimes. On my birthday, I got the word *grotesque*. I saved the library blog I'd been writing, even though it was only half-finished, and took out my cello. I wondered if I could play Elgar's "Love Greeting" better now I'd kissed someone. Okay, maybe I was being ridiculous. One kiss was not going to outweigh the thousands of hours of cello practice I'd done throughout my life. But I'd finally experienced someone liking me! I was allowed to be happy about that, wasn't I? And Evan was not bad-looking. Quite the opposite actually. He had heart-in-your-stomach, blotchy-rash-on-your-cheeks, plunging-into-a-blackhole, reading-poetry, gazing-at-the-clouds kind of looks. And he kissed *me*. It was all so unreal! So unreal I wished I'd taken a photo of him to show Nisha. And yes, Evan was probably at home thinking what a gigantic failure I was at kissing, that I had the driest lips on the planet and tasted of spicy hot dog sauce. And seeing him at the game next weekend would probably be majorly awkward. But here, in my bedroom, lost in the romance of Elgar's music, I could replay our kiss behind the hot dog van in my head as many times as I liked. Naturally imagining a slightly less unprepossessing response from me.

After cello practice, I finished the book blog and emailed it to Mrs Gordon. Then I shouted to Mum I was going to Nisha's, ignored Hannah asking, "What have you got that dumb smile on your face for?" and headed out of the door.

Nisha was in her back garden practising the splits. As soon as I walked out of the patio doors, she bustled me over to the shade under the big apple tree and gave me strict instructions to go over the entire kissing incident again from beginning to end – skipping out the boring bits about baseball obviously. Her mum brought us orange and pineapple smoothies, which we drank sitting on the grass as I went over every tiny detail. From Evan's brown curls to his slight obsession with photographing dead sea creatures.

"Three seconds definitely counts as a proper kiss," Nisha whispered. Her dad was inside watching cricket with the door open, and neither of us wanted him to hear our conversation. "And you'll see him next weekend, yeah?"

"Yes, although considering the kiss was kind of disastrous on my part, there is a chance Evan will quit the team to avoid seeing me again."

Nisha laughed, draining the last of her smoothie in

loud slurps through her straw. "I doubt it. It sounds as though he likes you."

"Maybe," I said. "But – you know what this means, right?" Nisha frowned. "It means The List can't be right!"

Nisha raised an eyebrow at me. "I thought we'd already agreed The List was idiotic."

"I know, we sort of did. But this proves it can't be *true*," I insisted. "It literally proves it."

"We knew it wasn't true already," Nisha said. "We don't need Evan Palmer to prove it."

Maybe Nisha didn't need actual proof. But she wasn't the one right at the bottom. Just then, my phone pinged.

Evan_pCoyote started following you

My heart began playing a symphony in my chest! "Oh my God." I turned my phone to face Nisha. We both peered at Evan's profile picture.

Nisha blinked a few times. "You never said he had a beard."

"That's someone who plays for the New York Yankees!" I scrolled through Evan's photos, which were mostly of his old baseball team and memes I didn't really get, until I found his picture. "That's him."

Nisha took my phone and studied it for a moment. "Oh, he looks nice. But listen – a boy kissing you doesn't change anything, okay. Even if he is a fast pitcher from

Wales. Your freckles have always been nice." She gently shoulder-nudged me. "And the rest of you."

"Thanks." I smiled, even though I knew Nisha was wrong. Besides, Evan following me meant that I couldn't have messed up the kiss as badly as I'd thought! I tapped to follow Evan back and scrolled through more of his photos. "I wonder where he lives."

"Okay, Amelia." Nisha took my phone and put it face down on the blanket. "Enough about Evan Palmer. I need you to watch the new section of my dance routine and tell me if my timing on the cartwheel is off. Then I thought you had a speech to write for Debate Club."

"I have a week and a half before the meeting," I said. "Anyway, I still need to do a bunch of research on the Great Pacific Garbage Patch."

Nisha frowned. "What even is that?"

"You don't want to know." I put my glass down on the little wall by their pond and sighed. Just the thought of Miles Friedmann and his sarcastically raised eyebrows made me nervous. He was captain of Debate Club and more irritating than mosquito bites. If I didn't love debating so much, I'd have quit the team ages ago. But there was something about standing up and speaking about stuff I believed in that gave me a buzz. Maybe because it was the only time anyone ever listened to me.

Besides, we had the final competition coming up and I was determined to make the team.

Maybe it was over-ambitious, considering my desperately sad social situation, but one day, I wanted to change the world. Like Amelia Earhart. Only considering I can't even get people in my own class to call me by my actual name, maybe I'd struggle with the wider population remembering me. But still, I wanted to do something significant with my life. Something important. Something that would make people notice me (for the right reasons). Something to impress my dad. Now that really would be something.

I'd had my sights set on becoming vice-captain of the debating team ever since I joined. When Margot Jackson quit last month to focus on athletics, I knew I had a shot. So as things stood, I had no choice but to put up with Miles Friedmann. And try my best to be nice to him. Even if I did secretly spend most Debate Club meetings wishing the giant strip light on the classroom ceiling would fall down and flatten him.

"I need my speech to be amazing," I said. "Good enough for Miles to make me vice-captain for the final. If that's not impossible, considering he hates me."

Nisha looked up as she stretched out her calves. "I'm sure Miles doesn't hate you."

"Last meeting he asked me where my mute button was."

"Okay," Nisha said. "So write a brilliant speech that he just has to love. 'Women, like men, should try to do the impossible'."

I laughed. "Are you quoting Amelia Earhart at me?"

Nisha stretched her arms and grinned. "You're not the only one who can memorize a few quotes, Amelia. Besides, I've only heard you say it about a million times. Now, tell me what looks better after my cartwheel – sliding into the splits or jumping?"

Later, I walked the long way home, along the beach. It was almost high tide, so I took off my shoes and socks and carefully trod a path over the thin strip of cold sand. My eyes scanned the ground as I walked. More out of habit than actively looking for stuff. I picked up a barnacle shell, then threw it back when I noticed a crack. I didn't normally collect shells anyway. I was more interested in rocks. I had a collection at home. Nothing like fossils or quartz or anything like that. I like rocks that remind me of other things. I had a pinkish one that had white stripes across it like lightning bolts. A grey pebble with so many perforations it looked like honeycomb, and one that resembled a crescent moon. Little symbols of the world captured in stone.

At the start of Year Seven, I took my best ones into school to show everyone. Ms Budnitz let me talk about them at the front of the class as they got passed round. DJ kept yawning in an over-exaggerated way, and every so often he and his friends would burst out laughing. Afterwards, I noticed some of my rocks were missing. Then at lunchtime, DJ shouted across the playground that I could find them in the Golden Fountain. I had no idea what he was talking about. Then someone told me he'd dumped them in the boys' urinal. Needless to say, I didn't retrieve them. Even though one of them was my absolute favourite. A perfectly round pebble with little indentations that resembled stitching, like a tiny stone baseball. My heart broke to think that DJ might have peed on it. I didn't cry at school. I didn't let myself. But as soon as I got home that day, I went straight to my bedroom and cried in silence until my eyes hurt. And I promised myself I would never show my stupid class anything I cared about ever again.

I took a seat in the alcove by the rocks that years ago me and Hannah had christened the Emerald Cave and claimed as our own. I used to think its walls were green from some kind of special sea magic. But it's only algae. Still, it's weirdly beautiful, if you don't mind the mouldy smell. Tucked out of the wind, you can just see the roof of our cottage over the top of the steps leading up the cliff. I usually combed the beach for another pebble like my baseball one. But instead I spent most of the afternoon scrolling through every single one of Evan's photographs. And watching all his videos on TikTok, although mostly they were baseball clips. Maybe I was being obsessive. But I'd never had this feeling before. A mixture of excitement and nausea. Like I was going through my own metamorphosis. I had this feeling I could be so much more than the Maggot people knew at school, if only I could figure out a way to show them. To impress people. To get them to like me. A three-second kiss should *not* change your life, I know that. But this one had. It made me realize that if people could just see me the way Evan saw me – Amelia with nice freckles who knocked his fastball out of the park – then my life would change dramatically for the better.

12

Twenty-four hours later I figured out what I could do to improve my popularity at school: improve my popularity *online*. It was after school on Monday, during my cello lesson, when my tutor Angela suggested we try something different. It was weirdly perfect timing. Because in all the time I'd known her, she'd never mentioned a musician who hadn't been dead for over a hundred years.

"So," Angela said, adjusting her piano music and tucking her bobbed hair behind her ears, "I thought we could give this a whirl today! Have some fun."

I took the music and read *Titanium – David Guetta featuring Sia*. Angela, who'd taught me Bach, Beethoven, Brahms, and made me listen to Classic FM, was telling me to play a pop song on my cello. It was like your maths teacher suddenly asking you to do the Floss.

"Are you sure about this?" I asked, reading over the

sheet music. But Angela's quick hands had already started playing. I began by plucking the same four notes, then I slid my bow over the strings. I kept my eyes on the music the whole time, but I could tell Angela's face was stretched into a smile. I felt every note resonate through my body, as though it was somehow reaching my soul.

When I got home, I looked up the lyrics online. As I suspected, all the stuff it says about titanium is a metaphor. The song is all about being strong no matter what life throws at you. As though you are bulletproof. And something happened to me when I was listening to that song, and when I was practising it again on my cello that night. It stirred something in me. Something that made me believe my life could be different. If only I could be a better version of myself.

"Woah, what's going on, dork?" Hannah asked, barging into my room. "You're playing something from this century! Should I be concerned?"

I shrugged. "It was Angela's idea. Do you like it?"

"Like it? It sounds cool! You should play more stuff like that." Hannah stood up, cleared her throat, and began singing "Titanium" a cappella. In the perfect pitch she was famous for at school.

And that's when I had the idea. This could be the song I played outside reception for my solo before *The Little*

Mermaid performance. Only, I'd need a bunch of others too because pop songs are way shorter than the classical music pieces Mr Giuliani had given me. But Hannah could help me choose some others. And that wasn't it. I could start dedicating my TikTok to playing cool songs on my cello. Let's face it – TikToks of stuff I found on the beach, Morph licking his eyeballs, and reviews of the books I was reading hadn't exactly shot me into social media stardom. But playing pop songs? That even Hannah said were cool? People at school would definitely see me differently!

You have to understand – I didn't decide to do this just because of Evan Palmer. Even with my head still spinning from our kiss. It's just that I figured, if Evan could like me for getting a lucky hit in baseball, maybe people at school could like me too. *If* they saw me doing something impressive. Nisha had said I didn't need anyone else to validate me. But I did. I needed it big time. I needed people to like me. I needed to get rid of the name Maggot, like Morph shedding his old skin. And, with Hannah's "Titanium" still ringing in my ears, I honestly believed I could do it.

The next couple of nights, I worked on learning "Titanium" off by heart. And by Thursday, I had it note-perfect. I'd never put any videos of me playing cello online before. So for this performance to make a difference to my reputation – to move a rung above "Maggot from Gossland Bog" on the slippery ladder of popularity – it had to be exceptional. I practised in front of the mirror again and again until my arms ached. I didn't stop until I played it five times in a row without any mistakes. I borrowed some of Hannah's eyeliner and lip gloss while she was downstairs, pulled on the coolest pair of jeans and T-shirt I owned, then set up my phone. When I was satisfied everything was perfect, I pressed *Go Live*.

The performance was the best one I'd done. I even remembered to keep my eyes open most of the time. It felt pretty good. To be at home in my bedroom but performing in front of, I don't know, maybe over ten people!

At the end, I tapped X on the screen and named it *"Titanium" performed by Amelia Bright*. Within fifteen minutes there were already eight likes. My heart ricocheted bullets with the excitement of it. When you start secondary school as Maggot, and you're heading towards the end of Year Eight in the Extreme Fug Zone, there really is only one way to go. And that's up.

13

TikTok didn't exactly turn me into an overnight internet sensation. But almost everyone in Orchestra had liked and shared my post. And there was one comment from Evan that I had to try really hard not to keep reading over and over and over.

Amazing 🤩

I hoped people at school would see his comment. And I really, really hoped they wouldn't think he was an old man with a beard like his profile picture indicated.

That weekend was the end of May and our first baseball league match of the season: Redcliffe Rockets vs Fairfield Falcons. Dad planned to take me and Hannah out for dinner afterwards, so I knew I had to win or sitting across the table from him in a restaurant would be unbearable. I had butterflies in my stomach the whole way there thinking about seeing Evan again. My Word of the Day was:

Nauseant: an agent that induces nausea.

It was weirdly prophetic. Because when Evan messaged saying, **Looking forward to seeing ya!** my stomach flipped over so many times I almost asked Dad to stop the car.

And yes, Evan had put "ya" instead of "you" even though he'd said English was his favourite subject. But still, there was a chance we might kiss again today, and this time I was going to be ready. I'd applied my ChapStick four times already and practised kissing on my hand so many times last night it was practically indecent.

When we pulled into the car park, Evan was already on the pitch practising catches. He stopped when he saw us arrive and lifted his arm up into a wave. All the blood in my body rushed to my cheeks. I straightened my glasses and pulled my cap down a little lower so Dad and Selina didn't notice.

"You see that, Amelia?" Dad said, waving back at Evan. "Evan's out there practising early. *That's* commitment to the game."

Evan told me later that actually his parents were clearing out their back garden today so had dropped him off extra early. But I didn't mention that to Dad.

I waited by the car as Dad unloaded bags of bats, gloves and helmets. I didn't dare look in Evan's direction. All I could think about was his crystal blue eyes and the electrical moment our lips touched. Then Dad yelled at me to get out of the way of the car door.

"Go pitch Evan some balls!" he added, tossing me a bat which I only just caught. "Get your head out of the clouds and in the game, Amelia. I need you at your best today. First game of the season. Let's start on a high."

"Yes, sir." I gripped the bat then slowly walked onto the field.

"Hey," Evan said, throwing a ball several metres into the air and catching it easily.

"Hi." I could feel my cheeks were bright red and I couldn't find a way to stand that didn't look awkward. Eventually I leaned on my bat and tried to think what to say. The only thing that came into my mind was, "Have you heard of Amelia Earhart?"

"I have since seeing your Instagram," Evan said, grinning. "Loved your TikTok by the way. You're really good. At cello, I mean. How long have you been playing?"

"Thanks," I said awkwardly. "About six years. Feels much more natural holding a bow than one of these." I tried to grab the bat I was leaning on, but it fell to the ground as soon as I moved.

Evan smiled and picked it up, then balanced it vertically on his hand. "Want to pitch me some fastballs?"

Fastballs are not exactly my speciality, but I nodded anyway and handed him the bat. My fingers brushed against his as I took the ball from his hand. He looked at me right in the eyes and for a moment I got the feeling he might kiss me again. I glanced over to check that Dad and Selina couldn't see, but when I looked back Evan said, "There's a bug on your glasses."

As if that wasn't bad enough, when I tried to brush it off, I accidentally squashed it with my finger. So then I had to clean its smudged remains off my glasses with the edge of my T-shirt. It was mortifying. By the time I'd put my glasses back on, people had started arriving, so I didn't even get a chance to redeem myself by pitching him a decent fastball.

Dad put me in to bat fourth. Which meant I spent the beginning of the game in the dugout. I was supposed to be concentrating on the game, trying to figure out the pitcher's technique, but instead I was watching Evan. He sat next to me on the bench and his leg kept touching mine. I hoped I didn't smell too strongly of suncream. Evan started doing a commentary on the game in a funny voice and even though it was silly, I laughed. By the time I went up to bat, I'd barely even noticed where the fielders were. Which probably explains why I was struck out almost immediately.

Dad shouted, "WHAT WAS THAT, NUMBER THREE?" so loudly even the players on the opposite team looked over.

"Sorry," I said. "The balls were too fast for me to hit." But even I knew that was no excuse. I swallowed the lump in my throat and kept my eyes on the ground as I returned to the dugout. I hated losing. But even worse was losing in front of Dad.

"Struck out before you even hit a ball!" Dad said to my back. "Unbelievable." I tried to mutter an apology, but it was like something was constricting my airway. I sat down without looking at him. "Your head wasn't in the game, Amelia!" I kept my eyes firmly on the ground. "That second low ball you could have knocked out the park!"

"I'm sorry," I called.

Poppy scooted up next to me on the bench. "Don't worry," she whispered. "You tried your best." And I felt the splash of tears on my shirt. My best doesn't cut it with my dad, unfortunately.

"You're up next, Number Nine!" Dad said to Evan, who winked at me as he stood up.

"It's okay," he said. "I can take this pitcher. I promise you, we're going to win."

I took off my glasses and wiped my eyes, feeling so

stupid for crying in front of Evan. I smiled at him, then pulled my cap down low and watched as he stepped up to bat, praying he'd score.

The first couple of balls were too low, but the third was perfect. Evan slogged the ball and ran as though his life depended on it. Everyone on our team had learned to run like that. Mainly because Dad yelled at them otherwise.

By the end of the game, we'd won by two runs. But Dad said my performance was "bush league". Meaning he wasn't even close to being impressed. As Dad was giving us his "You played like a bunch of amateurs today, Rockets" speech, Harry pulled out a bag of gobstoppers and offered me one. I whispered, "Thanks," and popped it in my mouth, glad to have something distracting me from Dad's disappointment. And to stop myself from reminding him that we were, in fact, amateurs.

When Dad had finally finished berating us, Evan grabbed my hand. "Is there somewhere we can talk in private?" I nodded and led him away from the dugout, behind the changing block and down these concrete steps. Weeds poked through the cracks and I was careful to point out a large patch of stinging nettles near the bottom. We were completely shaded from the sun and it felt cool compared to the dry heat of the baseball field. The hairs on my arms immediately stood up. I felt nervous. But also, I was acutely aware that I had a giant gobstopper in my mouth.

"We won our first game," Evan said above the sound of engines starting up in the car park. "That's pretty cool."

I smiled, feeling the tiniest speck of sunshine on my skin. I tried to think of something good to say, but my heart was beating at a million beats per second and all words seemed to have vanished from my memory. Whatever they say about love and romance, let me tell you – it is not healthy for your brain.

"That's a guillemot," I tried to say, pointing to a black and white bird above us as I lodged the gobstopper in my right cheek.

Evan only glanced up briefly at the sky then looked back at me. "Your eyes are like lily pads."

I blinked a few times, and blushed. I'd been out in the sun all day so hopefully it wasn't that noticeable. "Um," was all I could say in response. Just then, a car horn beeped and I jumped.

Evan smiled and moved closer to me. So I was expecting it this time. Unfortunately, I didn't have a chance to mention the gobstopper before Evan's lips were pressing against mine.

I tried to ignore the gobstopper in my cheek, but it was one of the really hot ones, and my mouth started producing loads of saliva, which I desperately tried to swallow. I put my hands on Evan's cheeks as he kissed me, which I'd seen someone do in a film once and it seemed appropriately romantic. It also distracted me from the fiery-saliva tempest going on inside my mouth. By the time Evan pulled away, my eyes were watering. I stood there for a minute not saying anything. I didn't dare crunch my gobstopper. I wondered how to get the stupid thing out of my mouth without him noticing.

"See you next weekend, Amelia Bright," Evan said and walked back up the steps.

As soon as Evan turned his back, I spat the gobstopper out and threw it like a fastball into the bushes.

In the car on the way home, Dad critiqued every second of my game. "And don't even get me started on your fielding!" he said. "A Little Leaguer could have caught that hitter out..." He went on for the entire journey home. Even Selina got sick of it.

"But, Mike, the Rockets *won*," she said eventually. I didn't tell Hannah, but I did smile at Selina after that.

"No offence, honey, but that's not the point," Dad said. "A win isn't an excuse for a poor performance."

I opened the window a fraction to feel fresh air on my

face. The sun was hidden behind thin, wispy clouds, casting orange stripes across the sky like spilled paint. I tried to ignore what Dad was saying and thought about my second semi-disastrous kiss. I mean, it would have felt really nice if it hadn't been for the gobstopper. I wondered if Evan had noticed. If he thought I was abnormal. All that kissing practice on my hand for nothing! I was never eating another gobstopper again. If our first kiss hadn't been enough to make Evan realize I was the most inexperienced kisser on Earth, this one surely had. I mean, he was a whole year older than me. Who knows how many kisses he'd had! Just then, my phone vibrated with a message.

Evan: Good to see you again Freckles 😃

And I felt so happy I swear I almost fainted right there in the back of my dad's Audi.

14

We pulled up outside our cottage and Dad told me to go get Hannah. She was supposed to be coming out for dinner with us, but I knew there was no chance she'd get into a car with Selina in it.

"I'll be a few minutes," I said. "I need to change."

Dad turned off the engine and rubbed his hand on Selina's thigh. I got out as quickly as I could and slammed the door.

"Hannah!" I called as soon as I got in. "Dad says you have to come to dinner with us!"

I ran upstairs and pulled off my kit, hearing Gramps say, "Oh, his master has spoken!" as I closed my bedroom door.

"Is *she* going?" Hannah said, opening my door without knocking.

"She's in the car so yes, probably." I pulled on a pair

of leggings. "She's actually not that bad—" I started, but Hannah glared at me. "I mean, she's only partially evil."

Hannah snorted. "Tell Dad if he wants to see me, he'll have to leave stupid Selina at home."

"Hey!" Mum called from the landing. "I already told you I do not want to hear you calling Selina that, okay? It's so unkind." She gave Hannah one of her looks. They're pretty tame really, but somehow they can still crush your heart. "You're supposed to be setting a good example for your sister. Turning Selina into some kind of senseless villain just isn't fair. She had nothing to do with your dad and me splitting up."

"But, Mum," Hannah said. "She has fake boobs."

"I don't care if her boobs are made from Swiss cheese! You show her some respect, young lady. You're the first to complain if someone judges you on how you look. Remember what Auntie Sal said about your nose piercing?" Hannah instinctively put her hand to the tiny stud in her nose. Last Christmas, Auntie Sal had said nose rings were for cattle. She'd also said that Mum should buy special cream to lighten my freckles. Needless to say, Hannah and I are not exactly fans of Auntie Sal. "Well, my darling, it works both ways," Mum said pragmatically. "You're going for dinner with your father and Selina and that's final."

"But, Mum—"

"*And*, you are going to be nice. Here, take this." Mum handed Hannah a mini scented pillow. "It's chamomile and bergamot."

"For Selina?" Hannah asked, furrowing her eyebrows.

Mum smiled. "For calm."

Gramps's voice came sailing up the stairs. "You'll need something stronger than a scented pillow to deal with that—"

"Thank you, Dad!" Mum called, then turned back to us. "Listen, girls, whether you like it or not, your dad is with Selina now. And it seems pretty serious. So try to be nice, okay. For me? Things will be a lot easier if we can all just get along. Goodness knows I try hard enough to bite my tongue around your father." Mum pulled us both into a hug. It was a bit embarrassing as I hadn't fully pulled my T-shirt down yet. "Selina's obviously trying to make an effort with you if she's sitting through those tedious baseball games!" Then we all laughed.

"I guess," Hannah said. "But she's way too young for him so don't expect me to like her."

Mum put her hands up like she was surrendering. "I'm not saying there isn't an age gap. But they've been together for a while now so maybe it's time you gave her a chance. Like Amelia has."

I gulped and looked at Hannah, then mouthed, "I haven't given her a chance," when Mum wasn't looking.

Mum gave Hannah the look again then peered into the laundry basket where I'd just stuffed my baseball kit. "It's a shame to miss out on time with your dad just because you've taken a dislike to Selina's boobs."

"Mum!" Hannah cried. "That's not what I've done at all!"

"Isn't it?" Mum said. "Because it certainly seems like that to me. I can't think of anything Selina's done wrong."

"Apart from liking that pillock," Gramps chipped in as he walked past the bottom of the stairs. "He's still got that poser car, I see."

"Thank you, Dad," Mum called. "I'm just trying to teach my daughters the importance of kindness here." She looked back at Hannah. "Please will you at least try?"

"Fine," Hannah said, putting on her best smile. The one she usually reserved for after a musical performance. "But I can't help it if *she* doesn't like *me*."

Mum laughed and kissed her head. "That's just not possible." She looked up and smiled, and I thought she was going to say the same applied to me. But she scooped a load of washing out of the laundry basket and told us to have a good time.

The meal wasn't actually too bad. Dad barely had a

chance to mention my terrible baseballing because Selina asked Hannah about the different singing ranges. Once Hannah starts talking about singing it is impossible to make her stop. But Selina seemed glued to every word she said. Which made it easier for me to ignore them and relive Evan's skin-tingling kiss behind the changing block.

Dad tried to convince Hannah to come back to the baseball league, but she lied and said she has a singing lesson on Saturday mornings now. I didn't say anything. But I did file that information away for the future in case I needed it. Anyone with a big sister knows you occasionally need dirt on them. Besides, if I wanted ideas for TikToks that got noticed, I was going to need Hannah's help.

15

The next day, the warm smell of cinnamon bagels and the smooth sound of Handel's "Harp Concerto" drifted up to my room. I stretched and got up to scratch off my new word for the day.

Apricate: to bask in the sunshine.

I smiled and pulled one of my curtains open. Closing my eyes, the music enveloped me as the morning sun bathed my face in light. Then Hannah yelled that breakfast was ready, so I shouted back that I was apricating.

I opened the lid of Morph's tank and he climbed onto my hand, his claws tiny hooks on my skin. "Hey, Morphy," I said and let him lick one of his food cups from my hand. Crested geckos don't have any eyelids, so they are constantly staring. Hannah says it's freakish. But I think Morph's eyes are one of his best features. They're the colour of honey, with a vertical pupil, and he cleans them with his tongue. Plus, the little spikes above them look like false eyelashes. I changed his water, kissed his scaly head, then carefully lowered him back in.

Downstairs, Hannah poured maple syrup over a stack of bagels then licked her fingers. "About time! It's really good, by the way."

"The maple syrup?" I asked, taking a seat and helping myself to a bagel.

"Your TikTok, dummy!" She began humming "Titanium" in the harmonious voice I've always envied. Hannah's singing is a big deal at school. I've lost count of the number of times she's sung in assembly. On my very first day in Year Seven, Ms Sharp, one of the music teachers, realized I was Hannah's sister because of my surname. She got all excited and asked me to sing a solo. Then after I did, she never asked me again. That kind of thing happened a lot when I first started at St Clement's. I seemed to exist in Hannah's shadow. Maybe that's why I tried so hard at everything. Hoping that one day I might be better than Hannah at something, instead of always playing catch-up. "I still can't believe Angela got you to play 'Titanium'," Hannah said. "I think it's the best thing she's ever done for you."

"Really?" I looked at her to check if she was being sarcastic. But she reached across the table and took my hand.

"Listen, you sound great. You should make some more. I'll share them." I ignored the fact that her fingers were still slightly damp from where she'd licked them.

"Okay, thanks." I smiled. "Because I was actually going to ask what you think I should record next."

"Hey, Gramps," Hannah said, ignoring me as Gramps shuffled in wearing Mum's dressing gown as usual.

"Good morning, princesses!" he said, planting kisses on our heads. Hannah's first, as always, then mine. I got a waft of minty breath. He'd obviously started on the Extra Strong Mints early. Mum was trying to get him down to one pack a day. But, like Gramps says, they're healthier than the cigarillos he used to smoke.

"So, what's the plan for today, girls?" Mum said, putting Gramps's napkin on his lap and two warm bagels on his plate. By "plan" Mum meant "work". On Sundays she liked us to do something constructive because she practised her harp in the conservatory, which meant we weren't allowed to disturb her for about four hours unless it was a life-threatening emergency. And even then we were under instructions to call 999 first.

"*Little Mermaid* solos. Zadie's coming over later so we can practise 'Poor Unfortunate Soooooooouuuuuls'," Hannah sang as Gramps applauded. "Just try not to freak her out this time, Amelia."

I rolled my eyes. "It's not my fault Zadie's scared of geckos."

"No," Hannah said sighing – we'd had this conversation at least ten times – "but it is your fault you brought him into my room to show off."

I sighed back louder, even though I still felt kind of embarrassed. For some reason I'd thought having a gecko might impress Zadie Ali. But actually, when she saw Morph, she'd screamed as though she was in physical pain. "It's not like Morph would cause her any harm," I said. "Unlike Barnacles, who's about as affectionate as Cerberus."

"Hey, that's enough, you two." Mum gently nudged my shoulder, then twisted my hair into a bun that sprang immediately back into frizz when she took her hands away. "So what about your plans for the day, Amelia? A couple of hours of cello and then…?"

"Actually, cello most of the day," I said and Mum hummed her approval. "I need to figure out what I'm playing for my solo and get practising."

"Didn't Mr Giuliani give you something?" Mum asked.

I was about to reply, but Hannah interrupted. "Haven't you heard, Mum? Amelia is taking on pop. She's going to be the next TikTok star." Hannah grinned at me so I know she didn't exactly mean it. But still, I felt a prickle of pride in my stomach.

"Is that so?" Mum said. "Just make sure you do your homework as well, okay."

"Like you need to tell Amelia to do her homework," Hannah said, laughing. "She sets herself extra."

"That's not true!" I said, even though it was kind of true.

Upstairs, I messaged Nisha, asking if she had any song ideas for my solo. But she didn't reply. She was probably already at dance class. I scrolled through my phone and my thumb hovered over Evan's name. My stomach dipped like I was on a roller coaster. I quickly wrote: **Hey, I'm making another TikTok. Any requests?** and pressed send before I could chicken out.

I watched the little grey dots appear and disappear for a minute or so, then Evan sent a link to a song called "Dynamite".

Evan: This seems appropriate for a Rocket with hot lips 😄

I wasn't sure whether he meant metaphorically, or if my lips had literally been hot from the fireball gobstopper. My cheeks flushed thinking about it.

The song was easier to play than "Titanium". And after practising "Dynamite" for the entire afternoon, I posted another TikTok. My stomach twisted with a mixture of nerves and excitement as I watched the first comments load.

Nisha: Love it. Amazing. 🔥🔥🔥.

Ju-Long: Awesome!!!!

And some others from Orchestra:

Mind Blown.

OMG Love this!

Best performance ever!!!

Even Benedict had put **Unreal**. Although admittedly that could be interpreted in two ways.

I lay on my bed refreshing my phone, waiting for a comment from Evan. I seemed to be lying there willing it to come for ten years. And finally it did.

Evan: nailed it 😃 **Incredible!!!**

I could not stop smiling.

Later, Nisha came over to show me a dance she'd been doing at the dance academy she goes to at weekends. I had to wake up Gramps from his nap in the living room so we could move the sofa out of the way, since Nisha decided my room wasn't big enough. As I started the music on Nisha's phone, Hannah and Zadie opened the door.

"What are you doing?" Hannah said, projecting her voice so it filled the room. She always spoke like that after she'd been rehearsing. "Oh, hey, Nisha."

I paused the music. Nisha put her hands down from their position above her head and looked over awkwardly. "Hey."

"Nisha's showing me a dance," I said. "It's called…" I hesitated, not wanting to pronounce it wrong.

"Bharatanatyam," Nisha said, smiling at me. "It's this traditional Indian dance, but the teacher at my dance school mixes it with street dance and we do it to modern music."

"Ooh, sounds awesome. Can we see?" Zadie asked, then she and Hannah plonked themselves down on the sofa before I had a chance to say anything.

Nisha shrugged. "Sure." She got into position and nodded for me to start the music again.

It's impossible not to join in a bit when Nisha's dancing. Even with my bad coordination, I couldn't help doing a few sways and head bounces. But after watching Nisha for less than a minute, Zadie leaped up to join in properly. "This is so amazing!" Zadie shouted over the music. "I love it!"

Afterwards, Nisha taught us how to create the different shapes with our arms and hands, and these steps, turns, stretches and jumps that I barely got my head around but Zadie seemed to pick up immediately. Even Gramps came in to have a go.

Zadie hugged Nisha before she left and said, "You have *got* to show this Bharatanatyam style to Ms Romero. It would be perfect for our 'Poor Unfortunate Souls' number."

"Do you really think she'll like it?" Nisha asked.

"Are you kidding?" Zadie said. "It will blow her away."

"I don't know if I could teach it though," Nisha said, her eyes darting from Zadie's to mine.

"Nisha," I said, "you just taught my gramps to express joy through all the major limbs of his body. You've got this."

Zadie added, "Exactly. You'll be great! It will be the best dance of the show."

I've never seen Nisha look so happy. I beamed at her and tried my best to contain my excitement that the most popular girl in Year Ten had actually been nice to us.

That night, I snuggled up next to Gramps on the sofa and showed him the TikToks I'd made. Afterwards he wiped tears from his eyes and hugged me.

"You're amazing, love."

And as I read even more comments…

you're a legend

can't stop watching this!!!

😍 obsessed 😍

jaw drops

BEAUTIFUL!

Can't wait for your next one 🖤 🖤 🖤

…my heart sang louder than Hannah in the shower.

I don't know what I expected to be greeted with at school on Monday. I'd researched meteoric rises to fame on social media, and although turning into an overnight sensation did seem unlikely, I didn't think it was entirely impossible. Especially considering Nisha and I had basically made friends with Zadie Ali. By the time I'd reached the school gates the next day, my "Titanium" TikTok had forty-two likes, but the "Dynamite" one already had sixty-eight! Okay, it was mostly Hannah's and Zadie's friends since they had shared it. But still, sixty-eight likes were significantly more than I'd ever had for anything. Not including The List of course. That had racked up hundreds before whoever created it took it down.

So put it this way – I was expecting a positive reception. I was running late, so I didn't have time to take my cello to the music room like I usually did. I said a quick goodbye to Hannah and waited by the English block doors until the bulk of the crowd had gone in. I went to go through the doors but I felt something tug my back. I thought my cello had caught on the door frame, but when I tried to turn around, I saw Madison and her friends Maggie and Grace holding on to my cello case. The first thing I noticed was how flawless they looked. Madison's hair fell in sleek golden ringlets and her eyeliner ended in perfectly symmetrical flicks. It was the same with Maggie and Grace. They didn't have so much as an eyebrow hair out of place between them. I wondered how early they had to get up every morning to look like that. But it wasn't just how they looked. They had this confidence about them. This energy that compelled you to watch. Like spotting a flutter of brimstone butterflies amongst the dull grasses of the dunes. No wonder the entire school adored them.

I smiled, hoping for…I don't know. A glint of newfound respect? But the three of them sneered at me in unison, like revolted triplets.

Madison said, "Saw your TikToks, Maggot." From the way she said it, I could tell she didn't think they were any good. I bit my lip, hating myself for being so stupid. Why did I think a couple of cello TikToks would make them see me differently? I waited, half-through the door, for them to let go of my cello case, but they held on, laughing each time I tried to step forward.

"It's literally the lamest thing I've ever seen," Maggie added. I thought about unstrapping my cello case and making a run for it, but I couldn't bring myself to abandon my cello. Then I spotted DJ heading towards us. My stomach dropped. Now I was really trapped. I tried to wriggle free from the girls' grip on my case, but it was impossible.

DJ's face cracked into a smile as he took out his phone to film me. He announced, "It's Maggot Movies!" I cast my eyes to the floor, wishing the grey carpet tiles would open like a portal and transport me into a parallel universe where people like DJ didn't exist. "Come on," he said, "play us something then."

I knew DJ wasn't exactly a genius, but I figured even he knew you can't play a cello when it's strapped to your back. I stayed silent, feeling the burn of shame on my cheeks.

"I am Titaniiiiiuuuuuum," DJ sang, completely out of tune actually, but I kept my mouth shut about that. He stepped forward so his nose was almost touching mine and sang, "*You are a maaaa-aaaa-ggot.*" His breath stank of sour milk.

Suddenly, Mr Malcolmson's voice sounded from the

stairs above. "DJ, hurry up, you're going to be late. And Amelia, stop dawdling! Madison, Grace, Maggie – go to wherever you're supposed to be, please."

"Yes, sir," they chimed politely.

As soon as they let go of me, I ran past DJ and all the way up the stairs to our form class. Everyone was reading their books in silence, but it's impossible to take a cello into a classroom without making any noise. At least Mr Malcolmson had listened to me about reinstating private reading on Mondays. He sighed as I tried to balance my cello against the wall then told me to sit down. I took my place next to Nisha. She smiled and wrote on the scrap of paper she was using as a bookmark, *Loved Dynamite!* And for some reason that made me want to cry. I took *Tess of the D'Urbervilles* out of my bag as quietly as I could. But as I started reading, I noticed my hands were shaking.

I tried to focus on the words, but it was like they were swimming across the page. *Sixty-eight likes*, I tried to tell myself. *That is really good!* But it was beginning to dawn on me that maybe those likes just gave people like Madison and DJ sixty-eight more reasons to hate me.

16

By the next day, I had 112 likes on my "Dynamite" TikTok and nearly a hundred on the "Titanium" one. I should have been feeling pleased. But virtually all the boys in my class had started calling them "Maggot Movies".

In science, Lachlan played clips followed by, "Maggot thinks she's gonna go viral" and "Ninety likes, lol". Until eventually Mrs King confiscated his phone until the end of the day. I wished she could keep it for ever.

In English, I was greeted by DJ asking, "What's next on your TikTok, Maggot?" Then he put on an American accent like the voice-over of an action movie as I sat down. "Coming soon! It's Maggot Movies: the trilogy. Nothing can save your eyes and ears from the horror of…THE MAGGOT! And her weird gigantic violin."

Humiliation rained down on me like a storm cloud. I felt like pitching my metal pencil case at his head. But everyone except Nisha was laughing along and I could feel my face turning red. I took my seat without saying a word. Then Tally, who never even spoke to me usually, said, "Maggot's got over a hundred likes, DJ. That's more than you've ever had." And for the tiniest fraction of a second, she smiled at me.

Okay, she called me Maggot. But I could have taken off I was so happy! Tally stuck up for me! She wasn't exactly in the popular crowd, but people in our class seemed to like her. DJ and Lachlan barely said anything to me after that. I mean, there was the usual, "Lend us a pen, Maggot," in history. And, "Out the way, Maggot," at the end of drama. But I was used to that.

Maybe it is working, I thought. *Maybe I just have to win over one person at a time.* If Tally sticking up for me was anything to go by, the plan to crawl out from the Extreme Fug Zone might actually be starting to work.

On Thursday, I began the day by scratching off a new word from my poster.

Charisma: attractiveness or charm that inspires devotion in others.

My face sprang into a smile. *This is the EXACT thing I need!*

While I was having breakfast, I read a couple of articles online about how to learn charisma. One idea was to ask people open-ended questions. It gave a list of suggested topics. So, in our art lesson that morning, I tried it out on Nisha.

"What do you think about zoos?"

Nisha looked up from her sketch of a fruit bowl. "Is this for one of your debates?"

"No," I said innocently, shading in the base of a slightly lopsided pear. "I'm just interested in your opinion."

She looked at me weirdly. "Because it sounds like a debate topic. And why are you looking at me like that?"

"Like what?" I asked.

"Like, all smiley."

"Okay," I said. "Then tell me what you think about banning cars from city centres."

Nisha put down her pencil and looked at me like I had just landed from another planet. "Are you okay?"

"I'm fine." I sighed. "I'm just *trying* to practise being *charismatic*."

Nisha laughed and patted my arm. "Maybe you need some more practice."

"Thanks," I said, rubbing out the wonky pear and starting again. "That was actually what I was trying to do."

"I'm joking," Nisha said. "Seriously, Amelia. You don't

need any more charisma. You're great the way you are."
But I didn't let that put me off. Maybe my charisma
wouldn't work on Nisha because she already knew me.

I decided to practise on Tyler Gordon instead. He
usually completely ignored me so I figured he would be a
good test subject. I went over to Tyler's table at the back
of the classroom and pretended to sharpen my pencil.

"Hi, Tyler, what kind of books do you like reading?" I
asked. "Want me to recommend some for the summer?"
Only Tyler burst out laughing. I wasn't giving up easily
though. *Brights don't quit!* was practically my family
motto. One of the articles I'd read had recommended
giving compliments. So, I tried, "I like what you've done
with your hair."

But Tyler responded, "Get lost, Maggot."

However, I knew that if you want something badly
enough, you have to be prepared to risk failure. So later,
in maths, I smiled at Tyler from across the room. And he
smiled back! Only then I noticed he was putting his
middle finger up at me. Which brought an abrupt end to
the Amelia Bright Charisma Experiment. My conclusion:
an epic failure. I'm talking *Icarus falling to his death*,
Prometheus repeatedly getting his liver pecked out by an eagle
and *Medusa beheaded by Perseus* level of charismatic
failure.

Luckily I had another chance to prove to myself that I wasn't destined for the lowest league of likeability for ever: Debate Club. If I could secure the vice-captaincy then I'd be guaranteed a place on the team in the final this month. And then, in September, our school would host the first round of next year's competition. I'd get to stand up in front of everyone at St Clement's Academy and show them what I was made of. I mean, if I could persuade Miles to make me vice-captain, surely I could win over the likes of Madison and DJ.

At lunchtime, I wished Nisha luck for her dance rehearsal and I headed to the English block where we held our Debate Club meetings. It was ridiculously sunny, so I walked the long way, through the shade of the leafy beech trees that line the playground, then cut through the history corridor. Most of the Debate Club posters I'd put up at the start of the year had been torn down. But there were still a few exclaiming *COME FIGHT WITH WORDS!* I'd thought up that phrase. Not that we'd exactly had any new members so far. But at least that meant there was a higher chance Miles would give me vice-captain. I wanted it so badly, I could feel my hands getting sweaty.

"Amelia, *finally!*" Miles said, ticking my name off on his home-made register. Mr Hall was supposed to take the register, but he'd stopped coming to meetings ages ago.

He'd said Miles's leadership was strong enough to not require a teacher to be present at every meeting. So I partly blame Mr Hall for Debate Club turning into Miles's dictatorship.

"I'm not even late!" I said, checking my watch.

"Right," Miles said, as though he couldn't be less interested. "Has everyone prepared their environment speeches? Because next week is the final and I need us to be *bodaciously rad* if we're to have any hope of beating the boys' school."

Miles always said things like "bodaciously rad" and "dynamite-astic!" and "Don't barf me out". His words were incomprehensible to me half the time. Plus, his nostrils flared whenever he was concentrating. At least I wasn't the only person in Debate Club who lacked charisma. Everybody took their carefully-folded speeches or cue cards out of their pockets and waited for Miles to call on someone to speak.

"Amelia, you're first up!" Miles said. "Since you were last in and all."

I don't know what he meant by "and all". But actually I didn't mind going first. I went to the front of the classroom and smiled at the audience. *Audience* is a bit of a stretch considering there were only eight people in front of me. There were only three places on the team, since

Miles always picked himself. So performing your speech well was crucial if you wanted to make it. And, as he likes to remind us, we could be dropped at any point. William Hamilton gave me a thumbs up. He's probably my best friend in the club. Meaning he's the only one who doesn't seem to actively hate me. He has a stammer, so he never wants to be picked for the competitions. He wouldn't even be in the club if his mum didn't make him join. I happen to think William is a terrific debater. But I don't have a say in the team unless I get vice-captain.

I took a breath, then nodded at Miles to start the timer.

"When I say the eighth continent, you may be wondering which planet I'm on. But, as you can see, my feet are firmly planted on Planet Earth. Made up of ninety-four per cent plastic, the Great Pacific Garbage Patch is considered—"

Just then, the classroom door flew open and smacked into the table behind it. "Sorry," a boy with dark, curly hair said. His bright blue eyes stared straight at me. A fierce heat crept up my neck and onto my cheeks as I recognized him. My cue cards dropped from my hands. Standing right there, in the doorway of Debate Club, wearing the St Clement's Academy uniform, was Evan Palmer.

17

"Amelia!" Evan said after he'd picked his jaw up from the classroom floor. "What are you…? I had no idea you were…"

But before Evan could finish a sentence, someone behind him burst out laughing. Some boys from the year above appeared in the doorway. I recognized one of them as DJ's cousin, Jayden. He'd cornered me once in the maths corridor, pretending he was holding a maggot. He shoved his dirty-fingernailed hand in my face and kept telling me to look at it until Nisha managed to pull me away. Jayden peered through the doorway and announced, "That's Dork Club."

I looked from Evan to Miles and then back to Evan, my speech cards lying on the carpet like used tickets. Flora Andrews, who's in Year Ten, broke the silence.

"This is *Debate* Club," Flora said. "And we're in the middle of practising."

"Right, sorry," Evan said. "It's just…I saw a poster saying you wanted new members?"

Jayden snorted. His nose expelled a greeny-yellow globule of snot which he wiped on his sleeve. "You want to avoid these losers at all costs, mate," he said to Evan. "Once they suck you in, your brain turns to pure nerd juice. Come on." He pretended to shoot himself in the head then disappeared down the corridor.

Evan waited a moment, then he smiled through the window as he closed the door. I noticed he wasn't quite looking me in the eyes.

"You can stop staring now, Amelia," Miles said. "He's gone. And so is your time."

I felt the heat in my cheeks intensify. The words *Evan Palmer goes to my school* whirled through my mind like a tornado. I shook out my shoulders to get rid of the terrifying feeling rushing through my entire body, picked up my cue cards and told Miles to start the timer again.

"I'm not starting it again, Amelia," he said. "You know the rules. Distractions happen. Remain on topic."

"Please, Miles," I said. "He just burst in!"

"You know what the head judge always says, Amelia," Miles said, in his annoyingly nasal voice. "*Even if a jumbo jet ploughs through the ceiling, keep speaking!*"

"This isn't the competition, Miles," Aakesh said, giving

me a sympathetic smile. "Let her start over."

"No way. The final is next week and we need to be tight-a-licious. Sorry, I'm pulling rank on this." Miles tapped the lapel of his blazer where his captain badge was pinned. "Not allowing yourself to be distracted is a key debating skill. I suggest you learn from this, Amelia. Better luck next year." He did a double eyebrow raise at me and flared his already cavernous nostrils. "Flora, you're up."

"But, Miles! That is so unfair!" I pleaded, on the verge of tears. I should have known it was useless to try and reason with him.

"Rules are rules," he said in his sneery voice and over-exaggeratedly crossed my name out on his list. "I can't take any risks for the final."

I took a seat at the back of the classroom and closed my eyes to stop the tears. I wouldn't give Miles the satisfaction of seeing me cry. I sniffed in a few deep breaths and told myself I was okay. Only I wasn't okay. I'd missed out on giving my speech. My chances of becoming vice-captain were completely ruined. But worse than that – *Evan Palmer goes to my school!* And he's hanging around with Jayden Gillingham! The home run and the awkwardness and the gobstopper kiss all came flooding into my mind. Surely it was only a matter of time before

Evan found out I wasn't an ace hitter with nice freckles. I was St Clement's Academy's lowest ranking maggot. And then, he wouldn't want to know me.

After Debate Club my phone was showing a message from him.

Nice speech 😉 had no idea you were at St Clement's!!??

But I was too upset to reply. I ran all the way to the library, colliding with Mrs Gordon, who was walking the other way.

"Amelia!" she said. "Goodness me, slow down! Surely you're not in that much of a hurry to get a book?"

But I couldn't breathe. I pulled off my glasses and put my hands over my eyes. They felt wet with tears. Mrs Gordon put down the gigantic pile of books she was holding and rubbed my arm. "Whatever is it, Amelia?"

But how could I explain? My head was flooded with nerves and fear and shock and failure. And one thought stood out among all the rest: Evan was going to find out I'm Maggot. How could he ever look at me the same way? But there was no way I was telling Mrs Gordon about it.

"I messed up my speech in Debate Club." I sniffed. "I won't make the final team."

"Oh, I'm sure it went better than you think. Miles would have to be mad not to put you on the team." Mrs

Gordon handed me a crumpled tissue. "Now, dry your eyes. There is no problem that the right book cannot solve! Here – I was about to put this one aside for you." She passed me a book from the pile she'd been carrying. *Speeches that Changed the World.*

"Thanks," I said. But I knew for certain there would be nothing in it about preventing your maggoty reputation from reaching the ears of the boy you liked. A book could not solve this unmitigated disaster. Even one with Nelson Mandela on the cover. The only good thing to ever happen to me was in danger of total annihilation. I wanted people at school to see me the way Evan did. But now the exact opposite was likely to happen! What if he found out about The List? Wouldn't he end up laughing at me like everyone else?

I blew my nose on the tissue Mrs Gordon gave me and shook my head. "I think it's too late to do anything about it."

"Oh, come on now," Mrs Gordon said. "The Amelia I know doesn't give up that easily! Where's that famous 'Bright fight' you put into everything?" She looked at me with unblinking eyes and it was impossible not to smile. "That's better!" She tapped the *Speeches that Changed the World* book she'd just given me. "You think these people didn't face the odd hurdle?"

I turned the book over in my hands then looked up at Mrs Gordon. Maybe she knew more than I gave her credit for. I'd never given up on anything in my life. And I wasn't about to start now. Evan was at my school. And if I didn't want him to see me for the maggot that everybody else took me for, then I had to act. And fast.

18

"Evan Palmer?" Nisha screeched as I tried to shush her. Mr Harding, our religious studies teacher, gave us both a warning look so I stuffed my head inside my textbook. "I cannot believe he's at our school." Nisha was whispering now, but Mr Harding kept looking over. I prayed to Saint Clement of Rome, who we were learning about, that Mr Harding hadn't heard.

"I know," I whispered back. "It's a total disaster! I don't even want to think about it. How did your dance go? Did Ms Romero like it?"

Nisha grinned. "She loved it. She wants me to choreograph a dance that fits with the song and teach it to the Unfortunate Souls group. I can hardly wait!"

"That's amazing!" I whispered, conscious that Mr Harding was watching us from his desk.

"So why is this Evan thing a disaster?" Nisha asked. "He likes you!"

"Only because he currently has no idea who I am," I replied. "As soon as he finds out, he'll stop seeing me as Amelia Bright and start seeing…" I couldn't even bring myself to say the word.

"Not necessarily," Nisha said. "Not if he's a decent person."

I took a deep breath and shook my head. "He will. That's why I need to think of something."

"Amelia, he is in the year above," Nisha said. "I'm sure he's more mature than the boys in our class. And if he likes you, he won't care what people think."

"Yeah right," I said. "For a start, he's hanging around with Jayden Gillingham. I may have to change schools."

Nisha laughed so hard she almost whacked me in the face with her plait.

"That's enough, you two," Mr Harding said as he looked over again. "You're usually my star students! What's going on?"

"Sorry, sir," Nisha said. Then a moment later she whispered, "The main thing is, what are you going to do about Miles?"

"Miles?" I whispered back. "How can I even think about Miles right now? He didn't even let me do my speech!"

"So?" Nisha dug me in the ribs. "The debate final's next week. You're just going to give up? I thought you wanted vice-captain."

"I do, but…"

"So try again," she said. "Make him listen to your speech." As if making Miles listen to a word I said was that easy.

I shrugged and tried to ignore the pencil sketch of a penis someone had added to the picture of Saint Clement in my textbook. "But what should I do about the Evan situation? That's the urgent thing right now."

"It's really not," Nisha said bluntly. "You've known Evan for less than two weeks. You've wanted to be vice-captain *for ever*. Sorry, but I think it's kind of dumb to give up so easily when Miles never even heard your speech. I don't see how Evan finding out about that stupid nickname is more important than you making the team for the final. Maybe kissing boys destroys brain cells."

"Nisha!" I said. "I'm not saying I'm not annoyed about the team. I'm just saying that this is the first time a boy has ever *liked* me. I have a chance to not be at the bottom of the popularity pile at school. A much better shot at being popular than being vice-captain of Debate Club. Which, to be realistic, would probably only impress my dad. Isn't being a somebody at school important too?"

Mr Harding walked over and warned us that we'd be in detention if we talked again, so we were silent for the rest of the lesson. But Nisha kept blowing out her breath really loudly and sucking her bottom lip. So I could tell she didn't exactly agree with me.

I didn't agree with her about the brain cells thing either. But I had to admit she was right about Miles. I couldn't let Evan's appearance at school stop me from achieving vice-captain. Also, the prospect of telling Dad I'd missed out on the final competition didn't bear thinking about. I had to make Miles hear my speech. I knew he couldn't care less about being fair. But he did care about winning. If I could just make him listen to what I had to say, I was sure he'd put me on the team.

As the bell rang for the end of school, I nudged Nisha. "You're right. I'll find Miles at breaktime tomorrow and get him to hear my speech."

Nisha smiled. "Good. I'm heading to the dance studio to come up with this choreography. Zadie said she'd help me. But listen – do not spend all night thinking about Evan Palmer." I laughed. "Or this popularity thing. Promise me. It's not good for your brain." She leaned forward so her forehead was touching mine and eyeballed me.

"Okay, I promise!" I said.

But I figured one more night of thinking about kissing Evan wouldn't do my brain cells any harm. I collected my things from my locker and headed outside. Only to find him standing by the school gates waiting for me. Immediately, it felt like the playground was spinning.

"Hey," he said. "Thought I'd wait and say hi properly. Sorry I interrupted your speech like that."

He put his hand on my arm and for a split second I thought he might try to kiss me right there by the gates! I adjusted my rucksack and tried to avoid looking into his dazzling eyes too deeply. "So, how was your first day at St Clement's?" I asked. "And, erm, what exactly are you doing here?"

Evan laughed. "I started here last week! I can't believe I've only just run into you. I swear I had no idea you lived in Ravens Bay. The baseball ground is miles away. Sorry if I wrecked your speech."

"It's okay," I said quickly. "You only put me off a tiny bit." *Good one, Amelia*, I thought. *The boy saw you drop your cue cards!* My heart was thumping and the wind kept blowing my hair into my face. How did anyone make talking to boys look easy?

"So," he said, looking kind of embarrassed. "I was thinking about joining Debate Club but…"

"Yes! You totally should!" I blurted out, way too enthusiastically. "I mean, if you want."

"Nah." He looked over to where Jayden and two other boys from Year Nine were getting bikes out of the racks. "I decided it's not really my thing. I'm trying to fit in, you know. Jayden and everyone play basketball most lunchtimes."

"Oh," I said, trying to hide my disappointment. "So, Jayden is your allocated buddy?" I tried to mask my disbelief that any form tutor could be so blatantly irresponsible.

Evan smiled. "No. It's supposed to be this boy called Benedict something. But Jayden said he's kind of weird so..." Evan let the sentence hang there. I wondered if I should tell him that I sat next to Benedict in Orchestra. But I decided, all things considered, it was best if I didn't mention it. "So, can I walk you home?" he asked, like it wasn't a weird thing to say. He headed over to the bike racks but I didn't follow. "I just need to grab my bike."

"Right," I said. But I didn't move. There was no way I was going over to the bike racks with Jayden there. "I'll wait for you here."

I don't know why I didn't tell Evan about the maggot thing straight away. Maybe I should have been more honest with him from the start. Then maybe none of this would have happened. But I wanted to impress him so badly that I couldn't bring myself to tell him what a massive loser everyone thought I was.

As Evan undid his bike lock, Jayden grabbed one of his friends and put him in a headlock. A few people watched, jeering and laughing, as the headlocked boy's face turned redder and his grunts to be released grew louder. I watched Evan, figuring he'd realize that Jayden and his friends ought to come with a warning label. But it looked like Evan was laughing too. I was just considering calling an ambulance when Jayden finally let the boy go. A loud whoop came from the small crowd surrounding them. Evan smiled as he headed back over. I wished I was brave enough to say something. Like, I don't know, that Jayden Gillingham belongs in a zoo. But I took a few steps backwards so none of them could see I was waiting for Evan, and sucked the sleeve of my blazer instead.

"My house is over there, on the Turnstone Estate," Evan said, wheeling his bike with one hand and pointing towards town with the other.

"Oh, that's the opposite direction to mine. So, you really don't have to walk with me..." I hoped Evan couldn't tell how badly I wanted him to say he would. Being with Evan was like climbing into a different world. Kind of how I felt when I played cello. Or read a really good book. Only now that world was colliding with my real one. It felt wrong, like two magnets repelling each other. Only somehow I had to make them fit.

"That's okay," he said, gesturing at the blue sky. "The day's pretty glorious, isn't it!" He followed me as I started walking down the hill. "I can't believe we go to the same school!"

"I know!" I smiled. I wondered if it would be possible for him to hold my hand and balance his bike at the same time. He didn't reach his hand out to mine so I guessed not. But as I reached for my water bottle, my arm brushed against his. People talk about chemistry – well, this was pure nuclear fission! I needed a radiation suit! I don't know how I managed to remain upright for the entire walk home. It felt like there was popping candy under my skin.

Just before we reached my cottage I stopped. I wanted to make sure we weren't too close in case he kissed me. Mum would be at the shop, but Gramps sometimes sat in the living room in the afternoon.

"So, this is where I live," I said. "You've officially walked me home!" And I wanted to slap myself in the face.

Evan squinted, the sunlight catching his eyes so they looked electric blue. We were standing far enough away from my cottage so no one would see if he kissed me. But there were still a few people from school walking past. Evan looked at me for a few moments and I hardly dared breathe. It was like waiting to see if you've got rid of the hiccups. Then he turned his bike around and said, "See you tomorrow?" and I watched as he rode off.

I spent most of that evening coming up with a variety of best- and worst-case scenarios about Evan being at my school. Worst-case scenario was he started hanging around with Jayden permanently, who informed him I was Maggot – a revolting school species that was certifiably sub-human – and Evan never spoke to me again. He'd ignore me at baseball, maybe even quit the team so he didn't have the humiliation of standing within ten metres of me. And every day he'd wonder how he ever touched lips with such a disgusting freckled maggot. I spent quite a long time thinking about this one.

But the best-case scenario – that was the one I pinned my hopes on. I'd be walking past the basketball courts where all the cool people hang out and Evan would call my name. Our eyes would lock over the crowd, and he'd smile like he did the first time I saw him. He'd take my hand and pull me towards him in front of everyone in the entire school. Everyone who matters anyway. Then he would kiss me. The name Maggot would instantly vanish from everyone's vocabulary. Like it never existed. And I'd be Amelia Bright, Evan's girlfriend. Obviously, I'd still hang out with Nisha and go to Orchestra and everything. But I could hang out with the popular people too. And no one would look at me weird or call me names or think I was in the Extreme Fug Zone. Or think that I ever belonged there in the first place.

I had to make this one happen before Evan figured out how grossly unpopular I was.

My daydream was interrupted by Mum calling, "Amelia! Could you come down here a second and help me with the shopping, please," as soon as she got home. "And I want to hear how your speech went!"

I dragged myself downstairs and I guess she saw the disappointment on my face because she said, "What happened?"

I heaved a shopping bag up onto the worktop and began loading stuff into the fridge. "I messed up my speech. But it wasn't my fault."

"I'm sure you didn't mess it up," Mum said. I couldn't see if she was smiling or not. "What did Miles say?"

I sighed. "He said I got distracted, but..."

"Ah, well that explains it." Mum thumped a shopping bag on the kitchen table and flicked the kettle on, giving me one of her looks. "I've been wondering if making these

TikTok things would be a distraction."

"They're not!" I insisted. "It was just...it wasn't my fault, Mum. Seriously. I was just getting started with my speech and these Year Nines burst through the door. It could have happened to anyone! But I'm finding Miles tomorrow and trying again. I really think he'll put me on the team if he hears my speech." I closed the fridge and leaned against the door. "You won't tell Dad, will you?"

Mum gave me a look. "Is that what you care about? What Dad will say?"

"No," I lied.

"Well, you can relax. I won't say anything." I sighed with relief and Mum flashed me a smile. "I know your dad can be a little hard on you, Amelia. But really – you should want to succeed for yourself, not anyone else." She cupped my chin in her hands. "Not even Dad. Although don't ever tell him I said that." I sighed with relief. Then Mum added, "Besides, Hannah's got her Head Girl interview with Mrs Weaver tomorrow, so I expect your dad's mind is filled with that." She kissed my forehead, only somehow it felt like a consolation prize.

19

The next morning, Hannah forced me to listen to the things she'd prepared to say to impress Mrs Weaver in her interview. Annoyingly, they were all true. I mumbled, "Good luck!" and headed to form time.

Mr Malcolmson called, "Go on in, girls!" as he saw Nisha and me walking down the corridor. "I've got word searches!" He waved the stack of papers he had in his hand and held the door open for us. Then, as we walked in, he announced to the entire class, "Let's see if anyone can complete this word search faster than Amelia!" A few people laughed, but definitely not everyone. Still, Mr Malcolmson chuckled to himself like he'd just made the Joke of the Year. Schools really ought to have some kind of complaints desk.

At breaktime, I tracked down Miles in the canteen and delivered my speech about plastics in the ocean. Word-perfect. I could tell he was impressed because his nostrils flared. I was kind of impressed with myself too. Miles slowly finished chewing on a Jaffa cake and looked at me.

"Not bad, Bright." It was the only compliment I'd ever received from Miles. "But let's see how you do on the theme of Minecraft."

"Minecraft?" I repeated, thinking I'd misheard. "That's not the theme, Miles. It's a game. You know the theme for the final is the environment."

Miles shrugged. "If it's too much of a challenge for you…"

"No, it's fine," I said. Even though I'd never even played Minecraft before. "Okay, I'll write a speech on Minecraft. You want to hear it on Monday?"

"No, not on Monday," Miles said, smirking. "The competition's on Tuesday. I have to decide on the team today so I need to hear it now. If you want to be in the final, Amelia, you have to be ready for anything. So, let's hear what you have to say about Minecraft." He folded his arms, leaned back and grinned. There were blobs of Jaffa cake stuck in his braces. His friends all gawped at me, sniggering, waiting for me to admit defeat.

"Fine," I said through gritted teeth. "But I need a minute to think." You're allowed up to a minute to think in competitions, so I knew even Miles couldn't disagree.

He nodded and I took a deep breath. I knew practically nothing about Minecraft. Only that it…hold on. When I'd gone to Ju-Long's house last summer, hadn't he played it? And didn't he have that Minecraft poster in his bedroom that turned 3D when you put those special glasses on? I remembered now…wasn't it all about world-building? I nodded to Miles that I was ready. He tapped the timer on his phone and I began.

"In many ways, the Minecraft world mirrors our own. It works on a building system, allowing players to create their own fantasy world based on the raw materials they find. This echoes the accomplishments of our ancestors – scavengers, problem-solvers, innovators, surviving on whichever terrain they found themselves, be it mountains, forests, caves. We remain a species of hunter-gatherers, creator-survivors, conquering the planet to make it our own…"

By the time his phone beeped, Miles's jaw was hanging open. His friends even gave a cheer. "*Respect-a-mondo!*" Miles said. "You know, Bright, you're a bit of a *marvellosaurus*. You're on the team."

"Thanks," I said, making no attempt to hide the smug smile on my face. "Oh and Miles?" I said as I was about to leave. "I want vice-captain."

Miles looked at me for a second, then did one slow nod.

I left feeling like wherever Amelia Earhart was in the skies, I was with her. I couldn't wait to tell Nisha. I pulled my phone out of my blazer pocket and messaged her. She replied, saying, **OMG I TOLD YOU!!! Awesome!!** Then I tapped out a message to my dad. Vice-captain wasn't the top position, but I still hoped he'd be impressed.

That lunchtime at Orchestra, Mr Giuliani asked me to bring my cello to the front. "We're going to play something a little special." He pointed to the music on the stand next to his piano and smiled. "As soon as you're ready, Miss Bright."

I let my eyes scan the music. I hadn't ever played it before, but I recognized it. "Running Up That Hill" by Kate Bush. Usually I hated playing pieces I hadn't practised in front of anyone. But Mr Giuliani gave me this look. Like he knew I could do it. That we could play it together. I picked up my bow, let my eyes study the first few bars again, then nodded. With my eyes closed, I brought my bow slowly over the strings.

I didn't play it perfectly. But it didn't matter. By the end, the entire orchestra was on their feet. I could hear Ju-Long calling, "Bravo! Bravo!" above the applause.

"Well, Miss Bright," said Mr Giuliani, "I think we've found your opening song for the production evening, don't you?"

* * *

Later, on the way out of school, Nisha was talking about how her dance was going. But her voice seemed to fade into the background as soon as I spotted Evan approaching on his bike. He was standing up on the pedals talking to someone in his year I didn't recognize.

"Amelia," Nisha said, nudging my arm. "Are you even listening?"

"What? Sorry," I said, trying to tune back into what she'd been saying.

"So that's him," Nisha said, following my gaze. "The famous Evan Palmer."

"Nisha!" I hissed. "He'll hear you!" But it was too late. Evan's brakes squeaked as he stopped just in front of us.

"Famous?" Evan grinned. "I'm not sure about that."

I glared at Nisha so she added, "I mean…Amelia said you're pretty good at baseball, that's all."

Evan smiled at me. "You're not so bad yourself!"

"Thanks…" I said, wracking my brain for something else to say and failing dramatically.

Evan let off his brakes and his bike drifted forward a little bit. "I was wondering if you fancied heading to the park. Some of my friends hang out there after school."

"Um, okay," I said – then instantly wished I could take those words back.

Nisha looked at me nervously. There was no way I could go to the park. It was where all the popular people from school hung out. I could just imagine what would happen if I showed up. It would be like a fawn walking into a nest of pythons. Unless...

"Great!" Evan said. "Meet you there in about half an hour?"

I swallowed. "Sure." I could see Nisha's eyes practically bulging out of her head as she tried to communicate telepathically *NO NO NO!* "Oh, actually," I said. "I just remembered, I'm hanging out with Nisha tonight."

Evan shrugged. "That's okay, you come too, Nisha."

Nisha and I exchanged a look. I begged with my eyes for her not to say anything.

"Okay, see you later!" I called, grabbing Nisha's arm and leading her through the gates before she had a chance to protest.

"Amelia, what were you thinking?" Nisha said. "Madison and her friends go to the park on Fridays! Not to mention DJ and Lachlan! There's no way we can turn up there."

I squeezed her arm in reassurance. "It'll be fine!" I crossed all of my fingers and prayed it *would* be fine. Better than fine. "Evan's invited us! How many times have we been invited to the park since we started at St Clement's?"

Nisha rolled her eyes. "Exactly zero. Because they hate us."

"But this could change everything!" I said. "I've got a good feeling about this, Nisha. Listen, I got vice-captain today, didn't I? I got a standing ovation at Orchestra. I'm getting loads of likes on my TikToks. Look –" I took out my phone and showed her – "157 likes!" Nisha blinked at me like it made no difference. "Evan likes me, Nisha! This could be my chance. If he makes it obvious that he likes me at the park then…they'll see me differently."

Nisha sighed and looked at me. Her silence spoke a thousand words. But I wasn't giving up.

"I know how it sounds, Nisha. But they all like Evan. He's popular. And he's *my* friend. This could be the moment I finally get accepted by all of them!"

Only, what happened was pretty much the exact opposite.

20

Nisha and I were running late for the park, since it had taken me so long to persuade her to come. And for me to decide what to wear. In the end I'd put on one of Hannah's hand-me-down denim skirts and a T-shirt Dad had got me for my birthday saying *Have a ball*. It has a picture of a baseball on it, which I thought might be lucky.

When I called for Nisha, she had the same troubled look on her face as she did when I left her earlier. "Are you sure you want to go?" she said. "Because you could message Evan and say something came up."

"Nisha!" I said confidently. "It will be okay. It's just the park! They are only human people!"

But when we got there, it didn't feel that straightforward. For a start, hovering over the crowd of people from our school was a gigantic cloud of smoke.

"Are they...vaping?" Nisha said, stopping dead in her tracks.

"Maybe there are some older people there," I said in my brightest voice. I carried on walking, but Nisha stayed where she was. "Come on, Nisha! It's fine. Evan's probably wondering where we are."

We looked over at the crowd again. It was hard to make anyone out, as they were all engulfed in a murky haze of vapour. "I can't even see Evan," Nisha said. "I think we should go home."

"But we only just got here!" I said. "Let's find Evan and if it's too smoky we can stand over there by the swings."

Nisha eyed the swings. Two of them were empty, but there were four people crammed onto the third, its chains heaving under their weight. Nisha looked at me.

"Okay, by the trees then," I said, pointing at a spot that was reasonably vacant. "But I'm sure it will be fine once we get there."

"Okay," Nisha said eventually. "But I want it noted that I think this is a really bad idea."

"Noted," I said and laughed as she took my hand. "But at least *try* and enjoy yourself. We're hanging out at the *park*!" She gave me an unimpressed look but stayed close to my side as we walked into the crowd.

"Oh my God, what are they doing here?" The voice was unmistakable. Madison Hart. I tried to ignore the icy feeling in my stomach, desperately searching for Evan's face. But Nisha stopped and faced me.

"I really think we should just go," she whispered.

"We can't go now," I whispered back. "What will they think?"

"I don't care," Nisha replied. "It's obvious we're not welcome."

Then, behind Madison, I spotted Evan's curls. He had his back to us. I was just about to call his name when the word "Maggot" was hurled at me like a slingshot. A boy who looked like he was in Year Ten or Eleven stepped forward and blew a stream of vanilla smoke in our faces. The people around us started laughing. I swallowed, closing my eyes to stop them stinging. But also to stop myself from seeing Evan's face.

A car horn sounded from the nearby road and when I opened my eyes, Nisha was half-waving at someone driving past. "Great. That's my next-door neighbour! She's the biggest gossip ever. She'll probably go straight round to tell my mum," she said, then tugged on my arm. "Please, Amelia, let's get out of here."

I was torn. I could see how desperate Nisha was to leave, but at the same time I didn't want to give up so easily. We'd only been there for two minutes. I hadn't even spoken to Evan. How could I ever fit in with these people if I didn't give it a proper try?

I turned to the boy who had blown smoke at us and smiled. "Hi, I'm Amelia and this is Nisha. Do you go to St Clement's?" I said in my cheeriest voice, like I genuinely didn't mind he just deliberately blew smoke in our faces. Even though the taste was stuck in the back of my throat and was probably already causing me lung damage. I can only assume the boy had never heard of charisma. Because he took a gigantic gulp of the can he was holding, leaned towards me and burped. The people around us burst out laughing. Behind him, Evan was about to turn around. I couldn't bear for him to see me being laughed at.

I turned to Nisha. "Okay," I said. "Let's go."

Someone yelled, "MAGGOT!" at my back as we walked away. But I didn't turn around. I kept Nisha's hand gripped in mine, feeling ridiculous for even considering coming here in the first place. Part of me hoped Evan might call my name. Run after us. Explain to everyone that he wanted us here. That I was his friend. But I didn't hear anything apart from laughter, and Madison's voice shouting something I can't even repeat. All I could hope was that by some kind of magic, Evan hadn't noticed us.

I hardly got any sleep that night. Mainly because Nisha

insisted on me staying over at hers, and was intent on making me try the moves from her new dance. Nisha did a backwards handspring over her beanbag. Then she made me have a go, creasing up with laughter as I landed on my backside. "I don't understand why your musical rhythm doesn't translate to your body."

"Neither do I," I said. "Hannah says it was lucky I picked an instrument you have to play sitting down."

Nisha smiled. "So, you feeling better?"

"Yes," I said. "Nothing makes me feel better about social humiliation than almost breaking my butt."

Nisha laughed. "It wasn't social humiliation. Those people are barbaric. At least we saw Evan's true colours."

"What do you mean?" I got up from the floor and straightened my pyjamas. "It's not Evan's fault Madison said that stuff."

"No," Nisha said. "But he didn't exactly stick up for you, did he?"

"He probably didn't even see us!" I said quickly.

Nisha rolled her eyes. "Amelia. I saw him. He looked right at us."

I chewed the inside of my cheek. "Well, maybe he did say something. After we'd gone. We left so quickly it didn't give him much of a chance. Anyway, he's new at school so…"

Nisha looked at me like she wanted to say something else, then her phone beeped. "It's my cousin, Kajri," she said, sitting down cross-legged on the floor. "I'm going to be staying with her for the holidays."

"You're going to India for the whole summer?" I asked.

Nisha nodded. "For most of it. Kajri's getting married. But Mum and Dad want to take me to Goa and Karnataka and a few other places. So we'll be travelling too. I can't wait. Look." Nisha tapped her phone and scrolled through pictures of sandy beaches, misty hills, elaborate temples, cascading waterfalls. It looked beautiful.

"I'm so jealous," I said. "I think the most exciting place I'm going this summer will be the inside of Mum's shop."

"To be honest, your mum's shop can be pretty wild." Nisha grinned.

That night, we watched the entire second season of *Extreme Dance*, until Nisha's dad banged on the wall and told us to go to sleep.

"You sure you're feeling okay?" Nisha whispered after she'd turned off the light. "Did Evan message you?"

I tapped my phone and watched its bluey-glow light up the room. "No. But he knows I'll see him tomorrow at baseball," I whispered back.

"And you're okay?" she said. "You sure?"

"Of course. It was probably a bit soon to introduce me to his friends, that's all. It's fine."

I didn't usually lie to Nisha. But that night, lying in the dark, I didn't let her see my tears falling silently into the pillow. Or how stupid I felt. How much of a failure I was. Probably because I didn't want to believe it myself.

21

The next morning, I was late getting back from Nisha's. Dad's car was already outside our cottage as I ran down the hill. So I knew I'd be in trouble. Dad stood on the pavement with his hands on his hips as I ran up to him panting.

"Sorry."

"I've been waiting almost ten minutes, Amelia!" he said. "Grab your kit and let's go!"

Only it wasn't that straightforward because I'd forgotten to pack my baseball bag before I went to Nisha's last night. I quickly pulled my kit from the bottom of my chest of drawers and stuffed it into my bag.

"Hey," Mum said, as I ran down the stairs. "Slow down! Did you even have breakfast?"

"There's no time!" I swear I could hear Dad's foot tapping impatiently outside. I dashed out of the door, still out of breath.

Dad said, "Finally!" so loudly the whole street probably heard. Then I realized I'd forgotten my glove. "Amelia!" Dad shouted after me as I ran back up the stairs. "That's the last time you have a sleepover the night before a game!"

"Mike," Mum said. "I told her it was fine. She's only a few minutes late. You'll make the game. Spending time with her friends is more important than bouncing a ball around."

"Bouncing? That's *basket*ball, Penny." I heard Dad's sigh all the way from upstairs and knew Mum had said it deliberately. "Hurry up!" he shouted. "We're going to be late!"

"Hey." Hannah stuck her head out of her bedroom door and blew me a kiss. "It's only a dumb baseball game."

And for some reason that made the tears in my eyes spill. I wished Hannah hadn't quit so we could go together. Downstairs, I had to rub my eyes so Dad wouldn't notice I was crying. It wasn't just Dad being mad at me. It was the thought of seeing Evan after yesterday at the park. How badly I'd wanted to impress him and how it had completely backfired. I should have listened to Nisha and avoided the park entirely.

The weather was sweltering but the air conditioning in the car gave me a false sense of security. As soon as we got to the field, I realized it was not a good day to be ginger. Mum had packed my factor fifty-plus, but suncream and sweat is not a particularly good combination for skin protection. Not for mine anyway. I'd only been out of the car for ten minutes before my arms felt like they were burning.

"Hey," came a voice from behind me.

"Hey!" I replied, only half turning round. There was no way I wanted Evan to see how embarrassed I was about yesterday.

"You okay?" he asked, bending down to help me with the bag of bats Dad had told me to carry.

"Fine!" I said as breezily as possible when you're lugging a bag of heavy bats in the scorching heat.

"Listen, about the park…"

"It's fine!" I said quickly. "Nisha wasn't feeling very well so we had to go."

"Oh, right. It's just—"

I couldn't bear to hear the word *maggot* cross his lips, so I made an excuse about needing to go back to the car, and left him to carry the bats to the dugout.

As the away team, we batted first. But after a few decent hits, it was one disaster after another. And by the end of the game, we'd lost by a mile. I'd seen Dad lose his temper over baseball loads of times, but it was always worse when it was the Rockets. I preferred it when he was just yelling profanities at the TV.

"That was lousy!" Dad shouted in the dugout before he let anyone go home. "Absolutely lousy! Harry, if I see you slow up before home base again, you're off the team! Amelia, your fielding was pathetic! Pathetic! What's the first rule of catching?"

I swallowed the fist-sized ball of shame in my throat. "Never fear the ball."

"Exactly. So what were you doing out there? It's a ball, not a bomb!" Every muscle in my body was clenched as he went through each of us one by one, telling us how lousily we'd played. Except Thomas Cornish. His mum complained last season after Dad called him a worthless lump of cheese. "And, Evan…well actually, you played pretty decently out there, considering." I accidentally let out an audible *phew*. "But to lose eight-two? It's embarrassing! I am embarrassed on your behalf," Dad said and put his cap back on. He really didn't need to be embarrassed on my behalf. I was already embarrassed enough for the entire team.

"Your dad doesn't like losing, hey," Evan said as we headed towards the car park. My stomach flipped like the ground was unsteady. What was it about Evan that made my stomach go weird like that?

"You can tell?" I said and Evan laughed. For the first time that day I started to relax.

"Want to hang out tomorrow?" Evan said. "Maybe you could show me the best beach." He still wanted to spend time with me? Maybe the park disaster hadn't ruined everything after all!

"Sure. That would be nice." I clamped my teeth onto the insides of my cheeks so my smile didn't go too wide.

As I got into the car I checked my phone. The screen was filled with messages from Nisha. I scrolled back to the first one so I could make sense of them all.

Nightmare!!!

Literal nightmare!!!

Neighbour told my parents she saw me at the park.

She said everyone was vaping!!!

OMG Amelia!!!

Mum thinks I am in with a BAD CROWD!!!

I tried to explain

That we were only there for a minute then came home

They just made me watch a load of YouTube videos

About the dangers of vaping!!

I told them a million times I would never

I messaged back:

What?!!! They believe you though, right?

I'm so sorry!!

I spent the rest of the journey staring at my phone, waiting for a reply that didn't come. It had been my idea to go to the park. I'd practically forced Nisha to come with me. Guilt sat in my stomach like bile. I was still looking at my phone as I got out of the car, willing Nisha to reply. Suddenly Dad shouted my name and turned as if to throw me a fastball. I was so surprised I dropped my phone and almost tripped over my own feet.

"Amelia, seriously," Dad said. "Never fear the ball."

22

That night, I posted a new TikTok and dedicated it to Nisha. It was a song called "Firework". If you listen really hard, you can hear Hannah singing in the background from her bedroom. It got over fifty likes almost straight away. Okay, most of them were Hannah's friends or people from Orchestra but still, it felt pretty good. My phone beeped with a message.

Nisha: Thanks for the song 😃 I'm okay.

Mum and Dad believe me about the vaping.

Amelia: Phew! Let's never go to the park again.

Nisha: Agreed. The park stinks.

I was about to reply when my phone beeped with another message. This time from Evan.

Evan: Awesome TikTok. Love that song.

Amelia: Thanks. What are you doing?

Evan: I'm already in bed 😌 You still showing me the beach tomorrow? 😁

My heart lifted like a hot air balloon.

Amelia: Of course! Message me tomorrow and I'll show you the sights!

Evan: You could show me some sights now 😊

I pointed my phone out of the window, but it was dark and you couldn't even see the sea, only greyish clouds. **It's too dark.** I figured I might already have something on my phone. **What do you want to see?**

Evan: Something interesting 😃

And this was it. The moment I misunderstood what Evan meant entirely. Because *he* meant a photo like The Photo. *Before* the summer holidays. We'd only kissed twice and he was already asking for That Kind Of Photo. I realize that now. But at the time, you have to appreciate I was brand new to all this. Evan was the first boy to even message me apart from Ju-Long about Orchestra practice. He was the first boy who'd kissed me. How was I supposed to know his idea of an interesting photo differed majorly to mine?

I feel kind of stupid saying this now, but I flicked through my pictures and sent Evan a photo of a velvet swimming crab. I'd found it on the beach last weekend and rescued it from a flock of circling seagulls. It's the kind of thing I find interesting. And that's what he'd said, right? I even added a message saying, **Clawsome or what!**

Evan: Woah! Wasn't expecting that lol.

Amelia: Maybe we'll see some tomorrow! My favourite beach is the BEST for rock pooling.

Evan: Clawsome!

And I went to sleep with the biggest smile on my face.

The next day, the skies were pouring down with rain.

I messaged Evan: **Should we leave the beach for another day?**

But he replied: **Are you joking? Rain brings out the best creatures!**

So I stuck my wellies on, pulled on Hannah's leopard print cagoule, checked my hair was held firmly in place with the silver grips she'd left in the bathroom, and ran out of the house before she saw me.

Evan was already outside my cottage when I opened the door. I was so glad he was wearing a cagoule and wellies too.

"Where's your bucket?" he called. I was just about to turn around and fetch one before I heard him laugh and realized he was joking.

"So, what makes this the perfect beach?" Evan said as we stood at the top of the cliff steps and looked down at the bay.

"Look," I said. "See the sand dunes over there? When it's not raining, they're the most stunning shade of yellow. Those spiky tufts of grass are called marram. They're really important habitats for insects. I saw a tiger beetle up there once. These cliffs are part of a Jurassic coastline, so you can find fossils and ammonites that have fallen onto the beach. And those rocks down there? The crevasses are really deep so they're the best in Ravens Bay for rock pooling."

Evan smiled. "Okay, you've convinced me." He grabbed my hand and we set off down the steps.

He was right about the rain bringing out all the good stuff. We saw starfish and prawn, all kinds of anemones and what I think was a long-spined sea scorpion. But we only glanced at it for a second before it darted under a rock. Waves crashed around us and the entire beach was deserted.

As we walked towards the steps to go home, Evan took my hand. It was wet and cold, and my fingers were half-numb, but it still felt incredible. I mean, he must have heard me being called Maggot on Friday. The entire park probably heard it. But it was as though the whole disaster had been completely washed from our minds, like the tide cleaning the shore.

Then, as we reached the bottom of the steps, Evan stopped. "I like you, Amelia."

I turned around. And I don't know what came over me (okay, I'd been repeating this Amelia Earhart quote about courage in my head a hundred times) but I kissed him. *I* kissed *him*. I'd completely forgotten about my ChapStick, but our lips met at exactly the right angle and I did it the way I'd practised. It felt magical. Like when I play a piece of music with no mistakes. Our faces were damp from the rain, but somehow that made it feel nicer. Evan had the biggest smile on his face afterwards. Probably so did I, but I was too blown away to care.

Evan put his sandy hand in mine and a tiny tremor went up my arm. And I got this feeling like it meant everything would be okay. If Evan liked me, there had to be a way to convince his friends to like me too. We were hand in hand on my favourite beach. Waves crashed like a percussion section in the background. My lips tasted salty from his kiss. I wanted to call out, "TO ADVENTURE!" like Amelia Earhart at the top of my lungs. But on reflection I am so glad I didn't.

* * *

When I got home, Hannah was mad about her cagoule being soaked and sandy. And Mum was annoyed I'd gone out in the rain. But nothing could bring me down from that cloud. My third kiss. *Lucky number three* – was perfect.

I pulled my phone out of my pocket and checked my TikTok. *204* likes for "Firework"! I tapped to see who they were. Loads of people from Orchestra. But also some people from the year above. People in Evan's year! And the comments were amazing.

This rocks!

So cool Amelia!

Love love love!!!

Obsessed

Bowing down!!

That night, I went to sleep imagining Evan kissing me at the top of the hill, in front of everyone from school. At my locker. Under the beech trees. Even in the music corridor! I imagined us kissing everywhere, like I'd seen some couples doing at school. I imagined everything. From meeting in the library at lunchtime to holding hands on the way home down the hill. I imagined us reading the same book. I even came up with different scenarios of him asking me to be his girlfriend. I was certain it would happen soon. And then the name Maggot would be gone for ever.

23

In science on Monday, we were learning about parts of the eye. "Turn your attention to the board, everyone, please," Mrs King said, as she displayed a picture of a dissected eyeball. "Who can tell me the names of the different parts?"

The entire class let out a collective, "Yuk!"

Mrs King blinked a few times then looked at me. "Amelia? Perhaps you can tell me."

"Only if it's a maggot's!" DJ shouted.

Lachlan added, "Maggots don't have eyes, idiot." And they both fell about laughing.

"Erm, gentlemen!" Mrs King said firmly. "I have no idea where this idea has come from, but I can assure you that maggots have eyes. All over their bodies, in fact, or at least light-sensitive cells, that are essential for their survival. People see them as insignificant grubs, but believe me, scientifically speaking, maggots are fascinating! They are of vital importance in terms of ecology, medicine, recycling. And not only that, they are useful in the world of forensic science too. The presence of maggots can help to determine the time of a corpse's death. So, dismiss them at your peril!"

By this point my face had gone bright scarlet. I felt Nisha's hand squeeze mine under the desk.

"Anyway, let's stick to human anatomy for now, please," Mrs King said. "Amelia – you were about to tell us the different parts of the eyeball."

Thankfully the bell went so everyone headed out to break. Nisha and I volunteered to stay behind to put the books away, which wasn't easy considering my hands were shaking with humiliation.

"Don't let DJ get to you," Nisha said. "He's such an idiot. You need to keep your confidence up for the competition tomorrow."

"Oh yeah," I said. With everything that was happening with Evan, I'd almost forgotten about the debate final. I collected the last textbook from the back bench and sighed. "I just wish there was something I could do to make them drop the whole maggot thing."

"You heard Mrs King," Nisha said as we headed out of the lab. "Maggots are actually vital and fascinating creatures."

"I guess," I said, trying to suck up the dejection I felt. Nisha linked my arm as we headed over to the library. "Mrs King said maggots help in forensics, right? Maybe I can handle being named after a creature that is essentially an honorary member of *CSI*."

But even as I said it, I didn't mean it. Now Evan was at St Clement's, I needed to lose the Maggot name and fast. But it was more than that. How was I ever going to get the popular crowd to like me if I still couldn't convince the idiots in my class that I was even human?

"GUESS WHAT?" Hannah screamed in my ear as she practically jumped on me walking home.

"You've finally figured out a way to deafen me?" I said, rubbing the side of my head.

"No, dummy. I got Head Girl!" I stopped walking. "Isn't it AWESOME!" Hannah's voice went a few octaves higher than usual. "Mrs Weaver pulled me out of maths this afternoon for a special meeting. Look – it's already on the school's Instagram." She shoved her phone in my face and I tried my best to smile. "I mean, it's going to be a lot of work," she went on. "There'll be meetings and I'll need to get prom committee organized and stuff but OH MY GOD! Can you believe it?"

"Yeah, amazing. Well done." I know I should have felt happy. I mean, she is my sister and everything. But it was like watching her star rise higher and higher, and all I could think about was how far I was below.

Needless to say, Mum cried. And I'm pretty sure the neighbours could hear Dad's voice over FaceTime shouting congratulations. Gramps put on an old jazz album and waltzed Hannah around the living room. I said I had to do some cello practice and go over my speech for the competition, and went upstairs to my room.

I played Mozart's "Requiem in D Minor", letting my fingers tremble on the strings to create the vibrato. I closed my eyes, and the melody lifted me out of my cottage and up into the clouds, where there was no such thing as maggots, or sisters who got Head Girl.

Later, I was rehearsing my environment speech when my phone vibrated on my desk. It was a photo of Evan holding *Pride and Prejudice*.

Evan: Just started this 😀

My stomach dipped like I was at the top of a roller coaster. That feeling kept happening when Evan messaged me. I thought that fancying someone meant you felt stuff in your heart. But actually, I was mostly feeling it in my stomach. I wasn't sure if that was normal or not. I tapped out a reply: **Awesome! I hope you like it.**

Evan: It's proper old fashioned lol

Well, obviously! I thought. I typed back: **It was written in 1813.** I reset the timer to practise my speech, but my phone went off again.

Evan: If you liked it I'm sure it's good 😄

I tried to concentrate on my speech, but now I was worried Evan would find *Pride and Prejudice* boring.

"Amelia!" Hannah said, bursting in. "The production is in three weeks!"

"I know," I said, feeling an extra flurry of butterflies in my stomach as she mentioned it. Hannah was the main part, but I was the one opening the evening with my cello solo. So we were kind of evens.

"Why aren't you practising?" Hannah picked up the music next to my stand and wafted it at me.

"It's the debate final tomorrow." Out of the corner of my eye, I saw my phone light up. I prayed Hannah wouldn't notice. I hadn't told her about Evan. I don't know why. Mainly because I didn't want Mum to find out and I knew Hannah would tell her immediately.

"The debate competition?" Hannah sighed. "The production is more important!"

"Fine." I pulled the music out of Hannah's hand, put "Part of Your World" on my stand and waited for her to leave. I readied my bow and found myself closing my eyes, falling into the music like it was a warm sea. By the time I had finished I had tears in my eyes. That happens to me with music sometimes. Mum says it's the sign that I should be a musician when I'm older like she was. Dad says that's a great idea if I want to be a poor, struggling artist my whole life. I just hoped the crying didn't happen during my solo. It would not be a good look.

Hannah was right. The production was more important than anything. My solo had to be good enough to fully reinvent myself. Obviously I'd pray for a terrible but non-fatal accident to befall DJ and his friends, meaning they had to be home-schooled for ever too. But maybe – just maybe – even they would be impressed.

I was reading my book in bed when Evan's name lit up on my phone again. I felt that familiar flip of my stomach.

Evan: It is a truth universally acknowledged that I am ready for bed 😀

Which was a *Pride and Prejudice* joke. Then a photo came through. It was Evan lying on his bed. His hair was spread across the pillow in a dark curly mess and he didn't have a top on. I felt a sort of flutter but not just my stomach this time, like the gentle beating of wings. Then another message flashed up: **Your turn.**

My turn for what? I replied. **I have not the pleasure of understanding you.** Which was also a *Pride and*

Prejudice joke. Only as soon as I sent it, I felt like an idiot in case he hadn't read that bit yet.

A photo, Evan replied. **Of you in bed** 😁

I sat up on my knees and looked at myself in the mirror on my bedroom wall. It is not an exaggeration to say it was a displeasing sight. I pulled my hair out of its untidy ponytail and wiped the spot cream off my forehead. It was a slight improvement. But my hair had a kink in it from the bobble, and my forehead was red from where I'd rubbed it. I leaned back against my bed and tried to arrange my hair into something that did not resemble a highland cow. I took a few selfies, added a black and white filter to the best one, then cropped out the giant rainbow on my pyjama top. **Goodnight x** I added and pressed send.

The next morning, I noticed Evan had messaged me back late last night. I must have fallen asleep before he sent it. **Cute. Do I get to see what's underneath?** I read it a few times, trying to figure out what he meant. Surely Evan didn't want to see what was under my bed? I was brushing my teeth when it dawned on me what he might have meant. A weird tremor ran over my body like a heat rash. Surely he didn't mean…?

"Hurry up!" Hannah shouted, banging on the bathroom door. "You've been in there for ages."

I spat out the remainder of my toothpaste and rinsed my mouth. "I'm coming!"

I thought for a minute about showing Hannah Evan's message. Asking her whether or not I was understanding it right. But she started singing "About Damn Time" and shoved me out of the door the second I undid the lock. So I decided to leave it.

Miles had thankfully listened to reason about the debate team for the final. (Reason being me.) It was me, Miles, Aakesh, Flora and William as sub. Between us we'd read practically everything there was to know about climate change, and Miles and I had practised our opening speeches until we knew them backwards.

The competition was at Atherstone Boys' School, so Flora and I were literally the only girls in the whole building. If you think that intimidated me, think again. I'd been playing baseball on mixed teams since I was in Little League with my dad yelling at me from the sidelines. Speaking in front of this crowd had to be easier than that. Besides, after Mr Hall's erratic minibus driving, I was thankful to still be in one piece.

Their head teacher welcomed us in the hall as the audience was filing in. A mixture of different year groups, including Years Twelve and Thirteen from the looks of it. Okay, maybe it wouldn't exactly be a piece of cake. But, like Amelia Earhart said, *Use your fear, it can take you to the place where you store your courage.* My fear, however, was only taking me to the bathroom. I shot to the nearest toilet and felt a little better with an empty bladder. I took a few deep breaths, removed my glasses to splash water on my face, and looked at myself in the mirror. I was ready.

Miles's opening speech went well. He timed it exactly so he finished just before the buzzer. Then it was my turn.

"When I say the words 'eighth continent', you may wonder what planet I'm on. But – as you can see – my feet are right here on Planet Earth. Our only home. The only hospitable home for thousands of light years, perhaps the only one that exists in our universe at all…"

By the time the buzzer sounded, a ripple of excitement went through my body. I'd done it. Word perfect. The only thing missing was my vice-captain badge which Mr Hall had forgotten to bring. I tried not to let it ruin the moment.

A boy sitting on the table opposite us stood up. "Climate Emergency," he began. I tried not to roll my eyes at the predictable opening. But then he launched into one of the greatest speeches I have ever heard. He talked about ice, wind, fire, the utter destruction of humanity. He painted the bleakest possible picture of Armageddon. Then halfway through his imagery switched. To waterfalls and plentiful fields and peace. It was incredible. I had to stop myself giving him a standing ovation. Miles's face looked almost green.

Their vice-captain's speech wasn't as powerful, but it was still very good. So it all rested on our debating skills. Anyone can write a brilliant speech, I told myself, but not everyone can debate.

The head judge stood up and declared the debate open. He put the first question to us, the visiting team. "St Clement's Academy, in your speeches you talked about the negative impact of human behaviour. Is that what you see as the greatest emergency facing Planet Earth?"

Miles was stumped. I nudged Aakesh while I thought of my own answer. Aakesh paused to take a breath then said, "Could one species really be responsible for the destruction of an entire planet? Well, when it comes to humans, I'm afraid the answer is yes. Already, humans have destroyed approximately seventy per cent of the world's wildlife..."

He went on to give the most brilliant answer. When the opposing team suggested that the climate crisis was partly due to natural climate change, I came back with a barrage of evidence that put them off their stride for the rest of the debate. I added that humans were destroying land on an unprecedented scale. The judges ticked something on their score sheet when I said "unprecedented". Mr Hall gave me a thumbs up. The New Word Every Day poster is worth its weight in gold when it comes to debating.

When we were announced as the winning team, an unenthusiastic applause rippled around the room. It always happens when you're not the home team. But I was elated. In the minibus on the way back I texted Dad saying we'd won.

Awesome Amelia! he replied. **I knew you could do it. So proud of you!**

And that was the icing on the cake. We'd won the debate final with me as vice-captain; Evan definitely fancied me; I had 223 followers on TikTok, Dad was proud of me, and Mrs Weaver was bound to announce our win in assembly. Especially considering it meant our school would be hosting the first round of the competition next year! It was a chance for Evan to see another side of me. The winning side. He'd see what *Vice-Captain* Amelia Bright looks like. Advocate of the Environment. Champion Debater. And I would probably officially be his girlfriend by then too. I couldn't wait.

24

The next day, Mrs Weaver told our debate team to come to the front of the assembly hall and made everyone give us a round of applause. She said we had "excelled ourselves" and that the entire school should be "enormously proud". Miles got to hold the trophy, but we all got special certificates and Mr Hall said it would be in the school newsletter.

I tried my best to bump into Evan that day so he could congratulate me in person. But it proved impossible. At break and lunchtime, he hung about on the basketball courts with everyone who was considered cool. I walked past a couple of times – even though it's the long way to get to the library and miles away from my locker. I looked over and I thought I caught his eye. But he didn't wave or anything, so I guess he didn't see me. I didn't tell Nisha about the message he'd sent asking to see underneath my pyjamas. She already thought the way he ignored me wasn't right. I dreaded to think what she'd say about that kind of message. But I didn't think Evan was ignoring me. Not exactly. Our paths just never seemed to cross at school. No matter how deliberately I strayed from my usual places. In a weird way I suppose it was for the best. The last thing I needed was for Evan to hear someone shouting Maggot at me again.

Every night, I practised my solo for the production until my fingers ached. I had to get it perfect in order for everything to go as I planned. I couldn't give a mediocre performance. This performance had to be the best thing the school had ever seen. I needed people to talk about it. To rave about it! To greet me in the corridors the next day and tell me how mind-blowingly amazing it was. Okay, maybe I had my sights set a little high. But I truly felt like everything – my survival at school and my potential relationship with Evan – depended on this one musical moment. The chance to turn my social life around was less than two weeks away. And I was going to grab it with both hands – literally.

On Friday, after school, Evan waited for me at the top of the hill. "Want me to carry your cello?" he asked as I approached.

I clutched the straps a little tighter. "It's okay, thanks.

I don't trust anyone with my cello. Don't take it personally."

There were a few steps of awkward silence, then he suddenly blurted out, "I heard people call you Maggot." It felt like being whacked round the back of the head with a baseball bat. I did not see it coming. "I figured it was random when I heard someone shout it that night at the park. But everyone calls you it, Amelia. What's that about?"

My heart dropped out of my body and rolled all the way down the hill. What was I supposed to say? I thought about lying. And decided that was my only option. "It's a running joke!" I said, laughing awkwardly. "This thing from ages ago."

Evan carefully wheeled his bike around a lamp post. "Are you sure about that?"

"Yes!" I said. "It's hard to explain how they came up with that nickname but it was really funny at the time." I laughed again, a bit louder this time. I did such a good job, I half-convinced myself it was funny. "It's just this thing from Year Seven."

"It doesn't sound that funny." I avoided Evan's eyes by keeping mine firmly on the pavement.

"I guess you had to be there." I felt kind of weird. Like I'd betrayed myself or something. The words from *Wuthering Heights* echoed around my head: *Why did you betray your own heart, Cathy?* I watched a seagull fly off from the side of an old, upturned boat and thought about running the rest of the way down the hill, away from this conversation. But it was no use. With the weight of my cello, I'd fall over before I reached the bottom. "I do honestly find it funny." I forced my face into a smile.

"Okay," Evan said, changing the subject about as subtly as he'd started it. "So when do I get to meet Morph?"

Then I smiled for real. "You want to meet my gecko? Really?"

"Of course!" he said. "You're the only person I know with a lizard."

It wasn't exactly the compliment of my dreams. But it meant Evan was coming to my house! It meant he knew about the M-word and still wanted to know me.

"So can I come round now?" Evan's hair caught the wind. For a few seconds I watched his curls dance in the breeze and his eyes shimmer in the sunlight.

My heart pounded like a storm at sea. I really needed to get a hold of myself. I smiled. "Sure."

Inside, Gramps was asleep in the armchair as usual. He half opened an eye as we walked in. "Is that you, Hannah?"

"It's Amelia, Gramps," I replied. "Hannah's at rehearsals. This is my friend Evan, from school. He plays on my baseball team."

Gramps sat up and wiped his mouth with a

191

handkerchief. "Baseball? Oh dear. And what do you have to say for yourself, young man?"

"Gramps," I said as I watched Evan squirm. "He just wants to meet Morph."

"Hi, erm, Mr Bright," Evan said. And the words that shot through my head were: *Big Mistake*.

"Bright?" Gramps leaned forward like he was considering giving Evan a "clip round the ear" like he used to threaten us with when we were little. "Bright is the name of Amelia's father, young man! My name is Mr Wilson, and I'd appreciate it if you remember that in future."

Evan looked mortified. I wanted to vanish into the wallpaper.

"Sorry, Mr Wilson," Evan stuttered.

"We'll be upstairs, Gramps," I said, and bundled Evan out of the room as quickly as I could.

"You bring that lizard down here!" Gramps called as we went upstairs. "I'm not having you taking strange boys up to your bedroom."

"Sorry," I whispered to Evan. "He's usually…asleep."

"Looks like he could do with a haircut if you ask me!" Gramps added, and I heard him chuckling as we got to my room.

"Sorry," I said again. "My gramps has a weird sense of humour."

Evan smiled awkwardly. "I don't think he likes me."

"You should see what he's like with my dad," I replied. "Anyway, this is Morph!" I felt like saying "ta daaaah!" but I stopped myself just in time.

"Woah," Evan said, peering into the tank. "He's wicked!"

"You can hold him if you want." I stood on tiptoes to open the lid and scooped up Morph from the branch he was sitting on. "They're nocturnal," I explained, gently stroking Morph's scaly back. "So he's really sleepy during the day and they can—" Suddenly Morph sprang out of my arms straight onto Evan's chest. "Jump." I grinned.

"Hey, little fella," Evan said, stroking his finger down Morph's nose.

"He likes you," I said. Evan looked at me and smiled, his eyes bright as cornflowers.

"He's unreal!"

"He was left in a shoebox outside the vets in town. My mum's friend, Yvonne, is one of the vets but they didn't have space for him. Mum and Dad eventually agreed to let me have him. But only because Hannah got Barnacles the year before."

"Barnacles?"

"Hannah's cat." Morph jumped back into my arms and I nodded for Evan to follow me. I pushed open

193

Hannah's bedroom door. As usual, it was absurdly tidy. Barnacles was curled up on Hannah's bed. His ears pricked as soon as we walked in. "That's him. He was abandoned too." Just then, Barnacles hissed at us. "He's still kind of angry about it."

"Why did you shave him?" Evan said.

"He's a Sphynx!" I laughed. "They don't have any fur."

"I know," Evan said. "I was joking."

"Oh." For a few moments it was kind of awkward. I felt like a complete idiot for not getting his joke. I could feel Morph's claws clinging onto me through my shirt and the thump of my heart like a bass drum. "I should put Morph back in his tank. He gets cold."

Only I didn't move and neither did Evan. We stood there on the landing looking at each other with Morph in between us. My stomach felt weird and my mouth went dry, then Evan stepped forward and kissed me again. It felt like being swept up into a cloud! I was Amelia Earhart taking off, the ground was miles beneath my feet and I was soaring. *No borders, just horizons – only freedom*. I felt Evan's hand try to slide underneath my shirt and I'm pretty sure my heart completely stopped.

"Oi!" Gramps shouted up the stairs. Evan leaped back so fast he almost fell over the banister. "I think it's time you were going, young man."

I said a quick, "Bye," to Evan, ran into my room and closed the door. I put Morph back in his tank then collapsed face-first onto my bed. Thoughts raced through my head: *Gramps saw me kissing Evan! I am literally going to die! Please God don't let him have seen the almost-hand-up-my-shirt!* But also: *Evan kissed me! Again! Even though he knows people call me Maggot. And despite what Gramps said about his hair!*

Okay, so I would never be able to look Gramps in the eye again, but my heart felt like it was stuck to the ceiling. And it would never come back down.

Later that night, I'd just finished recording a Tove Lo song I'd found on YouTube when my phone beeped. Evan's name glowed from my screen. I put down my bow and reached over to read what he'd sent.

Evan: Hey beautiful

Beautiful! I almost dropped my phone.

Evan: What are you up to?

My heart was doing the weird fluttering thing again and I couldn't help but message back immediately.

Amelia: Just about to upload a new song.

Hope you like it!

Evan was the first person to like my TikTok. We ended

up messaging for ages that night. I sent him the songs I was rehearsing for my solo. He even wanted to see pictures of the best rocks in my collection. I'd never shown anyone except Nisha before. But Evan liked the same kind of things as me. Nature, rock pooling, lizards, reading. It's not like he was officially my boyfriend. I mean, we barely even spoke to each other at school. But it definitely felt like that was the way it was heading. Just as I was about to go to sleep, my phone went off again.

Evan: Goodnight you Mighty Maggot!

My heart stung, as though someone had poured antiseptic all over it. I knew I only had myself to blame. *It's funny!* I'd told him. *Hilarious!* Or something like that. I must have been called Maggot a million times. But now, from Evan, that word hurt more than it ever had before.

25

The next day, the Rockets were playing the Boston Barracudas. I was sitting on the bench next to Poppy and, since the start of the game, I'd barely even looked in Evan's direction. Preston hit a home run and everyone except me leaped up and started cheering.

"Hey," Evan said, taking the spot next to me on the bench as Poppy got up to bat. "Are you mad at me?"

I don't know why that made my heart race so much. It's the weirdest feeling when you like someone in that way. It's frightening actually. Maya Angelou said love "jumps hurdles, leaps fences and penetrates walls". But to me, it felt more like tumbling down a cold well and occasionally being lifted up in the bucket. I kept my eyes on the field and said quietly, "I don't like being called that name, okay?"

It took a while for Evan to reply. "Sorry, Amelia. But

you said you found it funny. I was just making a joke."

"Of course I said that. I felt like a total idiot when you asked me about it."

"Oh." Evan was quiet for a moment. We both watched Poppy slog a low ball halfway across the field. People were jumping and cheering around us. But neither of us moved. "I'm really sorry."

I adjusted my glasses and moved a stray hair out of my eyes. "It's okay," I said. "Just please don't say it again."

"I won't."

There was an awkward silence. There was so much I wanted to say, but none of the right words came into my mind. But I knew there was no point trying to hide the truth when it was so unmistakably obvious. "It's just," I said eventually, "if you thought things were nice or even normal for me at St Clement's Academy, then you were wrong. Big time. Most people don't even like me."

"Yeah, I've started to figure that out."

That's all he said. And even though he didn't say the word maggot again, it hovered between us like a gnat. I waited for him to say, "You're a loser, Amelia Bright, and I cannot be associated with you." My heart suspended its beat while I waited to hear those words. Like a teardrop that hasn't yet fallen. But the weirdest thing was, he never said that at all.

"So, do I still get to hang out with you?" Evan asked. "Out of school, I mean. You want to do something tomorrow?"

"Yes, definitely!" I practically screamed. I tried to turn it into a cough so it didn't sound too enthusiastic. I could barely contain how happy I was. Evan still wanted to know me! Better than that, he wanted to see me! Tomorrow! And to make the day even better, we hammered the Barracudas 15-9.

Only I woke up the next morning to Mum reminding me I'd promised to help her at the shop. Summer is high tourist season in Ravens Bay, so Mum always does a stock take before the schools break up. It's usually a fun day. But all I could think about was having to cancel on Evan. Things still felt precarious now he knew about my maggot reputation at school. The last thing I wanted was to make things worse. I typed out a quick message saying I was sorry but Mum was making me work all day. I added about ten annoyed emojis so he'd know how I felt about it.

"Why are you in such a bad mood?" Hannah asked as she dusted off a box of tambourines. "You've hardly said a word."

"I'm not in a bad mood," I said. "I just have better things

to do than unpaid labour for Mum today, that's all."

Hannah raised her eyebrows. "Oh yeah, what kind of things? Extra maths?"

I threw her a sarcastic smile. "Nothing I'm telling you about."

"Ooooh," she said really loudly. "How mysterious." Then she called, "Mum! Amelia's got some kind of secret life she's not telling us about."

I chucked a lavender cushion at her just as Mum poked her head through the gap in the door. "What's going on in here, girls? You're supposed to be tidying up, not making it messier."

"Amelia says she's sick of doing unpaid labour."

"I didn't say that." I narrowed my eyes at Hannah.

"Is that so? Maybe it's time for a break," Mum said diplomatically. "Go sit in the window and get some sunshine. It's beautiful out there. But very quiet. I think everyone must be at the beach."

"Exactly where I should be right now," I muttered and followed Hannah to the front of the shop. We perched in the window, beside one of Mum's harps that was on display.

"You should play this," Hannah said, brushing her fingers along the strings.

"Oh, don't be silly," Mum said. "I couldn't play in the

window! Everyone would see me." As she said that, an old lady drove past on a mobility scooter.

"Mum," I said, "it's not exactly busy."

"It could be a good way of getting new customers," Hannah said. "No offence, but it doesn't seem like you get that many. We could live stream it. I bet you don't even have TikTok for the shop."

"Yeah, Mum," I said, feeling my mood lift a little. "You should play."

"Oh, okay," Mum said, a smile spreading across her face. "Why not? Let me see if I can tune it up."

Half an hour later, Hannah and I were outside the shop with the door wide open, watching Mum play her harp in the window. A small crowd of tourists had gathered to watch. Hannah was filming it live on TikTok. I'd put some clips on mine too. Mum was playing John Thomas's "Watching the Wheat". It sounds really boring, but it's dreamy and romantic and magical. And watching Mum play it in the window of Harp and Soul, with the wind chimes adding their own melody, I got tingles all over my skin.

Just then I felt a tap on my shoulder and Evan grinned at me. My heart nearly jumped out of my body.

"Amazing!" he said. "I saw it on TikTok. Had to come down and see it for myself. Your mum looks like a princess up there." That was the thing about Evan. He said whatever he thought and didn't care how weird it sounded. That was why I liked him, I suppose. It was kind of contagious.

I looked up at Mum, framed by the window, her hair almost gold in the light. "No," I said. "She looks like a queen."

Evan stayed for almost half an hour watching Mum and talking, then he said, "I'll see you tomorrow, at school?" and flashed me a smile before disappearing down the street.

At school? I repeated in my head. Did this mean he was actually going to speak to me at school? In front of his friends? And as much as I tried to stop it, my heart started doing somersaults. *It's happening*, I thought. *Evan and Amelia: The Official Relationship is finally happening.*

After we'd closed the shop, Mum flopped onto a beanbag in the back room and said, "Right – that's it. I cannot move my arms!"

"Look how much we took, Mum!" Hannah said, pressing a button on the till and showing Mum the receipt that printed out.

"My goodness! Who'd have thought it would make such a difference!"

"Should I order the takeaway?" I asked.

But Mum stopped me. "No, tonight we shall go out for dinner. I think Ravens Bay's best marketing experts deserve a proper treat."

We went to the Nepalese restaurant on the high street and Mum ordered their Ultimate Feast. It was amazing. The waiter kept bringing more and more little silver dishes of the most delicious food, all with a chilli spark or lemongrass tang or spicy sweetness. I ate until I was so full up I couldn't move.

"What a lovely day!" Mum said. "We should do this more often." She took my hand and squeezed it. "You know what I feel like?"

"Slipping into a food coma?" Hannah said with her hands on her belly.

Mum grinned. "How about a moonlight walk along the beach?"

"But, Mum," I said, "it's high tide."

She wafted my words away like they were flies. "Oh, live a little, Amelia!" I think she'd had too much wine. "A barefoot walk along the beach is one of Earth's most wonderful pleasures."

So that was how the three of us ended up with our

jeans pulled up and our shoes in our hands, wading through the sludgy sand all the way home. "This is not one of Earth's most wonderful pleasures," I said as we trudged across the beach. "It's freezing."

But Mum was in some kind of reverie since playing the harp. It was like she'd hypnotized herself. She didn't care that the bottom of her dress was wet, or that her handbag kept dipping into the seawater. She hummed "Watching the Wheat" all the way home, then pulled us both in for a goodnight kiss.

"Check on Gramps, would you?" she said, doing something that I think was supposed to be dancing.

Hannah and I watched as Mum swayed unsteadily up the stairs. "I am never drinking wine when I am Mum's age," Hannah said, and I agreed.

We opened the door to the annexe and Gramps's familiar snore was coming from the bedroom. We giggled, closed the door, then headed upstairs.

"So," Hannah said. "Now you can tell me about that boy you were talking to."

"What boy?"

"The one outside the shop. Don't think I didn't notice the way you looked at him."

I sighed. "He's just…" I was planning on saying he was just someone I knew from baseball. But I guess Mum's hypnotic music must have rubbed off on me because I said, "DREAMY!" and Hannah collapsed on the floor laughing.

"Oh my God, Amelia," she said, wiping tears from the corner of her eyes. "You cannot say that to anyone else, okay? Especially not him!"

"I won't! But…" For a second I wanted to tell Hannah everything about Evan. But I thought maybe I'd jinx it. So instead I said, "He likes geckos."

Hannah smiled. "If he came to Mum's shop to see you, I'd say it's not the gecko he's interested in." She picked up Barnacles, who had been clawing at her leg. "Just…make sure he's nice to you, okay? Goodnight, dreamer." Hannah kissed me on the top of my head, which was the first time she'd kissed me goodnight in years, then closed her bedroom door.

Despite my freezing toes, I went to sleep that night with the warmest feeling in my belly. Mum's harp melody resounded in my ears and Evan's dreamy smile played over and over in my head like a film.

During the next week, I had Orchestra every lunchtime to practise *The Little Mermaid* with the whole cast, so I didn't see Evan at all. But I did get to watch the section of dance that Nisha had choreographed. It was the bit where Ariel dies and gets turned into sea foam. Nisha and the rest of the dancers were playing the sea foam. They were essentially devouring my sister, but somehow Nisha made it heartbreaking and beautiful at the same time. I had tears in my eyes by the end and I stood up to give a standing ovation until Mr Giuliani glared at me.

When it was over, Nisha came over and squeezed my arm. "Can you believe we perform this next week! I just don't want it to end!" I knew exactly how she felt.

That Friday, we performed the dress rehearsal in front of the entire school. It was completely nerve-wracking. I wouldn't be performing my solo, as that was only happening at the real thing – but Tech Club would be filming that for the school social media pages, so everyone would still get to see it. My hands felt sweaty as the teachers ordered their forms to sit silently in rows.

We all played perfectly. There was only a slight hiccup onstage when one of Ursula's tentacles got stuck on the king's trident. Nisha's dance got the biggest applause. When the curtain fell at the end, Mr Giuliani cried, "Bravissimo!" and that's the highest praise you can get in Orchestra.

Mrs Weaver congratulated all of the actors, then she asked me to stand up. "I also want everyone to know that our talented cellist Amelia Bright will be doing a very special performance outside the reception lobby to welcome the audience to St Clement's Academy." Then Mrs Weaver led everyone in another round of applause. I tried my hardest not to look at the audience. The last thing I needed to see right then was DJ's gawping face. But I looked down too late and our eyes met.

He put his hand over his mouth and coughed out, "Maggot: the Musical!" Lachlan and the rest of the boys burst out laughing before Mr Malcolmson told them to be quiet. I did my best to ignore them. I figured once my solo was the talk of the school, they'd have no choice but to leave me alone.

I never dreamed in a million years they would actually *do* anything.

26

The following week, I was allowed to skip PE lessons to practise my solo with Mr Giuliani. He's usually pretty tough the week of the production. Last year, he made at least five people cry during the dress rehearsal. But when I played the pop songs I'd chosen on my cello to him on Wednesday, Mr Giuliani closed his eyes and breathed in, like he was inhaling the music. At the end, he simply said, "Perfetto." And I knew he wouldn't say perfect unless it was.

Finally, Thursday arrived – the opening night of the school production. We'd be performing three nights in a row, but everyone knew opening night was the most pressure.

I scratched off my Word of the Day and felt a new wave of optimism flood my veins.

Cerulean: a deep blue, the colour of a clear sky.

208

No one was going to ruin my solo. Tonight was going to be perfect.

I definitely had a few nerves, because I could feel them churning about in my stomach when I ate an early dinner of cheese on toast. But mostly I felt excited. And proud. That I'd been chosen out of everyone in the orchestra to play outside reception.

Even though she had her own hair and make-up to do, Hannah helped me get ready. She let me wear a black dress she'd grown out of. It came to my knees and was tighter than my usual Orchestra uniform of black trousers and white shirt. And it meant my freckled arms were bare. But Mum and Hannah said it was perfect for a soloist.

"A soloist is allowed to look glamorous," Mum said, taking photos on her phone. "You look amazing, my darling."

Gramps wiped his eyes with his handkerchief and drew me into a hug. "Beautiful, Amelia. Just beautiful."

And maybe it's big-headed, but I thought, for that moment, I actually was beautiful and amazing. I felt so giddy with excitement as we were leaving that I almost forgot my cello.

We had to be there an hour before curtain, so Mum dropped us both off outside school at six.

"Gramps and I will be right there, in the second row," she said, kissing us goodbye. "I am so proud of you both! *In bocca al lupo!*" It's the equivalent of "break a leg" in Italian. My mum's not Italian, but she's spent so long reading Italian musical directions that she's practically fluent.

"*Grazie!*" Hannah and I said back at the same time. "Thanks" and the phrases you find on sheet music were about all the Italian I knew. It was still warm outside, and the sky was full of wispy cirrus clouds that looked like waves, seeming to mirror the sea below. It gave everything this magical feel. I took a deep breath of the warm air as I got out of the car and prayed I'd play my best.

Hannah stopped for a moment just before we parted by reception. "You'll do great, little sis," she said. "No one can play like you."

I had to bite my lips together to stop myself tearing up. Seriously, Hannah is never this nice to me. "Thanks," I said. "You'll do great too. *In bocca al lupo!*" I watched her disappear in the direction of the hall then looked around for Mr Giuliani or anyone from Orchestra. I grabbed a chair from the huge reception lobby and took it outside into the cool evening air, going through my solo in my head. Just the idea of playing outside, in the open air, made my heart soar above the clouds.

I was setting up my music stand while Mr Giuliani and some people from Orchestra were chatting inside. I checked my reflection in the windows, and that's when I saw them. Three of them on bikes. Wearing masks. At first I thought they were just riding past to take a look. I even smiled at them. Then all I heard was, "CATCH!" And I don't know what happened – maybe it was the catching instinct that had been drummed into me since before I could even walk... Because I caught it. Or at least, I caught most of it. It's pretty much impossible to catch an entire bucket of maggots thrown at you.

I froze and squeezed my eyes closed, hoping this was some nightmare I could wake up from. Hot tears ran down my face as the maggots squirmed in my hands and the people on bikes rode off, laughing. I didn't know what to do with the maggots. So I stayed holding them like that until Mr Giuliani came running out.

I still don't know what happened to the maggots. I only know that Mr Giuliani acted like some kind of conductor-superhero. He wiped my hands clean with his silk handkerchief. Then he took me to the toilets to wash my hands, and sat me in the music office and bought me a hot chocolate from the machine.

"Do you want me to call your mum?" he asked. "I can call her right now."

I shook my head. I couldn't face Mum and Gramps seeing me like this. Not when they'd said I looked so good. What would they think? This was supposed to be my big moment. The absolute last thing I wanted was for Mum to discover the truth about me. To have to tell her I was nothing but a useless maggot. I put down the hot chocolate because my hands were shaking and anyway it was burning my fingers.

"You don't have to perform, you know," he said. "I can ask First Violin to—"

"No," I said. "I can play." But as soon as I spoke I started crying. I knew what I needed and it wasn't clean hands or hot chocolate. "Mr Giuliani," I said, "could you go and get my sister?"

27

Hannah ran into the music office and wrapped me in her arms. She smelled of stage dust and hairspray and face paint and big-sisterly love.

"I'm going to kill them," she said. Mr Giuliani coughed, but Hannah didn't care that he'd heard. "I am literally going to find them and kill them. You're so unlucky! To be stood there at that exact moment. I mean, seriously, Amelia."

I tried to laugh, but what came out was more like a snotty grunt. Hannah had no idea that the maggots were intended for me. I'd never told her about what people in my year called me. In fact, I'd done everything I could to hide it from her. I opened my mouth to say something but then closed it again. Maybe it was simpler if she thought it was some freak accident. It was definitely less humiliating. I guess it was one of the perks of being a nobody at school

– at least my sister had no idea I was their target.

"And Ju-Long said you caught them?"

I nodded.

Hannah squeezed me tight; the sequins from her costume pressed into my arms. "I think we both know Dad is to blame for that."

And then I couldn't help laughing. I blew my nose on Mr Giuliani's handkerchief and tried to shake off the knowledge that I was a total maggoty loser.

"Did you recognize any of them?" Mr Giuliani asked. "It all happened so quickly. I'll get the site team to check the CCTV." But he didn't wait for an answer. He bent down so his face was opposite mine. "Are you sure you can play?"

I looked down at my hands. They were still shaking. And my black dress had splotches of maggot juice on it.

Hannah gently nudged me. "Amelia's a Bright," she said. "Of course she can play."

So that's how I found myself back outside reception, this time maggot-free, but the ground still wet from where someone had cleaned up the maggots and a faint stench of disinfectant in the air. The front of my dress felt stiff from where the maggot juice had dried and I couldn't get my fingers to stop trembling. It took a moment to steady my bow. There were already some parents watching me tune up. And a small child running up and down the steps. Mr Giuliani was smiling, but I could tell he was getting annoyed about that. I took a deep breath, and played the first note of "Running Up That Hill".

After the opening bars I knew I would be okay. Mr Giuliani was conducting me by the not-so-subtle nodding of his head. I guess he couldn't help it. I was on the closing few notes when I spotted Mum and Gramps standing by the line of potted bay trees. Their eyes were glistening in the evening sun. I should have felt proud. But I was suddenly aware of the maggot stains on my dress, the smudged mascara underneath my eyes, and the worthlessness those boys must have seen in me when they hurled the contents of that bucket. I messed up the closing bar. I don't think anyone noticed. Except Mum. She would have noticed. And Mr Giuliani. But they still had smiles on their faces. Parents who had gathered around clapped and whooped and cheered. But my heart was like a wrecked ship, and I couldn't play my best when it was floundering.

I somehow made it through the rest of my solo performance.

Mrs Weaver shook my hand at the end. "That was *terrific*, Amelia!" she said. Relief flooded over me. I thought for a second she was going to say *terrible*. She waited for the clapping to die down then said, "Thank you to our wonderful cellist, Amelia, who is only in Year Eight! And already playing like a pro!" A few parents looked surprised when she said that. A tiny molecule of pride made its way to my brain. But it couldn't shift the fog of sadness that had already settled there. I stood and bowed as Mrs Weaver directed everyone to the hall.

Mr Giuliani didn't say "*bravissimo*". I'm glad he didn't because I would have known he was lying. But he did pat me on the shoulder and say, "*Fantastica!*" which I guess was the next best thing.

Everyone in Orchestra went quiet when I came to take my seat, so I knew they'd heard about what happened. Ju-Long gave me the biggest smile and mouthed "You're awesome!" At least I think he did. It was either that or "opossum" but under the circumstances I doubted he'd be telling me about an Australian marsupial.

Benedict sniffed as I rosined my bow and whispered, "What's that smell?"

I ignored him and deliberately angled my elbow so it pointed into his face as I was tuning up.

There was the usual shh-ing and hushing as the lights went down. Mr Giuliani stood up and tapped his baton three times on his rostrum. I cradled my cello, finding comfort feeling its weight in my arms, like an anchor

216

mooring me to the orchestra, letting me know I wasn't alone. There was something about being in that darkness. It was like being in an entirely different world. A perfect one. One where no one gets buckets of maggots chucked over them. A world where I could be swept away into the magic of the music, and not have to worry about who I was in the daylight.

The violins began, then the drums, then all of us as we played a short medley of all the songs in almost pitch black, with just a blue glow from the stage curtains and our tiny spotlights so we could read our music. Chimes played and the curtains opened to reveal Ariel sitting on a rock, centre stage. She was no longer my sister, but a mermaid with the most striking red hair and hauntingly beautiful voice. I tried to stay focused on playing, but the sheet music went blurry as tears flooded my eyes. It was a good job I'd learned everything off by heart, because I had totally lost my place.

She sang of belonging to a different world, a different place, a different life. I felt every note, every word as though it sank into my skin. In the orchestra, I was a different person. First Cello. Something of a pro and sister to the most incredible mermaid who trades her whole life for love. Even Benedict's conceited face couldn't ruin that moment for me.

28

The first half went by without another hitch. The final scene before the interval was Ariel making the pact with the sea witch to trade her voice for legs so she can date the prince. Or in this case, Andre Walker in Year Ten. I angled my body so I could see the stage better. I didn't want to miss Nisha's bit when she held up the scroll. Benedict's massive head did get in the way slightly, but I got to see Nisha's incredible "Poor Unfortunate Souls" dance before I felt Mr Giuliani's eyes burning into the side of my face.

By the time Hannah and the rest of the cast gathered for the final bow, I had almost forgotten about the maggots entirely. And the real world that I had to go back to. The one where I permanently played a worthless nobody.

It felt cold in the car park as we waited for Mum to find her keys. "You both did brilliantly, absolutely brilliantly!" she said, rummaging around in her handbag.

"Yes!" Gramps added. "What an amazing night! Just perfect!"

"Not exactly a perfect night," Hannah said. I gave her a look that said *DO NOT MENTION THE MAGGOTS!* but clearly she didn't get the message. "Some idiots chucked maggots over Amelia."

"What!" Mum and Gramps said at the same time. Mum almost dropped the car keys.

"I know," Hannah said. "Probably some Year Elevens. They sometimes come back after exams and pull pranks like that. Mr Giuliani is getting the site manager to check the CCTV."

Mum pulled me into her arms. "Oh, my poor girl." The familiar smell of her blossomy perfume felt like home.

"How awful," Gramps said. "I don't understand kids nowadays."

"Yeah, and you want to know the worst thing?" Hannah said, a tiny smirk on her face. "Amelia actually caught them! It's a shame Dad wasn't there to see it. He'd have been impressed. I wonder if we can arrange for them to come back on Saturday night."

"Hannah, stop!" Mum said, squeezing me tighter. "It must have been horrible. Maggots! I cannot imagine anything worse."

And that was probably what stopped me from telling

them the whole story. The words: *I cannot imagine anything worse.* How could I tell them that, actually, this is what everyone at school thinks I am? The worst thing you can imagine.

"It's no big deal," I said. "Just a freak accident. I was in the wrong place at the wrong time."

"Wrong reaction," Hannah added. "Next time, try to duck."

Mum nudged Hannah. "I'm sure there won't be a next time!"

"I hope the school is going to do something about these hooligans," Gramps said as Mum helped him into the car.

"They will, Gramps," I said. "There's CCTV outside reception so I'm sure they'll catch whoever it was." As if I couldn't guess who was behind it. "But honestly, it's not a big deal. No one got hurt." Which was probably the biggest lie I've ever told.

"Unless you count the maggots," Hannah said. "I'm guessing they didn't survive." Mum gave Hannah a look as we got into the back seat. "I mean, it's horrible," she added. "And you did brilliantly to play despite the, erm, obvious maggot residue."

"I think you'd better let your sister have a shower first tonight," Mum said, getting into her seat and squirming.

"Urgh, maggots. How utterly revolting! You really are unlucky, sweetheart. It's amazing you played at all tonight, let alone with so few mistakes."

My phone glowed with a message from Evan: **Heard what happened. You okay?** But I swiped it away. How could he ever bring himself to kiss me now? I even disgusted myself.

Mum pulled up in front of the school entrance and waited for the cars in front of us to pull out. "Maggots!" she said, tutting and shaking her head. "How cruel."

"I know," Hannah said. "I'm talking to Ms Romero about it tomorrow. I mean, what the hell?"

"Hopefully it will get sorted out," Mum said. "Try not to worry about it, Hannah. What's done is done. The main thing is that Amelia's okay."

"They ought to put maggots down their bleeding trousers!" Gramps said. "That'd teach 'em!"

I closed my eyes, trying to block out their words and imagine I was somewhere else. But I could feel tears forming behind my eyelids and my bottom lip wouldn't stop trembling. "Can we please just go home?"

"Well, they won't get away with it," Hannah said, typing something into her phone. "The school probably won't do anything, but I'll make sure no one tries to ruin our production night again." She leaned over and stroked

221

my head. "Oh, you do kind of stink, actually."

Maybe it should have made me feel better – not being told I stank, but Hannah having my back and everything. But it just made me feel even more worried. I'd managed to hide the maggot thing from her for almost two years and now there it was – clinging to the front of her old dress. I turned my head towards the window. It was dark enough that Hannah and Mum couldn't see the tears in my eyes, so I let them fall unnoticed. Mum said what a brilliant production it was and how she'd cried at the end when Hannah turned into sea foam. But it was like they were a million miles away. I was trapped underwater, in this reeking maggoty world, and there was nothing I could do to escape.

29

I cried myself to sleep that night. I hadn't done that since Year Seven. I could still feel the cold slimy maggots squirming around in my hands, even though I'd scrubbed them ten times. I had messages and missed calls from Nisha, but I couldn't face speaking to anyone. The knowledge that I had to go into school in the morning to face everybody collected like bile in my stomach.

As soon as I woke up on Friday morning, I genuinely felt sick. I pleaded with Mum to let me take the day off, but as usual the shop came first.

"Amelia, I'm getting a big delivery at the shop today. I can't possibly stay at home with you."

"I'll stay on my own!" I begged. "I really do feel sick."

"And what about the production tonight? And tomorrow?" She put her hands on her hips. This really was going badly. "You can't be sick for school then play this evening. Come on, up you get."

I got out of bed with a heart heavier than a grand piano. My mood was in no way improved when I scratched off my Word of the Day.

Repugnant: causing a feeling of strong dislike or disgust.

And a message from Evan saying, **Hope you're okay. Must have been disgusting** 🤮🤮🤮

An ocean of truth lay before me. I was *disgusting*. *Repugnant.* I was the sick emoji in human form. And people like that do not get to be liked. If people called me Maggot before, it was only going to get worse now I had actually touched maggots with my bare hands. Mrs King had said maggots were fascinating. But she wouldn't say that if she'd been the one to catch a bucketful of them. I sat back down on my bed, wondering if there was any way I could stay at home without Mum finding out.

"Hey," Hannah said, poking her head around my bedroom door. "Mum said you want to skip school."

I had a million words swimming around in my head, but the only ones that came out were, "Everybody hates me." And then about ten thousand tears.

Hannah sat down on the bed, wrapping her arms around me so my head was squashed against her chest. It must have been ages since she'd done that because her boobs felt a lot bigger. "Nobody hates you, sis," she said.

And handed me the tissue box from my desk.

I blew my nose and sat up. "They do. They think I'm a maggot."

"Amelia," Hannah said. "Nobody thinks you're a maggot. You were just unlucky, that's all! They could have landed on anyone."

I fiddled with the edge of my bedsheet, thinking how now would be the perfect time to tell Hannah the truth about the maggot thing. But for some reason I couldn't bring myself to say it out loud. I didn't want her to know how much of a gigantic failure I was. So I nodded, and wiped away my tears.

"Listen," Hannah said. "You're so talented. You played amazingly, even after what happened. Your TikToks are next level brilliant. Tell you what – let's make one together. After the production's finished, I mean. We could even film one down at the beach!"

I smiled. "The sea air would ruin my cello, but yes. I'd love to make one together."

Before she left my room, Hannah hugged me again. "You're awesome, Amelia, don't ever forget it. You can't let everyone in the orchestra down because of a few stupid maggot-tossers."

And it was sort of exactly what I needed to hear.

Tolkien said that courage can be found in unlikely

places. I guess he was right. Because somehow I managed to find some at the bottom of a bucket of maggots. If those idiots on bikes thought I would be defeated by some slimy multi-eyed grub, then they had another think coming. I put my uniform on, gave Morph's spiky scales a few extra kisses, grabbed my cello and left the house with my head held high. Okay, not exactly high, but not looking down at the pavement either.

Nisha messaged saying she'd walk to school with me, and just seeing her made me feel like I could handle anything anyone said.

"Remember," she said as we neared the school gates, "the production was a massive success. The audience loved it. Everyone was raving about your solo."

"And your final dance number," I added.

"Exactly," Nisha said. "You've got no reason to feel anything but proud."

But she still agreed with me that we should spend break and lunch in the library to avoid everyone.

It was breaktime when I saw it. I checked my phone while I was in the library office. Of course they had filmed it. I don't know why I was stupid enough not to consider the possibility of them documenting the entire event.

"Hey," Nisha said, watching my face fall. "What is it?"

"Maggot: The Movie," I said. "For real this time."

Nisha moved so she could see my screen and I tapped for it to play again. And there I was. In Hannah's black dress with my hair done specially, performing what can only be described as one of my best catches of the baseball season. But with maggots.

"Oh my God, Amelia. We have to show Mr Malcolmson."

"Are you kidding?" I said. "He'll probably make some sarcastic comment about me catching them."

"Mrs Gordon then?" she replied. "We have to tell someone! It's been uploaded by a new account. Look, Lachlan shared it, so maybe he knows who uploaded it. Don't you want them to get caught?"

"Yes, I do!" I said. "And given some gruesome punishment like maggots down their pants, as Gramps suggested, or the electric chair or something. But if I go to Mrs Weaver everyone will hate me even more than they do already."

Nisha smiled and pointed at Mrs Gordon by the photocopier. "So let's tell her. No one would know Mrs Gordon isn't on TikTok."

I sighed and stood up. "I guess."

* * *

"It's rather shaky," Mrs Gordon said, replaying the video as I relived my bucket of maggots moment for the third time. "I mean, you can barely tell what's happening."

"I know, Mrs Gordon," Nisha said impatiently. "But this Baby Nachos account has called it 'Maggot: The Movie'. And that's obviously outside school. There's the sign! That's Amelia, look at the cello case next to the chair. And you cannot deny that's her hair." At least being bright ginger had its uses.

"Okay, send the video to me," Mrs Gordon said, then tutted a few times as she tried unsuccessfully to log in to her email. "Although I have to say, I've never heard of this Baby Nachos. Do they go to a different school?"

"Just forward it to Mrs Weaver so she can investigate." Nisha smiled and squeezed my hand.

I sighed. "Do you really think she can find out who @im.baby.nachos is?"

"At least she'll see who's shared it," Nisha said.

Mrs Gordon tutted again as she polished her glasses on a tissue. "I don't know. If only young people would read books instead of going on these dreadful websites…"

We could tell she was about to start one of her "In my day" speeches, so Nisha nudged her hand towards the mouse and said, "Just forward it to Mrs Weaver. She'll know what to do."

* * *

I don't know how many times the video had been shared by the time Mrs Gordon finally sent the email. It hadn't gone viral or anything, which I guess is something to be grateful for. But by lunchtime practically the entire school knew me as "Oh my God, that's the girl who caught maggots". And even though the video disappeared an hour or so later, it's not like anyone was going to forget it. In between lessons, people shouted "CATCH!" as they walked past me in the corridors, and everyone laughed when I jumped.

During my maths lesson, Mr Harding appeared at the classroom door and asked to speak to me. Everyone knew what it was about. I followed him down to the Student Services office and had to write a statement about what had happened. One of the questions on the paper was, *Were there any other students involved?*

I hovered my pen over it for a moment, wondering what to write.

Obviously, my prime suspect was DJ. But there was no way of proving it. The video of the maggot attack wasn't even on his social media. He was keeping suspiciously quiet about the whole thing. Ju-Long had told me at lunchtime that Jayden's dad owned the fishing tackle shop in town. I assumed they sold maggots. I wondered if the shop had CCTV. Perhaps I should suggest it to the school to help their investigation.

Mr Harding watched me hesitating. "Write as much as you know, Amelia. It's a serious matter and we want to catch whoever did this. Sadly they were wearing masks, so the CCTV is rather useless."

He told me to take my time, but I didn't want to miss my whole maths lesson. Besides, my class had seen Mr Harding come and get me, so if DJ or Jayden got accused, it would be obvious it came from me. Wouldn't that make my life a million times worse?

I sighed and wrote, *I couldn't see who threw the maggots because they were wearing masks,* and told Mr Harding I was finished.

But on the way back to maths I couldn't get rid of this burning sense of injustice. I hadn't done anything wrong! I didn't deserve the name Maggot. And I certainly didn't deserve to have thousands of them thrown at me. The more I thought about it, the angrier I felt. With myself more than anyone. I should have named every one of the idiots who'd ever called me Maggot on Mr Harding's Incident Statement. Although I'd have needed a much bigger piece of paper.

Later, as I was leaving school, someone chucked a half-eaten doughnut at me and shouted, "CATCH!" Only then this heat bubbled up in my brain, and some words from *Jane Eyre* came bursting into my mind: *"Unjust!—unjust!" said my reason.* So I did catch it. Then I threw it back like a fastball, right at their head. A perfect hit.

Hannah laughed as she fell into step beside me and shouted, "Any of you try that again at my sister, and you'll have my pitching arm to deal with as well!"

And weirdly, no one threw anything at me after that.

30

I thought Dad would let me off baseball on Saturday considering Mum had told him what I'd been through with the maggots. Plus, I'd performed for two nights running and still had one more performance to go. I pleaded with Dad to let me sit this game out. But like I said – nothing matters more to my dad than baseball.

I knew as soon as I got into the car that he was going to mention the maggots. Selina had this sympathetic look on her face. The kind you might give an animal about to be put down. Which was slightly more reassuring than my dad, who looked like all the blood vessels in his face had burst.

"I don't understand how the school could let this happen!" he said, slamming one of his hands on the steering wheel.

"It was outside reception," I said. "It's not like they have security guards."

"Well, I'm not happy," he said, breathing out so hard I could hear it over the radio. "And what are they doing about it exactly? Your mother says they haven't even caught the little—"

"Mike," Selina said, putting a perfectly manicured hand on his thigh. "I'm sure Amelia would rather us talk about something else." She smiled at me over her shoulder. I felt like weeping, I was so grateful. "Like how well she did to play that night. And how much we're looking forward to seeing her and Hannah perform tonight." She did a sort of squeal and her shoulders rose up. "I can't wait!" It reminded me that I still hadn't mentioned to Hannah that Selina was coming. I wondered if Dad would let me borrow one of the baseball helmets to wear when I told her.

Dad sighed. "You're right, honey." He patted Selina's hand then looked at me in the rear-view mirror. "At least you didn't get hurt, huh?" I nodded, even though I did get hurt by those maggots. It's just the injuries were kind of internal. "So, are we going to whip these Wolves or what!"

"Yep," I said half-heartedly. The last thing on earth I felt like doing was playing baseball. Or seeing Evan. He hadn't replied to my last couple of messages. I had no idea if he was out of credit. Or if the maggots had finished us for good.

"So," Dad said. "Let me hear you howl!" I blinked a few times, not sure if he was serious. He was. "Come on, Number Three!" he said as we pulled into the car park. "Howl like we are gonna shred these guys!"

I don't know what possessed me to do it. Other than my dad was staring at me expectantly and I didn't want to let the side down. I also knew he'd never let up until I did it. So, I let out the loudest possible howl I could. And I have to say, it was weirdly gratifying. Like a primal scream. Only right at that moment Evan opened my car door.

"Hooooowl to you too!" he said, laughing. My face turned the exact colour of a tomato.

"Evan!" Dad said, slapping his back and filling his arms with as many baseball bats as he could carry. "Good to see you here nice and early. That's commitment! See, Amelia? Now come with me and we'll talk tactics."

So before I even had a chance to say hi, Evan was following my dad to the dugout, leaving me standing by the car with Selina.

"Want a protein bar?" she asked, taking one out of her bag. "I thought maybe you'd need some energy today. School productions are pretty tiring if I remember rightly!"

"Thanks," I said, taking the bar. "You did school productions?"

"I played Frenchie in *Grease* once, that was probably the highlight of my musical career."

"So you sing?"

She waved her hand in front of her face. "Oh, nothing like the standard Hannah's at. But, you know, I can belt out a power ballad on karaoke if I have to." She smiled and I smiled back, forgetting about the pact I'd made with Hannah to freeze Selina out. It's impossible to freeze someone out when they're as warm as Selina. "Did I tell you I used to get picked on at school?"

I did a double take. "What?"

"Yeah," she said, sipping from her reusable cup. "I had to change schools when I was fourteen, it got so bad."

I could not imagine Selina getting bullied. She was beautiful! "But," I said, "you're so…" And I didn't know why but nothing else came out.

Selina gently squeezed my arm. "I know you've got Mike and your mum and sister and everything, but you can always talk to me about stuff. If you want to. I hope you know that." I nodded, not wanting her to take her hand away. "School can be the pits. But, you know, life gets a lot better afterwards."

Just then, my dad's voice came booming over from the dugout. "AMELIA! WHAT ARE YOU WAITING FOR? GET OVER HERE!"

235

Selina frowned. "Mike takes it all quite seriously, doesn't he?" Which was the understatement of the season.

During the game, Dad turned practically tyrannical, shouting non-stop instructions from beside the dugout until the umpire had to tell him to lighten up. But somehow it worked, because we beat the Warrington Wolves 16-11.

"*Howl's* it going?" Evan said to me as I was packing up my kit.

"Funny," I replied, trying not to let him see that my hands were shaking.

"Sorry," he said, then, "I'm sorry about the whole maggots thing too."

"Thanks," I replied. "But it's hardly your fault."

"I know, but I'm friends with them and—"

I almost dropped my bag. "You know who did it?"

Evan's eyes widened and he stayed silent for a moment. Then he swallowed and said, "Well, not exactly. Not for sure. I just heard—"

"What did you hear?" The hairs on the back of my neck stood up and my heart began to thump so loudly I could hear it in my ears. "Tell me."

Evan rubbed his hand over his face. "It's just…they're my friends, you know. And I'm new to the school." He kicked the dirt around a little bit, then wiped his trainer on the grass. "I don't want to make enemies."

I could hardly believe what I was hearing. "You're not going to tell anyone? After what they did to me?"

"Amelia," Evan said. "It's just that…if they found out it was me…I can't say anything. I'm sorry."

My heart was being ripped apart. Evan was like two different people. One person to me and someone else to them. Maybe I was stupid for expecting him to put me first. But protecting the people who did that to me? My heart was yelling at me that THIS IS NOT OKAY! So, I can't really explain it – the difference between what I felt inside and what I said out loud. In one of his letters to Fanny Brawne, Keats said, "I have so much of you in my heart". Well, it's possible I had too much of Evan Palmer in mine. Because the words in my head got drowned out and the ones that came out of my mouth were, "It's okay. I understand."

"You do?" Evan squeezed my hand and dotted a quick kiss on my cheek. "You're amazing, Amelia! I'll message you later."

As soon as he was gone I blinked, and felt warm, useless tears slide down my face.

31

The finale of *The Little Mermaid* should have felt exciting. But instead I just felt numb. And relieved that I wouldn't have to go through it all again after this.

"Don't forget your dad and Selina are watching tonight," Mum said as she drove through the traffic lights by school. "Dad said they'll bring you home afterwards, so don't take ages getting changed, Hannah, okay?"

"Wait, *Selina's* coming?" I'd neglected to tell Hannah about accidentally inviting Selina along. Mainly because I valued my own life. "Stop the car."

"Oh, Hannah, please don't start this again. I'm sure Selina's looking forward to seeing you both perform. The poor woman's had to watch goodness knows how many baseball games." Mum caught my eye in the rear-view mirror. "No offence, sweetheart. But they do drag on and your dad gets unbearable."

"Fine," Hannah said. "I can handle sharing air space with Selina for less than a mile. I doubt she can apply fake tan on me in that time."

"Good. And no sarcastic remarks," Mum said. "Unless they're in the script. Now, *in bocca al lupo,* my darlings."

"*Grazie*," we both chimed. And we stood there for a moment while Mum drove off.

Hannah batted me on the arm. "I take it you knew Botox Brain was coming tonight?"

"I had an inkling," I said. "But I was hoping she'd have realized she's not welcome." Even as I said it, I felt like I was betraying Selina. It was really hard to remember I wasn't supposed to like her.

"I know, right. Probably too much for her pea-sized brain," Hannah said, putting her bag on her shoulder. I doubted Selina's brain was actually pea-sized considering she was a fully qualified accountant, but I didn't contradict her. "Anyway, hope it goes well tonight, little sis. *In bocca al lupo*."

"*Grazie*," I said.

Hannah turned back around. "And even a sniff of fish bait tonight, you…?"

"Run." I smiled. "I know. Or use Mr Giuliani as a human shield."

"You got it." And I watched her walk down the corridor.

239

* * *

That night, I tried to play my solo outside reception better than I'd played on the other two nights put together. But my heart just wasn't in it. The belief that this solo might somehow change my life had disappeared. And it suddenly felt a bit meaningless. I spotted Dad and Selina in the crowd listening to me. Selina's blue dress was more sequined than Hannah's costume, and it sparkled in the sunlight. I closed my eyes and allowed the music to wrap itself around me. I knew every note, every pause, every movement. My cello and I were perfectly in sync. But it didn't feel magical. The atmosphere was probably electric, but it was like I'd been unplugged.

I stood up and smiled as Mrs Weaver said the exact same thing about me that she'd said the past two nights, word for word. Like she'd learned a script. Then Dad hugged me so hard he lifted me off my feet.

"Sensational, Amelia! You smashed it!" He gave me a one-person round of applause which was probably louder than when everyone was clapping. It felt really good. Dad heaping praise on me like that without a "But..." was pure sunlight, and I must have grown a foot taller just in that second. Then he added, "But you gotta keep your eyes open, kid," and broke the spell.

"It was amazing, Amelia!" Selina said, pulling me towards her and kissing me on the cheek. "I cannot believe you can play like that at thirteen. It's unreal! You must work so hard."

"Thanks." I waited for her to add something negative like Dad, but she didn't. "I have to join the orchestra in the hall now."

"Hey, don't let us hold you up, honey," Dad said. "Looks like it's time for us to go in anyway." He leaned down and kissed me on my head. He probably got a mouthful of hairspray but he didn't complain. "Listen – make us proud, okay? Meet you here after the show."

"We're already proud of you," Selina whispered. She took my dad's hand and they headed towards the hall.

And as I carried my cello to the hall, dodging parents and children, that word stuck in my head. *We. We* are already proud of you. Dad and Selina were a "we". And she was proud of me as well? Selina wasn't just a temporary glitch. Temporary glitches didn't feel proud of you after a cello performance and kiss you on the cheek.

Selina *loved* Dad. Maybe she even loved *us*. Or me at least. I hadn't heard her say anything like that to Hannah. Although she probably would if Hannah gave her the chance. I watched them wait in line to get into the hall, laughing about something and gazing at each other so hard they hadn't even noticed the queue had moved forward. Selina looked back at me and smiled, holding up two crossed fingers. My heart felt weird. Because I was supposed to hate Selina. That's what Hannah said anyway. But actually, right then, I wanted nothing more than to run over and hug her. Lose myself in her sequins and her warmth and ask her to shield me from the entire world.

To celebrate the end of the show, Nisha invited all the dancers over to her house for a party the next afternoon, and Hannah and I were invited too. I was ridiculously excited. It was the first party I'd been invited to when there would be actual popular people there. Nisha was used to it because she got to hang out with them at Dance Club. But for me, this was legendary. Hannah helped me select my outfit – jeans with the T-shirt Mum's friend Yvonne had bought me for my birthday that said *Fearless Girl*. Not that I was exactly fearless. My track record at befriending popular people was exactly zero. It would have been more appropriate if it said *Girl Scared To Death*.

Nisha hugged me excitedly as she answered the door. Her parents had made about a hundred different dishes, and the house smelled like one of those restaurants that makes your mouth water as soon as you walk in the door.

All the dancers were there. Even the ones in Year Ten. Nisha went to speak to some girls I recognized from the production, then Zadie Ali and Andre Walker started walking towards me.

"Hey, Amelia," Zadie said. "You okay?" I nodded, trying as hard as I could to swallow the onion bhaji I'd just put in my mouth without moving my lips. It was definitely a choking hazard. But when one of the most popular girls in school talks to you, you have to risk these things. "We heard what happened on opening night," she said, "with the maggots." My heart slowly sank, like the bhaji making its way down my oesophagus. "I'm so mad about it," Zadie added. I felt like I should apologize, as though it was my fault it happened. But I still had bits of bhaji in my mouth and anyway, she said, "If you find out who it was, let me know, okay?"

"Yeah, and me," Andre said. "They won't get away with ruining opening night like that."

"And you know that cleaner at school who's like ninety years old?" Zadie said. "She had to clean it up, apparently. It's just wrong." Zadie shook her head. One of her black curls got stuck to her lip balm. As she moved it, I noticed she had brown freckles over her nose. Some of them were joined up like mine. I smiled at the thought that I had something in common with Zadie Ali.

"Thanks," I said. "Hannah thinks it was some Year Elevens pulling a prank. I guess I got caught up in a random drive-by maggot hurling! I am seriously unlucky," I said, laughing. Only they gave each other a strange look and neither of them laughed.

"We know they call you Maggot, Amelia," Andre said, at the exact moment the song finished. Everybody in the room looked over. "My brother's in your class."

"They call you Maggot?" Hannah called from the other side of the room. "What do you mean, they call Amelia *Maggot?*"

I forgot all about the warm spices on my tongue, and the sunlight beaming through the living room windows onto my neck, and the gentle chords of the next song starting. Because as soon as Hannah said those words, I felt like I'd been split right open. And my worthless insides were visible for all to see. I dropped my plate on the table and ran out of the door as quickly as I could.

Hannah shouted at me to wait, but I didn't stop. I ran down the cobbled steps at the end of Nisha's street and onto the beach. I didn't care about missing out on Nisha's party, the only party I was ever likely to attend with Year Tens. I needed to feel the sea breeze on my face, squash myself into the big split in the rocks at the end of the bay, and pretend what Hannah heard wasn't true. That the word *maggot* didn't even exist. As though I could rub it out like I did with my mistakes on paper. But there it was. Attached to me like a shadow. And no matter what I did or said, no matter how hard I tried, or how good I was at anything, I would never outrun it.

There was a message from Evan on my phone asking how my solo went last night. But I didn't feel like replying. He was probably just checking his stupid friends hadn't done anything else.

It didn't take long for Hannah to find me. We'd named the split in the rocks as our alcove years ago, so I guess she knew where I'd be. Only one of us could fit in it at a time now so Hannah sat on a nearby rock and looked out to sea. The wind caught her hair, and she looked like Ariel all over again.

"You're going to miss my song," she said. "Nisha's asked me to perform."

"Sorry." I picked up a smooth black stone and brushed off the sand. "I need some fresh air."

Hannah put her head on one side and smiled at me. "That's what Gramps says when he goes out for one of his cigarillos."

"Gramps still *smokes*?"

Hannah smiled. "Seems like he's not the only one keeping secrets." I looked down at the sand, too ashamed to meet her eye. "You could have told me, you know," she said. "About the name they call you. Because now I feel really bad about all the stuff I said about you catching them."

I hated that Hannah knew. But I loved that she didn't say the word. I guess her big sister intuition could be pretty strong sometimes.

"You're supposed to tell me this kind of stuff," Hannah said, passing a stone to me. "That's the whole point of having a big sister." I looked at her for a moment, then looked away. I got that weird itchy feeling in my nose so I knew I was about to cry. I turned the stone over in my hands, examining the white speckled pattern, like tiny raindrops. I put it in my pocket.

"I couldn't," I said. "Every time I hear that word I feel like the world's most gigantic loser."

"Well, you're not," Hannah replied. "They're losers for calling you that."

"It's not just that," I said, squinting into the sun. "They made this list about the girls in my year."

"A list?" Hannah said. "What kind of list? Or do I really need to ask?"

"The worst kind," I replied. "It's been deleted now. But I was at the bottom. The very bottom. *Part reptile, part fungus* is what it said next to my name."

Hannah breathed out and bit her bottom lip, like she was stopping bad words from coming out. "Did you tell anyone?"

I shook my head. "I mean, there were horrible things written about loads of us. Nisha too. But no, it's not like any of us decided to broadcast it."

"Oh, Amelia. I would have stuck up for you if you'd told me! I could have helped."

"I didn't want you to know how much everybody hates me. I thought I could get them to like me, to change their minds, only…" I scraped a piece of flint along the wall of the alcove, listening to the waves and the distant shrieking of gulls. "Nothing works."

"You know, when I first started at St Clement's I used to get 'ginger' shouted at me constantly. Jackson Reed in my class said I was a genetic mutation."

"But I thought you'd always been popular…I mean, you got Head Girl."

"That doesn't mean that everybody likes me," Hannah said. "I told you and Mum and Dad that everything was fine when I started. Same as you, I guess. I didn't want them to think badly of me."

"So how did it stop? How did you change their minds?"

"It didn't stop, Amelia," Hannah said. "There are still people who say the same stupid stuff now. Even more so whenever I do a performance at school. But you know what I call it?" I swallowed and looked into Hannah's eyes. I thought maybe she was going to cry or something because her eyes were watery, but she didn't look upset. She looked defiant. "I call it background noise. That stuff is in the background and I am centre stage. I'm the one who is doing what I want, what I love, in the spotlight. Background noise will only ever be that. And you know what drowns it out?"

"What?"

"Applause. Come on." Hannah dusted off her hands and stood up on the rock. "As you don't want to come back to the party…"

Oh God, I thought. *She's going to sing.*

There were loads of families nearby, and a few people paddling in the water. Hannah smiled. And I knew immediately what she was thinking. *An audience.* I moved a little further out of our alcove. Hannah cleared her throat, hummed her scales, then began. I immediately recognized the opening words. "Titanium".

She held out her hand to pull me up on the rock. I shook my head. There were way too many people around. "Come on!" Hannah urged then practically pulled my arm out of my socket.

And at that moment, as me and my big sister and her

even bigger voice sang on that rock, my skin went all goose-pimpled. But not from the cold. By the time we had finished, every person on the beach was clapping. And I felt like, with every word we sang, with every bit of applause, a tiny bit of titanium went into my heart. I didn't exactly feel like I was bulletproof or anything. But I didn't feel like a maggot either. I felt like a Bright.

32

The next week at school was full of that excitement and chaos you get when it's almost the summer holidays. Teachers let us watch movies, and generally tried to pretend they weren't as excited as us to get out of St Clement's Academy for six weeks. Mr Malcolmson let us have a mini party in form time. This mainly involved listening to really loud rock music and watching him play air guitar. DJ and his friends took it in turns to down cups of Coke to see who could burp the loudest. The kind of memories you can never erase from your mind no matter how hard you try.

Nisha was flying to India the weekend we broke up. Even though I was not looking forward to her leaving, I couldn't wait for the final bell to ring. It meant I wouldn't have to hear the word *maggot* for six weeks.

What I didn't know was that soon I'd be wishing for

that name back. Because the words it was replaced with were a million times worse.

On the first day of the summer holidays Hannah woke me up early to make a TikTok. Now school had finished, I could focus on boosting my popularity online. And hopefully undo some of the damage the maggot video had done. Only it didn't work out the way I'd hoped. The piece Hannah wanted me to play was way harder than anything I'd ever played before and she kept getting annoyed with me when I made mistakes.

"Sorry, Hannah, but this piece is way above my grading," I tried to explain. But Hannah had basically turned into our dad overnight.

"I don't want to hear excuses, Amelia," she said. "Just play the right notes!" As if it was that simple. My fingers were practically red raw and my eardrums were ringing from playing the same section again and again.

"It's easy for you," I said, resting my bow arm on the side of my cello. "All you have to do is sing."

Hannah glared at me. "*All* I have to do is sing?"

"I mean, not *all* you have to do," I said. "I know singing is really, um, hard."

Hannah sighed and massaged her temples with her

fingers. "Singing is a form of *art*, Amelia. It's not like I was *born* being able to sing soprano."

I thought back to our childhood. I was pretty sure I could remember six-year-old Hannah singing "Let It Go" so high it made my ears hurt.

"Come on," she said. "Try this section one more time and pay attention." She tapped my sheet of music and hummed the tune.

I took a deep breath, resisted the urge to salute, and readied my bow. But as soon as I began I messed up again.

Hannah looked at me like I'd done it deliberately.

"Sorry," I said. "It's just it's basically impossible to play Lady Gaga on the cello. Can't we do something else? A bit easier? Please? Otherwise we'll be practising this all summer."

"Okay," she said. "Forget 'Born This Way'. What about 'Shallow'?" I looked at her blankly and she rolled her eyes. "That duet from *A Star is Born*?" She began singing the chorus as she typed into her phone.

"Oh yeah, I like that one," I said. "But…a duet? Really? I mean my voice is *okay*, it's just not exactly amazing, but if you think…"

Hannah coughed. "Obviously I'll sing both parts."

"Right!" I said, trying not to show how deflated I felt. "That's what I was going to suggest."

I spent the afternoon practising and by dinner time

we were ready. Which meant that our first recording had Mum yelling, "Dinner's ready!" halfway through so we had to delete it.

"Whatever you were playing up there sounded wonderful," Gramps said as he twizzled his fork into his spaghetti.

"Thanks, Gramps," I said.

"We're making a TikTok," Hannah added.

"So do we get to see you live or do we have to watch it on one of your little screens?" Mum asked.

Hannah looked at me. "Want to do it after dinner?"

"Sure." I nodded.

"In that case, I might dress up for the show!" said Gramps.

"You mean give my dressing gown the night off?" Mum asked. "This is a special occasion! Should I break out the champagne?"

Gramps laughed. "How about I make us some minty lemonades? It's been ages since I've done that."

Mum got up, put her arms around Gramps and planted a kiss on his head. "That sounds perfect, Dad."

After dinner, Hannah and I practised a couple more times then she let me get ready in her room. We decided to wear matching colours. Well, kind of. Hannah instructed me to wear black. Then she put my hair up in a messy bun the same as hers and put this sparkly gel on my eyelids that stung a bit.

"There," she said, taking a step back and looking at us both in the mirror. "Okay, ready. We'll do 'Titanium' as an encore. You know that off by heart, right?" It was a good job I did because Hannah didn't wait for an answer.

The evening sunlight poured through the living room windows, creating a pinky-orange glow. Barnacles padded in and hissed at me for no reason. Hannah scooped him up in her arms and he immediately began purring as she covered his face with kisses. She went to put him on the sofa between Mum and Gramps but they said, "No way!" at the same time.

"That cat can watch from a safe distance over there," Mum said, pointing to his basket in the corner.

"Fine," Hannah said. "But it's no wonder he doesn't like any of you when you don't even treat him like part of the family. Ready?" she asked me. Like I hadn't been sitting there in position for the past five minutes. "Okay, Mum, you can start recording."

I began playing the introduction and felt the room dissolve away. My bow felt light as air and I barely needed to glance at the music. Like it was already part of my DNA. Hannah began singing and I felt the little hairs on my arms creep up. I opened my eyes and saw the smiles on Mum and Gramps's faces. I looked over at Hannah. She reached her arms up along with the climax of the chorus as she belted out the lines. Even Gramps was singing along and I'm pretty sure he'd never heard the song before.

Just as Hannah predicted, Gramps and Mum called for an encore the second we finished. I nodded at Hannah and began the opening section of "Titanium". I closed my eyes. It felt like my heart was soaring out of the window and all the way up to the sky. The music went through me in waves, resonating through my body, enveloping me with its magic. I felt untouchable then. Sort of special. Like I was part of Hannah and she was part of me and we both belonged in this moment.

"Beautiful," Mum said, wiping her eyes. "Just beautiful."

My eyelashes felt a little damp too. Hannah took my hand and we did a bow. Mum and Gramps whooped and applauded while Barnacles gave me his standard one-eyed glare. And later, when Hannah squealed that our TikTok already had over four hundred likes, it felt like the best ever start to the summer. Okay, so tomorrow Nisha would be heading to a completely different continent. But Year Eight was finally behind me and I could spend six glorious weeks becoming the best ever version of Amelia Bright. And work on never having to hear that M-word again.

33

Later, I went round to Nisha's to say goodbye. I'd made her a card with a photo of us on the beach last summer. The sunlight created a golden aura around us. *Have a great time in India! I am sure going to miss ya!* I'd written inside. It wasn't my best poem but literally nothing rhymes with India.

Nisha hugged me tight and said, "I'll message you when I can."

I sat on her bed while she packed, wishing there was space for me in her suitcase. The thought of the entire summer without Nisha was like imagining the sea with no beach. Last summer she hadn't gone for the whole holidays. We'd camped in her garden for almost a week when she got back.

"You'll have an amazing time," I said, trying my best to sound enthusiastic.

"Hey!" Nisha said. "You'll have a cool summer too. I'm sure you'll hang out with Evan and I bet you won't miss me at all."

"Ha!" I said, my stomach flipping over like a fish at just the thought of seeing Evan. "And you'll be so busy you won't miss me."

Nisha smiled. "Maybe you'll be his girlfriend by the time I get back."

"Do you think so?" I asked, trying to sound like my entire life didn't depend on it.

Nisha pulled a long silk scarf out of her wardrobe and carefully folded it. "I have absolutely no idea what goes through that boy's mind. I mean, is that what you want? Even though he's been ignoring you at school?"

"Yes, obviously!" I said. "It's not Evan's fault his friends don't like me. They've had it in for me since the start of Year Seven."

Nisha sighed as I helped her fold a sari embellished with gold embroidery. It's fair to say we didn't exactly see eye-to-eye about Evan. "I just think that if he likes you, he should act like it at school."

"Well," I said with probably a little too much glaring optimism, "maybe this summer will change all that!"

"Okay…" Nisha said, drawing me into a hug. "Just don't pin all your hopes on Evan. And don't undergo some dramatic transformation while I'm away. I want to recognize my best friend when I get back. Be yourself."

I nodded. "Of course!" Although I had pretty much decided by then that being myself might be the main problem.

"Nisha!" her mum called from downstairs. "Have you finished packing yet?"

"Almost!" Nisha called back.

"I'd better go," I said, wishing there was a way I could be folded up and taken with her. Although I'm not sure I'd be able to last six weeks without my cello.

"You know," Nisha said, as I hugged her one last time on the doorstep. "There's nothing stopping you from asking Evan to be your boyfriend." I rolled my eyes. "That way at least you'd know."

I laughed and waved as Nisha blew me kisses before she closed the door. I didn't want to think about what she said. What was stopping me asking Evan to be my boyfriend? About a million things, starting with a bucketful of maggots. I picked up my phone and tapped on the TikTok Hannah had uploaded.

You rocked it Han!!!
Beautiful!!!
LOVE!!! Make some more please 🙂
Hannah you are 🐥🐥🐥

You can hardly even see me playing in the background. Half of my body is completely blocked by Hannah. And every time she moves her arms, they cast shadows over my face. Performing next to Hannah, I may as well be invisible. I sighed and put my phone in my pocket.

Hannah and I spent the following week practising another TikTok. Only this time I made sure I was sitting next to her and not in the background. It was called "Happier Than Ever". I'd never heard it until Hannah played it for me. It was slower than the songs I'd put on TikTok before, and I couldn't find the music score online. But it was a simple and beautiful melody, hypnotic even, and it didn't take me long to learn. The second half of the song gets louder and heavier, and Hannah's voice sounded so incredible I didn't mind that she made us record it ten times before she was happy.

On Saturday, I woke up to the doorbell ringing non-stop, and Dad's voice yelling, "Amelia! Get down here!" I sat up in bed and rubbed my eyes, then leaned over to look at the time on my phone. But I barely noticed the time, because I had three messages from Evan.

We're gonna smash the All Stars today.

Last game of the season.

Bring it on!

"Amelia!" came Dad's voice again.

Mum must have left for the shop already. I vaguely remembered her voice telling me to get up, but I must have gone back to sleep.

Dad rang the doorbell again and Hannah shouted at me to answer the door. I groaned. The last thing I wanted to do today was smash the All Stars. My arms were aching from all the cello practices I'd been doing. The idea of swinging a kilogram bat a hundred times was in no way appealing. But I really, really wanted to see Evan. It was a week into the summer holidays already and the closest we'd come to a conversation was him commenting on my TikToks.

"Coming!" I shouted as the doorbell rang yet again. I ransacked my room searching for my baseball stuff, then brushed my teeth as fast as humanly possible. I was out of breath when I got to the car.

"Finally!" Dad said, then added, "Hurry up!" as I struggled to find the buckle for my seat belt.

Selina winked at me. She had a reusable cup in her hand that said, *Whatever happens, keep smiling.* I challenged myself to keep smiling the whole way. Which turned out to be impossible. My face was falling before we even left Ravens Bay. I leaned my head against the half-open window and scrolled through the comments on TikTok.

Hannah omg amazing!!!

You're so talented Han!!

EPICNESS!!!!

Hannah Bright you are a LEGEND ☆

I know I should have been happy for her. I mean, it's true – she does sound amazing. But it would have been nice if just one person had noticed me.

"Amelia!" a voice called as I got out of the car. I squinted into the sunlight as Evan walked towards me. It was boiling hot and I could feel blobs of sweat on my forehead.

"Evan!" my dad said, slapping him on the back. "Appreciate your commitment, son. Are we gonna smash these All Stars today or what?!" Dad got Evan in a headlock and rapped his knuckles over his head. I wanted to get back into the car and die.

"Mike," Selina said, combing her fingers through her hair. It was Champagne Blonde. I know because she told me she was thinking of switching to Absolute Platinum for the summer. "Can he breathe?"

"Oh, he's all right!" Dad said. "He's a tough kid! Aren't you, Evan?"

Evan nodded. But his face had turned a distinct shade of purple. "Want to hit a few practice shots?"

I grabbed my kit. "Sure."

Then Dad yelled, "Swing for the fences!" as we jogged onto the field.

The day only got hotter. It must have been over thirty degrees by the time we started the game. My baseball shirt was clinging to me, my hair felt sweaty under my cap and my glasses kept sliding down my nose. I could feel my skin burning even though I'd applied suncream. The dugout was only partially shaded, so I had to push myself right into the corner to sit in the one cool spot. It was majorly uncomfortable.

"You're up, Number Three!" Dad hollered at me from the sidelines. We were two runs down and I could tell he was agitated. He kept rubbing his eyes and screwed his face up any time someone missed. "Hit some big ones!"

I touched the front of my cap and nodded. *Hit some big ones, Amelia,* I told myself as I walked to the home plate. *One big one, even. Just whatever you do, hit a ball!* Only the All Stars pitcher threw like someone out of the Major League. It was like being hit by a fighter jet. I didn't stand a chance. And when the umpire shouted, "Strike three!" I felt so ashamed I couldn't even look up at Dad.

"Hey," Evan said as I slunk back to the sliver of shade in the dugout and closed my eyes. "None of us could have hit those."

"Thanks," I said, feeling him edge a tiny bit closer to me. Evan hadn't kissed me properly since before the bucket of maggots incident. Part of me was worried it might have put him off me for good. So when he squeezed my hand and said we should hang out next week, all I could feel was this enormous sense of relief flooding through me.

Needless to say, we lost the game. Which meant we only finished third in the league. The silence in the car on the way home felt heavy, like it was constricting my chest. Even Selina had stopped talking. The only noise was the occasional sigh from my dad. Why couldn't I have hit just one stupid ball? I opened my book and tried to read, but nothing was going in. I read the same page three times then gave up.

"Last game of the season," Dad said eventually, shaking his head. "A strikeout."

"Mike," Selina said. "It was really unlucky."

As soon as she said the word "unlucky" I knew I was in for it – Dad's *It's got nothing to do with luck* speech that I'd heard over and over again. The soundtrack of my childhood.

"*Unlucky?*" Dad said. "Baseball has nothing to do with luck and everything to do with control and nerve. You lost your nerve out there, Amelia."

I know, I thought. But I knew better than to interrupt him. I watched the back of his head as he went on about skill and rookie errors and not blaming my failure on bad luck. Even though it wasn't me who'd said it.

"You gotta acknowledge your failure today, Amelia. That wasn't bad luck; that was you."

"I know," I said, aware he was watching me in the rear-view mirror. I turned my book over in my hands and felt tears pooling in my eyes. I sniffed, hoping they would go away. But before I could stop them, they had spilled over onto my face. I didn't dare wipe them away in case Dad noticed. I tried to hold on to Helen Keller's words: *self-pity is our worst enemy, and if we yield to it, we can never do anything wise in the world.*

If I yield to it, I can never do anything wise in the world, I repeated to myself again and again. And eventually my eyes got the message and stopped crying.

34

When Dad dropped me home, he turned the engine off and got out of the car. I thought he was going to give me another lecture, tell me how much of a failure I was again. But he leaned down and wrapped his arms around me.

"I'm sorry," I said.

"Hey," he said. "I'm sorry too. I don't mean to be so hard on you. It's just…" I bit my lip and braced myself for whatever was coming. "I know you can do better. You got it in here." He gently thumped my chest. "You're a Bright. That means you're a winner." I nodded, even though right then being a Bright felt more like a curse than a gift. "And listen, I'm crazy busy with work this month. But I've sorted it out with your mum so you can stay with me for the last two weeks of the holidays, right?"

"And Hannah?" I asked carefully, trying not to make it sound like I didn't want to go without her.

Dad made a face. "I'm still working on Hannah. Maybe she'll come for a weekend or something."

"Okay," I said, hiding my disappointment with a smile. "Bye, Selina!" I called, then headed into the house. The familiar smell of lavender and cedarwood candles felt like a welcome hug. I leaned my head back on the closed door and sighed.

"What's he said now?" Gramps asked, padding into the hallway in the shark slippers Hannah and I had bought him for Christmas last year.

"Nothing," I said. "I messed up. We lost the game. Finished third in the league."

Gramps tutted. "There's nothing wrong with coming third. It's not even a proper game. Come and play a game of chess with me."

I smiled. The idea of playing chess with Gramps was weirdly appealing. Even though there was little chance I 'd win. Somehow it didn't matter when I was playing Gramps. If I made a stupid move or missed something obvious it was just part of the game. I wished baseball could be like that. Then maybe I wouldn't feel like I'd let down the entire team.

We'd been playing chess for a while when Hannah came in and sat on the sofa next to Gramps. I was sitting on a cushion opposite him and she almost stepped on my hand. Her toenails were painted bright orange, like the feet of an Atlantic puffin. I wondered if she'd let me borrow her nail varnish.

"Hey," she said. "Bad baseball game?"

"You heard already?" I said, keeping my eyes on the chessboard. Gramps had moved his bishop and I was trying to figure out why.

"*Selina* messaged me."

"Selina?" I said, looking up. "I didn't know you messaged each other."

"We don't. She must have got my number from Dad's phone. Look." Hannah held up her phone and my eyes swept over the message.

Hi Hannah, it's Selina. Sorry to randomly text you like this. I hope you don't mind but your dad was a little tough on Amelia today. They lost the game and she seemed really upset when we dropped her off. Could you check she's okay? X

My heart teetered, as though it was too close to the edge of a cliff. I thought for a moment that I was going to start crying again.

Hannah raised her eyebrows at me. "So?"

"I'm okay," I said. "We finished third in the league. Dad's not exactly delighted."

"That's not what I meant." I looked at Hannah, confused. "I meant, why didn't you tell me Selina might be *kind of* a nice person?"

"Oh," I said. "I kind of did."

Hannah sighed and leaned back on the sofa. "It's going to be harder to be horrible about her now."

"I'm sure you'll manage it," Gramps said, winking at me. He pointed to my queen and suddenly I saw what he was trying to do.

"So, does this mean you'll stay at Dad's?" I asked. "I'm going for the last two weeks of the holidays."

"I can't," Hannah said. "I promised Mum I'd help in the shop. Plus I have a ton of revision to do for the mock exams. But I guess I should message Selina back. You sure you're okay?"

I nodded. "I am now." I slid my queen across the board, beating Gramps at chess for the first time ever. "Checkmate."

"What?" Gramps said, his jaw gaping open in fake surprise. "You've hustled me!"

I laughed. Gramps had obviously let me win. But still. It felt really, really nice to not lose.

That night, I practised "Running Up That Hill", the song I'd played in Orchestra and got a standing ovation. Hannah heard me playing, but she didn't burst in as usual.

She quietly opened my door and listened to me, a whisper of a smile on her face.

When I'd finished, she said, "Want to play again and I'll sing?"

And as my big sister sang about having thunder in her heart and running up roads and hills, I pictured us together on the beach when we were little. Jumping into the sea, trying to catch the tide. I could see in Hannah's eyes that she was picturing the same.

After we'd recorded it, I watched the likes and shares flooding in on Hannah's phone. She squeezed my hand.

"We make a pretty awesome duet, little sis, don't we?" And even though her massive head was blocking me during the second chorus, and I had to move my bow so I didn't stab her waving arms, I had to agree.

A couple of days later, I was waiting to meet Evan in town. My stomach was revolving like bicycle pedals. It was late afternoon, and if everything went as I had planned, we'd be on the beach together at sunset. This was my first official date with Evan (not that either of us had called it this) and I wanted it to go perfectly. I'd messaged him saying to meet me outside the library. It's pretty much in the centre of town, so not too far from where he lived.

Plus I figured he'd want to get some books out for the summer, same as me.

I spotted him just as a gust of wind blew my hair in front of my face. My arms suddenly felt all goose-pimply. I couldn't tell if it was the breeze or the fact that Evan was smiling at me. I tried to swallow my nerves.

"Hi," I said. Blood rushed to my face and I immediately put my hands up to cover my cheeks.

"You okay?" Evan asked.

"Yes!" I said quickly. "The sun's just getting in my eyes. Let's go inside, shall we?"

The air inside the library was cool, and there was that dusty-papery smell I loved. I wandered down a row of books, immediately feeling more relaxed. My eyes grazed the spines, stopping every now and then to read a blurb.

"This library was built in 1953," I whispered. "We did a project on it at primary school."

Evan smiled and pulled down a copy of *Ostrich Boys* from a display. He flicked through it a couple of times then put it back and stuffed his hands in his pockets.

"Shall we get out of here?" he said. "I thought we were going to explore the beach."

"Oh," I said. I'd assumed we'd be in the library for at least an hour. I wanted to impress Evan today. And already I felt like I'd failed. "Okay, it's just that it's still a couple of hours until low tide so…" Evan looked up at the domed ceiling. I stopped myself from pointing out the engraving of ravens in the centre. "We could walk around town, if you like? But there are tourists everywhere."

Evan shrugged. "I don't mind. I want to explore outside."

I really wanted to stay and choose some books. But it seemed like he was bored already.

As we walked down the library steps back outside, I mentally scribbled out half the places I'd planned on taking him today. If he didn't feel like seeing the library, I very much doubted he'd be into the lifeboat museum.

"Okay," I said, as we stepped out into the sunshine. "Shall we go to BonBons? It's the old-fashioned sweet shop on the corner. They have every sweet you can imagine! They put them in these red and white stripy bags just like the Rockets' kit."

Evan laughed and followed me down the cobbled street. It was busy with tourists, and the streets are really narrow, so it took a while to get there.

"Woah," Evan said as we walked in, and my heart did a little quiver. Evan bought pineapple cubes, and apple liquorice twists. I got strawberry sherbets and went bright red when I spotted a jar of gobstoppers. I would definitely be avoiding those today.

After walking around town for half an hour or so, Evan grabbed my hand and pulled me towards the sign saying *Beach*.

"Come on, Bright," he said. "You know where the best rock pools are."

Neither of us had brought a towel, so after we'd exhausted all the rock pools, we sat on the sand letting the sun dry our feet. I dug in the sand with a lollipop stick, watching Evan out of the corner of my eye, in case he leaned over to kiss me. He tossed a pineapple cube in the air and caught it in his mouth then grinned at me.

"So, how do you like living in Ravens Bay?" I asked.

The sea breeze was ruffling Evan's curls. "It's awesome," he said, pointing to a pair of surfers a little way out to sea. "I might learn to surf this summer."

"You should meet my friend Ju-Long from Orchestra," I replied. "He's into surfing and kayaking. His parents have a boat on the marina. Last summer he had this huge garden party and some of us played at it."

"Oh yeah, what's he play?" Evan asked, moving closer to me.

I felt a prickly heat move up my neck and I had to concentrate really hard to remember what I was talking about. "Um, the trumpet," I said.

Evan crunched a pineapple cube between his teeth,

swallowed, and leaned over to me. I felt his warm pineappley breath on my lips. I closed my eyes. All the tourists, all the kids playing, the faint music from the cafe a little way along the beach, everything seemed to evaporate. It was just me and Evan, and the sound of his breathing getting faster.

We stayed kissing like that for ages. Evan kept trying to brush his fingers through my hair, but the wind had knotted it and they kept getting stuck. But even that didn't matter. We talked and laughed and shared our sweets and Evan buried our feet in the sand, then we kissed again for ages until my lips tingled.

Later, we walked down to the shore. Evan grabbed my hand and held on to it for ages as we explored the shallow rock pools again. He walked me home, and I stayed on the doorstep for a while, hoping, willing, wishing for him to say that I was his girlfriend. I felt so close to him. But he gave me a peck on the lips and said, "See you later."

And that was how I spent most of that summer. Recording TikToks with Hannah and hanging out on the beach with Evan. In our TikToks, Hannah stood shining at the front and I sat next to her like a backing track. But they got more and more likes and shares. When we did "House on Fire" it was viewed almost six hundred times! Hannah was invited to a multitude of sleepovers and parties and barbecues and went to the new Escape Room in the next town. Whereas I divided my time between the library, cello practice, helping Mum out in the shop and kissing Evan on the sand dunes of East Cliff Beach.

It was a few days before I was due to go to Dad's. Hannah still hadn't changed her mind about coming, so it would just be me, Dad, Selina and the American Major League Baseball. I wanted to make the most of my last few days of freedom. I waited for Evan by the concrete steps that led down to the beach. We were supposed to be getting ice creams, but the wind had picked up and it felt kind of cold. By the time Evan got there I had my hands inside my hoodie sleeves and my teeth were chattering.

"Hey, sorry I'm late," he said, leaning forward. I closed my eyes ready for him to kiss me but he touched the end of my nose. "Your nose has gone red."

I instinctively covered it up with my sleeve. "Yeah, it's kind of cold today. I thought we could skip the ice cream and get hot chocolate instead."

Evan grinned. "Why of course, Miss Bennett," he said, pretending to be Mr Darcy from *Pride and Prejudice*. He stuck out his arm for me to link. "I have not the smallest objection!"

I laughed, my heart exploding with excitement that he remembered book quotes, and let him guide me down the steps.

Later, we sat up on one of the sand dunes, looking down at the sea. I'd taken off my trainers and was burrowing my feet into the sand. Evan was standing a little way off, finding stones and hurling them out towards the water. Then suddenly I heard a voice that made my heart stop.

"PALMER!"

Evan's head jerked up and he turned around. I stopped burrowing my feet in the sand, but I didn't turn around because I felt frozen to the spot.

"PALMER!" came the voice again.

Evan walked past me, dusting the sand off his hands. Some of it went into my eye. I took off my glasses and tried to rub it out.

"Hey, DJ! Jayden!" Evan said. "How's it going?"

I didn't turn to look. I just stayed there facing the ocean, wishing for some kind of disappearing spell. Anticipating the inevitable hit that was coming.

"What you doing with Maggot?" Jayden said.

DJ snort-laughed. "Yeah, she stalking you or something?"

I waited. Not because I expected anything. Although I

suppose if I was waiting to hear what Evan said in reply then I must have been expecting *something*. But not this. Not what he actually said.

"Oh, I'm not with her," Evan said, dusting off sand from his jeans. "I was…she was already here and just started talking to me."

It felt like the tide had come all the way up to the dunes, taken me in its cold grip and was dragging me under the water.

"Maggot talks?" Jayden said.

Waves washed over my head and I was looking up at the rippled surface of the sea.

"I guess," Evan said. "So, what are you doing?"

Time had almost completely stopped. And there was only the gentle movement of the waves as I sank further and further into their depths.

"Fancy a kickabout in the park?" DJ said. Then he leaned so close to me I felt the heat of his breath in my ear. "Get out of here, Maggot."

And in that instant, I became part of the icy ocean, my flesh and bones dissolving into sea foam. I was nothing.

I picked up my bag and trainers without looking back and ran as fast as I could down the dunes, until I reached the concrete steps. I let go of my breath, looked up at the steel-coloured clouds. And only then did the tears come out.

35

Two days later, I held the book I was reading and felt numb. I just sat there staring into space, flipping through the pages, thinking about what happened on the beach. And how Evan hadn't even sent me a message saying sorry.

Mum called to say Dad was here and I was dragged back to reality. I'd be staying at his house in Middlesbrough for the next two weeks. Two whole weeks on my own because Hannah wasn't even coming.

"Hurry up, sweetheart," Mum said, opening my bedroom door. "You know what he's like if you keep him waiting." I closed the book and stuffed it into the front pocket of my suitcase. "Hey!" Mum said. "Don't look so glum, you'll have a brilliant time."

"Yeah," I said. "If the Yankees win the championship."

Mum laughed. "If they lose, you have permission to call me to come collect you." She pinched my chin and lifted my head up so my eyes met hers. "Listen, if you need me, call." I nodded. "And do try to cheer up. Your dad's looking forward to having you."

"You're quiet," Dad said after we'd been driving for twenty minutes. I was surprised he'd even noticed. "You're not upset that Hannah's not coming, are you? Because we're gonna have a great time!"

"I'm fine. Just a bit tired. I stayed up late reading."

"Well, that's great! In fact, Selina picked you up some books. She says my bookshelf is a disgrace to literature." I smiled. Dad's bookcase was made up entirely of sports biographies. "That's better!" Dad said. "There's the Bright Smile!" And slowly my smile turned into a laugh. But my heart stayed as it was – a rotten piece of driftwood washed up on an empty shore.

When Hannah stayed, we shared a room at my dad's house. But as she wasn't there, I got the bed instead of the squashy fold-out chair. It was almost midday, and now and again a cloud would pass in front of the sun and cast the room into darkness. I heard Dad downstairs saying he needed to pop out for some shopping and he'd be back later. Selina brought me a glass of apple juice and said she'd be in the garden if I fancied coming out. Only I could practically feel my skin burning through the windows, so I politely declined.

I decided to unpack later and curled up on the bed. I pulled out *Knife Edge*, the book I was reading. And that's when my phone beeped. With three messages from Evan.

Sorry about what happened at the beach

the other day.

Feel really bad.

I'm an idiot.

I looked at the messages for a while, trying to figure out how I felt. Part of me wanted to call him a *skunk cabbage*, a phrase I'd read years ago in *Anne of Green Gables*. But another part of me – the part left wounded on the beach – was just really happy he'd apologized. Even if it did take him over seventy-two hours.

It's okay, I wrote back. *But also kind of not okay*, I thought. Because no matter who came onto the beach that day, I'd never in a million years have pretended I didn't like a friend. Especially not someone I had spent the best part of the summer kissing. But I also knew that I wasn't just anyone. I was Maggot. The girl rated bottom out of everyone in my year. The girl worthless enough to deserve having an entire bucket of maggots chucked at her. And stupid enough to catch them. I was trying my best not to be her ever again. Evan liking me felt like an escape route. If I could just get things right – get him to not be ashamed of me – then everything bad at school would go away. But the Maggot name was like the blood on Lady Macbeth's hands. No matter how hard I scrubbed, I just couldn't get it to disappear.

Evan messaged me almost every day while I was at my dad's. Photos of a clam he'd found on the beach, and what looked like a strawberry anemone. A picture of him with no T-shirt on, standing on the rocks where we'd gone rock pooling. Maybe that's what did it. Maybe it put me out of my mind. Or maybe it was the fact that the summer was almost over and he still hadn't said I was his girlfriend. I couldn't go back to school and have him ignore me again. I couldn't survive another year of being Maggot. Of him keeping us a secret from everybody. I needed to do something.

It was the weekend before we went back to school and I was watching the baseball with Dad and Selina. I was messaging Evan, holding my phone close to my chest so Dad and Selina couldn't see. Then he sent:

I want to see you. Send me a photo.

Dad leaped off the sofa as the Yankees scored a home run, grabbed me and twirled me round. I said I had to go to the bathroom.

Upstairs, I pulled off my baseball hat and looked at myself in the mirror. I didn't have any make-up on and my hair was flat around the top from wearing my hat. I peered over the banister to check Selina and Dad were still glued to the screen, then snuck into Dad's room. Selina's make-up bag was gigantic! It was like hitting the jackpot. I quickly applied some eyeliner, blusher and lipstick then went back into my room and took a few selfies. I angled the phone and pulled my top down a little so you could just see my cleavage. Even if it was kind of minuscule. I chose the best picture and sent it to Evan.

I went back downstairs and waited, half-watching the baseball and half-watching my phone.

Evan: Beautiful 😊

I'm not lying when I say it felt like there were fireworks in my stomach. *Beautiful.* I traced the word with my finger, feeling like this could be it. This could be the moment he says he wants me to be his girlfriend. But he sent:

Can I see some more?

I went upstairs again and tried to capture another selfie at a more flattering angle. But I'm really not that photogenic. Also it was hard because I took off my glasses this time so I could hardly see what I was photographing. I swiped through my filters and eventually found one that lit my face up pink.

Evan: You look amazing

But I want to see more of you.

Something I haven't seen before. More than
your face.

Your body.

Take your top off.

Take my top off? And that's when I started feeling worried. Not scared or anything. Okay, maybe a little bit scared. I was out of my depth, like I'd swum too far out and I couldn't quite see the shore. The baseball commentator was droning on and Selina was feeding my dad nachos. My phone vibrated again.

Go on please.

Come on Amelia.

I really want to see you.

It disappears after a few seconds.

I was just writing, **I'm not sure...**when he sent another. And another and another.

I sent you one of me.

Aren't we more than friends?

Don't you trust me or something?

Just one photo. Go on.

I so want to see you.

I won't show anyone.

I dare you Amelia Bright.

Dares don't usually work on me. And his didn't. I mean, that's not the reason I sent it. I desperately wanted to be his girlfriend. I thought, if I just sent him this picture, if I could prove I was attractive enough then I could show him I was worth more than the Extreme Fug Zone and maggot hurling and loserville status at school. If I could be less of a child then everything I imagined could come true. If I was with Evan, the name-calling would stop. All of it would stop.

Who knows what I was thinking, really? But the truth is, I snuck back into Dad's room and rifled through the chest of drawers until I found Selina's underwear. I am not exactly proud of myself for this. But I had on this white bra that was about as attractive as the underwear my mum wears. So I had to borrow something.

I found a pink lace thing with underwire, quickly ran back to my room and closed the door. I stayed there for a moment taking deep breaths. Part of me was excited. The part that wasn't terrified, I mean. Like when I got a new project or challenge at school. I wanted to do it right. If I was going to send Evan a photo with my top off, it was going to be the best photo he had ever seen.

It took me a few minutes to research how to do it. To see what kind of pose made me look the most grown up. And the whole time, Evan was messaging saying he wanted to see me so bad. I put on Selina's bralette thing. It was way too big for me. But it wasn't like I had time for a boob job. I twisted the straps until it was tight against my boobs, then tied it at the back so you couldn't tell. It was completely see-through. I pointed my phone at the mirror and tapped. It was simple really, in a way. I ignored the trembling in my fingers and the waves of fear running over my skin like electrical currents. And then it was easy. I double-checked the photo would disappear a few seconds after I sent it, then I messaged Evan.

Okay, are you ready?

And then I did it. Photo sent. No going back. It only took a few seconds to get his reply.

Evan: OMG Amelia you look amazing 🔥

The knot in my stomach slowly started to loosen. I'd done it! It was sent. Evan liked it. And now, the picture would vanish. Like a firework. That was how it worked. That's why I wasn't worried. Because no one would ever see it except Evan. I could just pretend it didn't exist. I could put Selina's lacy bralette thing back in the drawer, wipe off her make-up, go back downstairs and watch the baseball with a secret smile on my face. Because I had nothing to worry about. The photo would already have disappeared. I'd completely deleted it from my phone. It no longer existed.

Only that's not what happened at all.

36

The next day, Dad dropped me off at home and kissed me goodbye. "I'll see you next weekend, okay?"

I waved to Dad and practically levitated into the house, I was on such a high. Evan had messaged me that morning saying, **Can't wait to see you**. I was certain he would say I was his girlfriend today. Before we went back to school. Meaning I'd start Year Nine as Evan's girlfriend and never have to hear the M-word again.

After lunch, I ran over to Nisha's and rang her doorbell with that fizzing excitement in your stomach that you only get when you haven't seen your best friend all summer. I practically pounced on her as soon as she opened the door.

"You're back!" I cried, hugging her as tightly as I could.

Nisha laughed in between taking big gulps of air like she couldn't breathe. "I've been to India, Amelia, not the moon!"

"I know," I said. "But I missed you. How was it?"

Nisha smiled. "It was so good! The wedding was amazing, and look, my cousin got me this." Around her wrist was a delicate gold bracelet with a green heart dangling from it. Nisha turned it round; the clasp was engraved with her name in Gujarati.

"It's beautiful." I slipped off my shoes and followed Nisha upstairs. "I'm so happy you're back!"

When we got to her room we sat on Nisha's bed scrolling through her pictures. "It looks incredible!" I said, gazing at photos of Goan beaches.

"It was incredible!" Nisha said. "I know we visit India every year but this time felt different. We travelled so much and I got to see so many amazing places. It's made me so much more determined to get into dance school over there."

"You will, Nisha. You're an amazing dancer."

"I mean, there's a university in Jaipur where you can study dance and choreography and oh my God, you should see the library!"

"You visited it?"

Nisha laughed. "No, silly. I've been looking online."

"At universities?" I asked. "Nisha, we're literally only about to start Year Nine."

Nisha looked at me. "Okay, what's happened?"

"What do you mean?"

"What do I mean?" Nisha sat up and put her hands on her hips. "*We're only about to start Year Nine* from the girl who made a speech in Year Four about wanting to change the world?" She narrowed her eyes at me. "What's happened?"

"Nothing's happened!" I said, breaking into a smile. "I just think it's better to focus on what's going on in the present. Seize the day!"

Nisha frowned. "What do you mean?"

"Well," I said. "Obviously we're going to be Year Nines now and I've been thinking about this whole popularity thing." Nisha put her hands over her face and groaned. "Just hear me out, okay! My followers on TikTok have quadrupled over the summer, so already that's a good sign. I'm vice-captain of Debate Club, which means at the end of September everybody in the whole school will see me make the best speech they've ever heard."

Nisha smiled. "Now that I can believe."

"And, let's just say, I don't think DJ and his idiot crew will be such a problem this year."

"Why not?" I smiled at her. "Has something happened with Evan? Are you two official?" She screeched and launched herself at me. "How could you not tell me?!"

"Not exactly." I laughed and wriggled myself out from

underneath her, trying to hide my embarrassment. Evan and I had spent almost the entire summer together and still nothing had been said. I tried not to think about the photo. Each time I did I felt weird. I couldn't tell anyone about it, not even Nisha. I don't know why I kept it a secret like that. Probably because I knew what Nisha would say. Which was exactly why I didn't tell her about him pretending not to know me at the beach. I just knew she wouldn't understand. But if Evan acknowledged me at school tomorrow, if he asked me out, it was worth it. "But it's only a matter of time," I said. "And once I'm his girlfriend – officially – DJ and everyone won't say anything to me. I'll finally be Amelia Bright, member of the popular crowd and not… you know…a Gossland Bog sub-species."

"Amelia…" Nisha looked at me. "You know you've never been a sub-species. And honestly, you shouldn't even care what DJ and people like him say. Has Evan actually said anything about what's going on between you? Because you know you can't control—"

"But that's the thing!" I replied, not waiting for her to finish. "I've tried not to care what they think, but it's impossible. Besides, I don't need to worry about them any more because being Evan's girlfriend will change how they see me. I know it will! And I just know he's going to say something. Probably tonight."

Nisha smiled weakly at me. "It's just that Evan hasn't exactly been…" She paused, watching me as I tried not to let my face fall. "I just mean, don't *change* yourself, okay? Because I happen to like my best friend exactly how she is. And if things don't work out with Evan, then you've still got me. And you're still awesome."

But one person thinking that, even if it was my best friend, wasn't enough.

"Thanks," I said and hugged her. "But you don't have to worry. Evan's not said the exact words 'girlfriend/ boyfriend' yet but seriously, that's basically what we are." I'd already convinced myself that it was going to happen. That I was speaking the truth. That everything was somehow under control.

That night, Hannah and I made a TikTok of "Levitating" by Dua Lipa. It was the most upbeat song we'd done and really hard to learn. But after reading the lyrics online, I knew it was what I wanted to say. It's about blasting into the stars with that perfect person, gliding through the moonlight, getting lost with them for ever. It didn't take a genius to figure out I was playing it for Evan. As I watched my phone glow with notifications, I felt like I was really up there, amongst the stars, heading towards the light.

37

In the morning, Hannah waltzed downstairs wearing a plastic tiara. "What do you think?" she said. "Too much?"

I gave her a sarcastic smile. "You're Head Girl, Hannah, not the queen."

Hannah replied with a fake laugh.

"Girls," Mum said, appearing from the kitchen with her phone out. "Stand by the wall; let's get a photo."

"Why do we always have to do this?" I asked as Hannah dragged me towards the wall for the annual "new school year" photograph.

"For posterity," Mum said, her phone clicking. "And because your dad wants a picture."

Mum finally managed to take a photo that wasn't blurred and we escaped. At the top of the hill, I stopped and waited for any sign of Evan.

"You coming?" Hannah asked impatiently.

"I'm just waiting for someone." I checked my phone for the millionth time to see if Evan had replied to my **Meet by the corner of Chapel Street?** message. He hadn't.

"For your boyfriend?" Hannah said in the most annoying voice I'd ever heard. I looked around to make sure there was no way Evan could have heard her. There wasn't, since he was still nowhere to be seen. "Come on, you'll be late for school."

"Hannah, you're not the boss of me just because you're Head Girl now."

"Okay, wow. You're in a good mood this morning," Hannah said. "I'll see you later then."

I waited until Hannah was out of sight. By the time Evan replied saying: **Sorry, already here**, I had to run the entire way to school. I'd had this daydream about Evan kissing me and holding my hand in front of everybody, on the first day back. It was annoying as I'd been practising so much I could probably give him the best kiss of his life! But I suppose it was for the best. My cheeks were probably red from sprinting to school. Anyway, the bell had already gone.

As I walked into form, Mr Malcolmson greeted me with, "Ah, nice of you to join us, Amelia!" It was not the slick start to the year I'd been planning. He must have left the Boston fern I'd given him in the classroom all summer, as the leaves had turned almost completely brown. I was wondering if it would be rude to give it some water from my bottle when Mr Malcolmson told me to sit down.

"A new school year is an opportunity for a fresh start!" he was saying. "*Organization* is the key to success in Year Nine..." I almost laughed. Even I knew organization had nothing to do with being successful at St Clement's Academy. It was all about popularity. Being someone everyone liked made your life a million times easier. I don't know why teachers couldn't just admit that. Even my Word of the Day this morning had hinted at it.

Perpetuality: the state or quality of lasting for ever.

That was what I wanted. To really be someone. To be remembered for something good. To get my yearbook signed by more people than Nisha and Mrs Gordon.

I caught Lachlan's eye and smiled. He stared through me like I was invisible, then went cross-eyed at me. But already that was an improvement on last year.

At lunchtime, I went to the library the long way, taking the path that ran parallel to the basketball courts. I watched Evan through the wire fence, willing him to turn around and see me. But he was taking it in turns to score baskets with a group of other Year Ten boys, and his eyes never strayed from the ball.

293

"So, how was your summer?" Mrs Gordon asked as I arrived in the library. "Read anything good?" I was about to tell her I'd finished the *Noughts and Crosses* series, but she didn't wait for an answer. "Meet Bruce!" she said, holding up the latest addition to her llama collection. "Now, I've had an email through from my friend at the council that I wanted to talk to you about. They're doing a beach clean-up next weekend. I thought it might be nice if we could organize a group of students to take part. I'm sure you can use your persuasive powers to get a nice big group of litter pickers. Perhaps you could make an announcement about it in assembly."

"It's just..." I knew full well the last thing I needed was to start Year Nine by announcing The Great Ravens Bay Litter Pick to the entire school. "I'm already really busy. There's the debate competition in a few weeks and I'm vice-captain. As Amelia Earhart said, *There is so much that must be done!*"

"Yes, I know, my dear," Mrs Gordon said. "But I think she was talking about the war."

I smiled. "Maybe you could email Mr Malcolmson. Ask him to announce it?"

"All right, dear, but I do need you to write a blog about it for the school website. It would be great to get a good turnout. Do sort out the fiction shelves for me, will you?

I had a group of overenthusiastic Year Sevens in this morning and they've ransacked the place."

I waited until she'd turned back to her computer before I snuck out. I felt kind of bad. Like I was leaving a piece of me behind. But as soon as I got back to the basketball courts and saw Evan, I knew I'd made the right decision. My life should be happening here, with him. With people who are considered popular. Not in the library with Mrs Gordon and her tiny llamas.

I stood there for a minute willing Evan to look over. I kept saying to myself, *if he looks over now, everything is going to work out.* I admit, I had to repeat it a few times before he finally looked in my direction. But when he did, he gave me a quick smile. I waved and waited for him to come over, but he turned straight back to his friends.

I messaged him later asking how the first day back went, and he replied with a picture of a Sphynx cat yawning. I waited in case he decided to follow this up with something more romantic. But he didn't. I thought back to that morning, waiting for him on the corner; willing him to look over at me by the basketball courts.

I went to sleep that night with a strange feeling, like there was a hand inside my chest squeezing my heart. It wasn't sadness exactly. I think it was fear.

* * *

The next morning, I finally collected my vice-captain badge from the history office at breaktime and I could not help feeling proud. I'd had to email Mr Hall over the summer to remind him about it. I was trying to pin it to my blazer, so I wasn't exactly looking where I was going, when I heard, "Watch out, Maggot!" I looked up and it was a group of Year Tens. I recognized Jayden at the back, then Evan came round the corner. "Yeah, get out of the way, Maggot," another of them said as I sidestepped them.

My cheeks reddened as I carried on down the corridor, trying to ignore their laughter. I waited to see if Evan came after me. But he didn't.

I reached Mrs King's science lab but the corridor was empty. There was still about five minutes before the bell. I dumped my stuff on the floor and sat down with my back against the wall. I should have been feeling proud. I was vice-captain of Debate Club! But all I could think about was "Maggot! Maggot!" and the silence from Evan that followed. And I felt mad. We'd been so close over the summer. He'd even persuaded me to send him a photo of my boobs! And now we were back at school, he was acting like he didn't even know me. Like I was nobody.

I pulled my phone out of my pocket, typed: **Thanks for sticking up for me!!** Then pressed send before I could change my mind.

When Nisha arrived she took one look at my face and asked what was wrong. I told her about the maggot thing in the corridor. She sat down next to me and looked at the wall opposite for a minute.

"Evan should have said something," she said eventually. "He knows that name upsets you."

"Yeah," I said. "I mean, maybe he did. Like after I'd gone?"

"Maybe," she said, but neither of us were exactly convinced.

When the lesson started, Mrs King put us into pairs again so I had to work with DJ. We were testing different foods for starch content using an iodine test. It should have been straightforward. Only nothing is straightforward when you're working with DJ. For a start, you have the added toxic ingredient of having to talk to him.

"DJ, would you pass me that banana, please?" I asked as pleasantly as I could.

"Get it yourself, Maggot," he replied, munching on a piece of apple we were supposed to be using for our experiment. I wanted to slap him on the head with the metal tongs. But I took a deep breath and cast my mind back to the articles I'd read about having charisma. *Smile from within.* I tried my best to smile from within as DJ ate his way through half of our starch experiment. Number five on the charisma list was *Phrase everything positively*. So when Mrs King came over and asked how it was going I said, "DJ has certainly got an appetite for science!"

Only he swore at me as soon as she'd gone, then ate our raw potato.

By Friday, Evan was still pretending I was invisible at school. And I'd had enough. The prospect of becoming his girlfriend was slipping through my fingers like sand. I had to do something. I messaged him saying: **Can we meet at lunch after Orchestra?** And waited for as long as I could after the bell went for a reply that never came.

Orchestra practice that day was the worst. I could barely make it through twelve bars without making a mistake. And when my bow squeaked for the third time during a solo, Mr Giuliani said the string section could finish early. I could hear Benedict sniggering. But for once I didn't care one iota about what anyone at Orchestra thought. All I could think about was speaking to Evan.

I found him sitting with his friends on the picnic benches near the hot chocolate machine. I smiled casually, like it was a total coincidence I'd wandered into the Year Ten hang-out. I had my cello on my back and hadn't tightened the straps so it bashed me on the back of the head as I stepped forward.

"Evan!" I called, and immediately about twenty people turned round. Evan jumped out of his seat like he'd seen a ghost.

One girl smirked at me.

Another said, "Oh my God, it's that maggot girl."

"Amelia, hey," Evan said, guiding me backwards towards the double doors. "Don't you have Orchestra?"

"We finished early," I said. "Mr Giuliani wants to work with the wind section. So…can we talk?"

He let out a nervous laugh. "Erm," he said, visibly squirming. "It's just…I'm with my friends, you know."

"Okay, well, you could come to mine after school? Morph's shedding his skin at the moment, which is a pretty fascinating process to watch." Evan hesitated and looked back at his friends. All of them were staring at me. I swallowed the lump forming in my throat and carried on. "He eats it. His skin, I mean."

"That's…gross. I mean, great," Evan said. "I'll message you, okay?"

I could feel tears balancing on my lower eyelids. I didn't dare blink in case they spilled over. "Okay," I said quietly.

Evan headed back to the picnic benches and sat down. As the double doors swung back I heard a wave of laughter erupt from his table. A sudden bolt of anger shot through my veins. Maya Angelou described anger as being like fire. Right then, I felt like I could expel molten lava from my eyeballs and burn the entire school to the ground. And as much as I wanted to scream at Evan, scream at all of them, I didn't let myself look back.

38

"Amelia!" Nisha said as she nudged me for the third time. "Please stop staring at your phone and eat something!"

We were in the canteen and the air felt heavy with the smell of greasy chips.

"Sorry," I said, pushing my plate away. "I thought he'd at least have messaged me!"

Nisha sighed. "I know. The boy is being an idiot."

I let out a weak laugh. "I shouldn't have gone to speak to him in front of his friends. I've probably ruined everything. But I feel so annoyed with him!"

"Good!" Nisha said firmly. "You should be annoyed with him. Sorry, Amelia, but I don't think Evan is treating you very well. Pushing you out of the doors! I mean…"

"It wasn't quite that bad," I said, looking up at the canteen doorway, willing it not to be empty. "Anyway, I suppose it's not Evan's fault. I can't expect him to declare undying love for me right there in front of the Year Tens."

"Why not?" Nisha's fork clattered onto her plate. "If that's how he feels then why shouldn't you expect that? Why should you be okay with him ignoring you?"

"I'm not! It's just," I started, "it's just…" And for the first time in my life, I couldn't think of an answer.

When I got home, I knocked on Hannah's door. She was singing as usual, and her room smelled of the lemon and honey drink she always had before bed.

"Can I ask you something?" I said, after she'd finished the final bars of a Christina Aguilera song. She bowed and signalled for me to applaud. "I've kind of got this problem."

"Okay," Hannah said. "But if it's a crush on Mr Giuliani then you probably need actual therapy."

I rolled my eyes. "It's Evan."

Hannah's face lit up. "Oh, the boy you're trying to keep a secret from everyone."

I sat down on her bed and picked up a cushion. "It's not me trying to keep it a secret."

"What do you mean?" Hannah's eyes narrowed.

"It's just, we message each other a lot and, erm, kiss, and stuff."

"Wait," said Hannah. "Is he trying to pressure you to do anything? Because I will literally—"

"No!" I felt my face flush with embarrassment. "God, Hannah, no, not that. It's just at school he acts like he doesn't know me."

Hannah watched my face for a minute. "What do you mean? He ignores you at school?"

"Not ignores exactly. I mean, he's in the year above anyway and he hangs around with different people but…" I thought about Evan flashing me the quickest smile possible at the basketball courts. Pushing me out of the double doors and then sitting back down on the picnic bench. His silence after his friends called me Maggot. "Actually I suppose you could say he is ignoring me. Sort of."

"And this is your boyfriend?"

I shrugged. "We're not technically anything. Not officially. I thought we might be. But now I think he just wants me to go away. I can understand why he'd be embarrassed about me. I've tried everything but whenever his friends are there it's like I don't exist."

Hannah shifted until she was squashed right up next to me on the bed. It was kind of nice. "Listen, he should not be embarrassed about you, Amelia! So forget that for a start. You're amazing! You're my little sister, so it's a proven fact that you have awesome genes." Hannah gave me her performance-smile. I sighed. "You're talented, you're super smart, you have THE cutest face in the universe. If Evan's ignoring you at school then maybe *you* should ignore *him*. Permanently."

Just then, my phone beeped with a message.

Evan: Sorry about today. You took me by surprise. I'd love to see Morph's shedding skin this weekend!

"Is that him?" Hannah asked, grabbing my phone. "Oh, he's sorry, is he? That's big of him." She started typing.

"Don't, Hannah! Please! What are you saying?" I cried.

"Oh, just telling him that the only skin likely to be shed this weekend is his, if he comes anywhere near you."

"Hannah, no!" I tried to wrestle my phone out of her hands, but she held it up over her head.

"Yes, Amelia. I'm doing this for your own good. You're worth more than this. You know you are. And if Evan doesn't have the genitalia to stand up to his stupid friends, then he doesn't deserve any more of your time." Only she said something else instead of genitalia. And for the first time that day I actually laughed. "Come on, let's work on a new TikTok." Hannah dropped my phone on her bed and put her arm around my shoulders. "I think 'abcdefu'

304

by Gayle should be perfect. And yes, you are so joining in on vocals."

The funny thing is, on Monday, ignoring Evan was exactly what I intended to do. I'd already ignored the messages he'd sent apologizing again. Saying Hannah was right that he deserved to lose his skin, but that he did want to see me. And asking if I wanted to meet at the beach. But I had not even replied. If Evan wanted to act like I was invisible, then that was exactly what I was going to be to him. In a weird way I was looking forward to seeing him. I wanted him to know exactly how it felt to be completely ignored by someone who said they liked you.

Even when I scratched off the gold to reveal the word *Tohubohu: a state of chaos and confusion* on my New Word Every Day poster, I didn't take it as a bad sign. I genuinely thought ignoring Evan would be all I had to worry about. I mean, it would be hard not to feel embarrassed if I saw him. He had basically seen my full boobs. But Nisha and Hannah were right. If he was going to pretend he didn't even know me at school, and let his stupid friends laugh at me, then I had to try and forget about him. Even if it did mean abandoning that particular plan for climbing out of school's unpopularity pit.

So I wasn't expecting it. Even when I noticed people staring at me on the way to school. Even when I heard Arran Parsons hurl "slag" at me from all the way up the hill. But when Hannah pulled me aside and asked me why everyone was gawping at me and why my phone was going off non-stop, I just knew.

"Amelia!" she'd said. "Tell me what's going on." Only how could I tell her? I couldn't even look at her.

Because even then, even with all the irrefutable evidence facing me, I didn't want to accept that everything – my entire life – was about to go horribly wrong.

39

I put my head down as I walked into the music block, ignoring the people shouting and laughing behind me. I wiped the tears from my face with my blazer sleeve. Some Year Sevens were in the foyer dropping their violins off. They went silent as I walked past. I had no idea if it was because they knew about The Photo or because I was crying. At that point I hardly cared. All I wanted to do was find an empty room and hide. I peered through one of the practice room windows and then went inside. I didn't switch the lights on. I just dropped my bag by the piano stool and sat down next to it. The bell rang for form time but I didn't move. My stomach churned over and over like a rough tide and my hands shook as I looked at my phone.

Over fifty notifications. I held my breath as I tapped the first one. And there I was. Standing in my bedroom at

Dad's wearing Selina's see-through bra. Someone must have zoomed in and cropped it because you couldn't see the outline of the mirror, or the top of my head. I started reading the comments, feeling fresh tears slide down my face.

LOLOLOLOL CHECK OUT MAGGOT

what the actual hell

lmao is that real

OMG she's a SKANK

literally the grossest thing I've ever seen

"Amelia?" Mr Giuliani's voice came floating across the music room. "What are you doing in here? Shouldn't you be in form?"

I'm hiding, I thought. But no words came out.

"Are you unwell?" He put down his briefcase and moved a music stand out of the way so he could sit on the piano stool. "What's going on? Has something happened? You can tell me."

I let out a laugh. As if I could tell Mr Giuliani about The Photo. I took off my glasses and wiped my eyes. "Thanks, Mr Giuliani. I'm okay." I put my phone on silent, but I could still feel it vibrating in my hand.

"Come on. Things can't be that bad! Not when we have music!" He reached over to the piano and played the opening to Beethoven's "Ode to Joy". As I sat there with my head resting against the wall, listening to Mr Giuliani play with my phone going off in my pocket, I don't think I have ever felt so sad. Or so ashamed. "Now, you'd better head to form before the bell goes."

Outside, there weren't many people around, so it was easy to avoid their eyes. I walked as fast as I could to the English block, trying desperately to drown out the horrible thoughts inside my head by humming "Ode to Joy". But with every refrain, I wanted to disappear.

As I walked up the stairs a boy coming down shoved his phone in my face. The Photo was right there on his screen. "That you?" He laughed and said he wanted to see the real thing. For a moment I thought he was going to lift up my shirt right there on the stairs. I don't know, maybe me bursting out crying put him off. But I ran as fast as I could to our form class. As soon as I walked in everyone went silent and I could feel all their eyes on me.

I quickly sat down and pulled a book out of my bag. I leaned down as far as I could over the desk without my face actually touching it. I could hear laughing and sniggering coming from behind me, but I didn't dare turn around. Nisha slid her homework diary towards me. On a blank page she'd written, *What's going on?*

So Nisha hadn't seen The Photo. That was something. I checked Mr Malcolmson wasn't looking, then unlocked my phone. I tapped on the screenshot Ju-Long had sent me, along with a message saying, **Thought I'd better send in case you didn't know. This is going round group chat. I haven't shared, I promise.** I handed my phone to Nisha.

Her gasp made Mr Malcolmson look up. She turned it into a cough, but everyone else knew what was happening so they burst out laughing.

"What is going on with you lot this morning?" Mr Malcolmson said with a smirk. But everyone just laughed even harder. Mr Malcolmson joined in, saying, "Well, I'm glad you're enjoying yourselves."

"It's Amelia who's been enjoying herself, sir," DJ said over the laughter.

"Oh, is that true?" Mr Malcolmson said. "And what have you been up to, Amelia? Anything worth sharing?" And the entire class erupted with laughter.

My face burned red with shame and regret and anger. I shoved my chair back and ran out of the room. I didn't know where I was going, only that I had to get out.

"Amelia!" Nisha called down the corridor after me. "Wait! Amelia!"

But I couldn't even face her. That stupid photo that was supposed to vanish was everywhere. Everywhere! Where could I go? How could I face anyone ever again?

I sobbed and ran down the stairs and out into the walkway that leads to the library.

Mrs Gordon didn't seem too surprised to see me. She didn't even look up from her computer. "Amelia!" she said. "How lovely!" Then she must have seen my face. "Is everything all right, dear?"

I sniffed, trying to hold back the ocean of tears about to break. "I have stomach ache. Do you mind if I stay in the library this morning?"

"Yes, of course. Just make sure someone lets your teacher know. If you have a bit of spare time before your first lesson you could tidy up the biographies. I didn't get around to doing it on Friday."

"Sure," I said, my voice quivering with tears. I headed to the biography section and sat down. The rough carpet felt prickly on my knees. I'd left my bag in my form room so I searched my blazer pockets for a tissue. It's quite impressive how silently I cried that morning. Sitting in front of books written about people who were truly inspiring. People who achieved incredible things. People who accomplished the impossible. Truly great people – the best of people – staring out at me from the shelf like a jury. Knowing that now, I was barely fit to hold their stories in my hands.

By breaktime I had messages from boys I didn't even know asking for nude photos. And about ten missed calls from Hannah. Nisha was trying to comfort me in the library office, but people kept coming in to use the printer and sniggering when they saw me.

"Oh, Amelia," Nisha said, her eyes glistening with tears. "We have to tell Mr Malcolmson."

"No!" I said. "I don't want to tell anyone."

"But he can help!" Nisha said.

I looked right at her. "Mr Malcolmson can never find out about this. Promise me."

Nisha stroked my hair. Typically today it was looking extra frizzy. "I just think it's serious and—"

"Please, Nisha," I said. "I don't want anyone else to find out."

"There you are!" Hannah said as she burst into the office. "Amelia, what the hell have you done?"

Then she hugged me. And I couldn't get any air into my lungs. I thought I was going to pass out and die, right there by the library printer. And I can't lie – part of me actually wanted it to happen. Because then I wouldn't have to face them all. And they could put a plaque up on the library wall saying *Here Lies Amelia Bright: Total Failure At Everything*. And that would be my legacy. I glanced up at the library shelves and I thought about all the books I wouldn't be able to read if I died, and somehow that made me take a breath.

"She's having a panic attack." It was Zadie. "Sit her upright."

"Amelia?" Hannah said.

"Just breathe," Zadie said, rubbing my back. "Don't think about anything except your breath." She held my hand and breathed with me while I slowly took longer and longer breaths and my heart felt less like it was trying to escape my chest. "There, that's it," she said. "You're okay. You're okay."

And for a few minutes I was okay. I was with Ursula under the sea. Only instead of stealing my soul she was saving it.

"Thank you, Zadie," I said when I could finally find my words. "I feel so stupid." And the tears rolled out again.

"Hey," Hannah said. "I'm calling Mum."

"No!" I cried. "Please!" If I had to form a line of all the people in the world I wanted to see The Photo in order, Mum would be right at the back. Maybe just in front of Dad. I felt sick.

"Amelia," Hannah said, tapping her phone. "I'll tell her you're sick. Come on, let's take you to Student Services."

"I'll bring your stuff," Nisha said.

"Please don't tell Mum, Hannah, please." But Hannah just shushed me and rubbed my arm.

"It's going to be okay," she said.

I don't remember much after that. Only that Hannah, Nisha and Zadie walked me to the Student Services office and then waited with me outside reception until Mum's car pulled up. Nisha squeezed my hand and said she'd call me after school. I could see from Mum's face she was annoyed. She must have had to close the shop. But as soon as she looked at me properly her expression switched to concern.

"Oh gosh, Amelia, you don't look well at all." She felt my forehead and I got into the car feeling like a bit of rubbish that had washed up from the sea. Or one of those Poor Unfortunate Souls who have given their whole life away for nothing.

40

I spent the rest of that day in my bedroom, my eyes stinging from crying so much. Mum went back to the shop, and Gramps called up to me a few times to check I was "still breathing". There was no way I could tell them what had really happened.

Nisha messaged saying, **It will be okay. Try not to think about it**. But how could I think about anything else? The entire school must have seen my photo by now. A photo that was supposed to vanish. The thought of everyone seeing me like that made me feel sick.

I dreaded to think what people were saying about me. But at the same time, I wanted to know how bad it all was. I knew Nisha wouldn't want to look at any of it. So I messaged Ju-Long, asking him to send me screenshots of group chats he'd seen.

You sure? he replied.

Amelia: Definitely, I want to see what people are saying about me. I promise I won't message anyone. I just want to see.

Ju-Long: Okay. But I don't think any of this.

My hands trembled as I waited for the screenshots to come through. And when they did, it was like someone had opened a trapdoor underneath me and I was plummeting down and down and down.

This should be her profile picture lmao

Scrubbing my eyes with soap

Maggot actually thinks she's attractive

I cannot stop laughing 😂

Maggot nude omg

How do I put this on Google?

There must have been over a hundred comments. Most of them included swear words. And then there were the messages. Loads of them. On TikTok and Snapchat, and even sent straight to my phone from numbers I didn't recognize. All asking me for photos. I read and reread them, each time watching them get blurrier with tears.

I heard Hannah's feet running up the stairs as soon as she got home from school. "Can I come in?" she asked, already pushing open my bedroom door. "Want a drink or something to eat? I'll bring it up here if you like."

"I'm not hungry," I said to the wall. I was lying on my bed with *The Great Gatsby* open in front of me, mostly unread.

"Listen. You should know that I reported it today. You know, the photo. Student Services are looking into it."

"Have they called Mum?"

"They'll probably call her soon," she said. "You might want to speak to her before they do."

I blinked and felt warm tears slide down my face. "She's going to kill me."

"She's not going to kill you," Hannah said. "But better for her to find out from you rather than that woman in Student Services who wears blue eyeshadow, right?"

I sniffed. "Everyone's seen it, Hannah. Literally the whole school. What's Mum going to think?"

"Not everyone's seen it, Amelia," she said gently. "And not everyone has shared it. Most of us think it's disgusting. I'm sure Mum will—"

"That's exactly how I feel," I said, not letting her finish. "Disgusting." I curled into a tighter ball, gripping the edge of the bedsheet in my hand.

"I mean, it's disgusting that it's being shared." I felt her sit down on the bed. "You're not the one who's disgusting."

"Well, I feel like it. You should see what people are

317

saying about me." I put a pillow against the headboard and sat up. "Everyone thinks I'm some kind of…" I left the sentence hanging there unfinished. I couldn't even say the word. One I'd seen plastered all over the comments on my photo.

"I could kill Evan Palmer," Hannah said. "He said he never shared it but obviously no one believes him. I mean, he must be lying."

"You spoke to Evan?"

"Of course!" Hannah said. "I'm your sister, aren't I? He swore he never sent it to anyone. He even let me check his phone."

"He must have shared it," I said. "I didn't send it to anyone else. I'm not totally stupid. He wasn't even supposed to *save* the picture. It was supposed to delete."

"Is that what he said?" Hannah asked. "He said he wouldn't save it?"

"Yes!" I shouted, hot tears streaming down my face. "He said it would disappear! But the only thing that's disappeared is my entire life. Down the toilet." I turned over and cried into my pillow. It was already damp from where I'd been crying before Hannah got back.

"Hey," Hannah said. "Your entire life hasn't gone down the toilet. You trusted Evan not to share a photo. I mean, clearly that was a massive mistake. But it was just one mistake. *One mistake*, Amelia. You're not responsible for all the people sharing the photo. That's their mistake. You believed he wouldn't save it. Obviously, that was idiotic. And where did you even get that bra?"

I lifted my head up a little. "I found it in Selina's stuff."

"Wow. Okay." Hannah laughed. "*Selina's* bra? I mean, talk about a betrayal."

I tried not to laugh but I couldn't help it. So then I was laughing and crying at the same time which felt like a major body disfunction.

"Listen," Hannah said. "Are you going to lie here like some kind of wet blanket and cry all night because of one mistake? You've read *Anne of Green Gables*, haven't you?"

"Only a million times."

"Well then. You know what she says, now where is it?" Hannah scoured the bookshelf for my copy of *Anne of Green Gables* and flicked through the pages until she found the bit she was looking for. "Here: *tomorrow is a new day with no mistakes in it yet.* See?"

I looked at the page, the words blurry through my teary eyes. "But tomorrow will still have my mistake in it," I said and turned back to face the wall.

"At least you're not Amelia Earhart," Hannah said.

I sat up and looked at her. "What's that supposed to mean?"

Hannah smiled. "Didn't she set off on a solo flight around the world and die? I mean, that was a *huge* mistake right there. She literally died."

Hannah had said bad things to me before, but this was a new low even for her.

"A mistake?" I said. "Attempting to become the first woman to complete a circumnavigational flight round the globe, a *mistake*? I don't think so!" I gestured at the giant Amelia Earhart poster I had on the wall above my bed. It said *Everyone has oceans to fly, if they have the heart to do it.* Words I could practically recite in my sleep. "Amelia Earhart is a pioneer and a legend, Hannah! You can't call her greatest adventure a *mistake*! She had oceans to fly! She faced the possibility of not returning and decided it was worth the risk. *Adventure is worthwhile in itself.*"

"There you go then," Hannah said as she stood up and walked towards the door. "You took a risk. You crash-landed, Amelia, but you haven't actually died." What she was saying was technically true. But only because Dad hadn't found out yet. "What would Amelia Earhart do?"

I hated to admit it but Hannah was right. Amelia Earhart would not have been crying into a pillow. I waited until Hannah had gone back to her room then I got up, wiped my eyes and went downstairs to face Mum.

41

Mum was leaning against the kitchen table when I went downstairs, waiting for the kettle to boil. "How are you feeling, sweetheart?" she asked as I walked in. "I have to say, you don't look great." She felt my forehead and my cheeks then planted a kiss on the top of my head. "Think you could manage some soup?"

"Actually, Mum, I need to tell you something."

"Oh dear, that sounds serious!" she said jokingly, but her smile disappeared when she saw the look in my eyes.

"Something's happened," I said and handed her my phone. The photo stared up at me like a digital ghost.

"Amelia, who took this?" she asked. "What is this about?"

I swallowed, as shame crept over every inch of my skin. "I took it."

Just as I was about to tell her more, the kettle boiled.

Mum put my phone on the worktop and poured herself a tea. "Really, Amelia. I have no idea what you expect me to say. Why on earth would you take a picture like that? It's...*indecent.*" She cradled the tea in her hands. It smelled strongly of liquorice. "I sincerely hope this isn't a new TikTok idea of yours because let me tell you – that bra leaves nothing to the imagination! Where on earth did you even get that? Is it one of Hannah's?"

"I sent the photo to a boy," I said quietly. Mum looked at me blankly so I repeated, "I sent it to a boy, Mum. And he's shared it with everyone at school."

Mum looked confused. "I'm sorry, Amelia. I don't understand. You sent what to a boy? Surely not that picture?" I closed my eyes so I didn't have to see her face and nodded. "You sent *that picture* to a boy? But you're half-naked!" I nodded again. "And what? He's sent it to other people?" I sniffed and screwed my eyes shut tight to stop too many tears from coming out. "Oh God, no. Amelia!" I heard Mum put down her tea and felt her draw me into a hug. "What the hell were you thinking? How could you even think of doing something like that?"

"I thought he was going to delete it," I said into her chest, and I felt her sigh with her entire body, as though it was the most stupid thing she'd ever heard. Just then, her phone started ringing.

"It's the school," she said after she'd fished her phone out of her bag. "I take it they already know about this?" But she didn't wait for me to say anything before she answered.

I sat down at the kitchen table so I could listen, but she went into the living room and closed the door. I could only hear low muffles, then what sounded like Mum crying, so I quietly went back upstairs to my room.

"How did it go?" Hannah said, poking her head around the door. "You're still alive, so that's a good sign."

I wiped my eyes with my sleeve. "She seemed pretty shocked. And upset. And disappointed. And probably wants to disown me."

"I'll gather up the lavender pillows."

And despite the circumstances I couldn't help letting out a laugh. Then I remembered Mum was downstairs crying on the phone, probably to Mr Harding, and I felt like someone had sucked all the air out of the room. I couldn't breathe. I caught sight of my reflection in the mirror and felt sick. How could I ever face anyone again? How could I even face myself?

"Hey," Hannah said. "Mum will be okay. She'll be on your side." Then she added, "It's Dad you need to worry about."

And no amount of lavender pillows could make me feel better about that.

* * *

The next morning, I told Mum I couldn't face going to school. "Please let me stay at home," I begged. "Just for today."

"Oh, Amelia. I honestly think the best thing to do is to go into school and face everyone." I seriously have no idea what kind of school my mum went to.

"Please, Mum! Just today!" I begged as she practically dragged me out of bed. "This is inhumane." As soon as she let go, I crawled back under the covers and shouted, "Please!" for the hundredth time.

Mum sighed and stroked my hair. "Okay, sweetheart. But just for today. I'll call school and tell them you're not up to coming in today." I sat up and wrapped my arms around her, crying with relief. "But I mean it – just today. Let the dust settle and tomorrow you'll get out of this bed and face up to what's happened."

"Thanks, Mum," I said into her hair. "I promise I'll go in tomorrow."

"Oh, and I should warn you, I'm telling your dad about it this morning. I just couldn't face telling him last night."

"No, Mum, please." A shudder of terror went over me. "He'll kill me!"

"He won't kill you, Amelia. But I can't keep something like this from him. Besides, I've already seen some comments about it on the school Facebook group. So it's only a matter of time before he hears about it."

"The school Facebook group?" My heart pounded inside my chest like it had packed its suitcase and was trying desperately to leave my body.

Mum rubbed her temples and sighed again so I knew it was bad. "Some parents are expressing concern." She looked at me, tucked my hair behind my ears then said, "It's nothing you need to worry about. Just some parents convinced that sending photos like yours might become some kind of epidemic. And a few comments about how I'm not exactly Mother of the Year." Mum looked like she was about to cry again.

"I'm sorry," I said, because I didn't know what else to say.

"Oh," she said, wafting her hands like she was trying to swat the whole situation away. "I was tempted to put a link to our online shop. Seems like there are several St Clement's Academy parents who are in dire need of the products in my de-stress range." Mum smiled, but her glistening eyes told me a different story. After finding out people had seen my photo, I didn't think there was any possible way I could feel worse. But when Mum left for the shop that morning, I felt as though I'd accidentally swept my entire life off a cliff, and all of us – me, Hannah and Mum – were drowning in the thick waves of the icy sea.

I stayed in bed all day, only getting up to go to the bathroom, or slip downstairs to get a drink. I couldn't even bear to open my curtains. Like I could somehow pretend the world outside wasn't happening. I didn't bother getting dressed. I just stayed zipped up in the zebra onesie I'd got last Christmas, as though it could somehow protect me, stop everything from falling apart.

When Mum got home she called, "Amelia!" up the stairs. But I ignored her. Until she added, "Your dad's on his way over!"

And it was like being hit by a truck. One of those giant American monster ones.

42

"Mike, we've been over this," Mum said, slumping back on the sofa and rubbing her forehead like she was in pain. "Amelia made a stupid mistake and she's paying for it, isn't she?" The word "stupid" echoed around in my head. I hadn't said anything for a while. There was no point. There was no explanation that would be good enough for my dad. I fiddled with the zip on my onesie, regretting that I'd decided not to get changed. I don't know what outfit would have felt appropriate, but it felt seriously weird for my dad to be talking about people at school seeing my boobs while I was essentially dressed as a zebra.

"No, no, no," Dad said, shaking his head as if he needed to add another negative. "What I want to know is why, *under my roof*, you thought it was okay to behave like that."

His words rained down on me like hail. I was in the

middle of a storm with no umbrella, no cagoule and no one shielding me from it. I found myself wishing Selina was here.

"I'm sorry," I said for the millionth time.

"You know, this is going to haunt you for the rest of your life!" Dad said. "You do know that, don't you?"

"Mike!" Mum said. "That's enough. I think it's best you go. There's no point in making Amelia feel even worse than she does already. She is actually the victim here, remember."

Dad took a deep breath and got up from the sofa. He held his hands up then rubbed his eyes. I'd never seen my dad cry before. It was the weirdest feeling. Like the world had turned on its axis and everything was the wrong way up. "You're right, Penny. You're right. So, where does Evan live? I need to pay him a visit."

"Mike. That's the absolute worst idea. You need to calm down. Here." Mum grabbed a box from the shelf and handed Dad a mini lavender-scented pillow. "Take a few deep breaths of this." For once, Dad did what she said. "It's bad, yes. But it's not the end of the world. It could be a lot worse. I mean, we could be talking full nudity."

Dad pulled the pillow away from his face. "Oh God, Penny. Really?"

And that was enough to convince him to leave.

I hardly slept that night, and I woke up really early. I could hear the birds singing their dawn chorus as though nothing in the world had changed.

"Listen, Amelia," Mum said to me at breakfast. "I'm not going to lie, today will be tough. But you've had tough days before and you'll have them again. The important thing is to keep your head held high and rise above it."

Rise above it, I thought. How do you rise above anything when you're so low you're practically below sea level?

"If anyone says anything out of line, report it to Mr Harding."

"Or me," Hannah said, grabbing two apples from the fruit bowl and chucking one to me. "Seriously, if anyone says anything to you, just remind them your big sister is Head Girl. I have the power to make their life a misery."

"Hannah," Mum said, "I don't think abusing your power is the answer to Amelia's problems. Oh, and that reminds me," Mum said, holding out her hand. "Phone."

"Are you serious?" I asked.

"Your dad and I agreed that you'll have to manage without your phone for a while until we can...well, until this whole thing has blown over at least."

I sighed and dropped my phone on the kitchen table. "Fine. But I thought you said I was the victim. So why am I being punished?"

Just then my phone beeped and glowed. Someone had sent me a meme. It was a cartoon boy with gigantic bulging eyes, saying **Millionth time I've seen your boobs.**

"Looks like Mum's doing you a favour," Hannah said. I grabbed my phone and switched it off before she could see anything else. Then I put my head in my hands.

"Listen," Mum said, rubbing my shoulder, "if you can survive a bucket of maggots being thrown at you then you can survive whatever words people throw at you today. Right?"

"Right," I agreed, only because I think Mum was genuinely trying to make me feel better.

I walked into form time with Nisha and a strange kind of roar erupted. Nisha clamped her arm in mine and didn't let go until we sat down.

"All right, everybody!" Mr Malcolmson was saying. "Let's settle down, shall we?" Then he started talking about some theatre trip the English department was planning. I'd usually have felt excited, but today I felt nothing. Worse than nothing. I wanted to somehow scrub myself out. Now everyone had seen me in Selina's see-through bra, I felt like that was the only thing I was wearing. No matter how tightly I pulled my blazer around me, I couldn't shake the feeling of having my skin on display. I sank as low as I could in my chair and tried to block out the thousands of pairs of eyes pointing in my direction.

In science, Mrs King made us work with our allocated partners again, which meant I had to sit next to DJ. The whole time he kept saying, "All right, Maggot! Keep your clothes on!" making everyone look over. It was like he could read my mind. I did feel like I had nothing on. But I still wanted to stick the spatula up his nose.

At lunchtime I had planned on hiding in the library office. But I saw Flora rushing towards the English block.

"Haven't you seen?" she said. "Miles has called a meeting."

I guessed he'd posted in our group chat, but as Mum had my phone I'd missed it. I ran straight back to my locker to get my notepad then all the way to the classroom we used for meetings.

"Sorry!" I said as I burst in. "I didn't see the message.

What did I miss?" But no one answered. Not even Flora.

Miles pursed his lips, glanced around at everyone, then fixed his eyes on me. "I've called this meeting because we've had a reshuffle. Under the circumstances, we can't risk having you on the team, Amelia."

"Under what circumstances?" I said, suddenly feeling dizzy. I looked at Flora and she gave me a sad shrug. Aakesh and William stared at the floor.

"We know *all about your photo*, Amelia. How can you debate serious topics and advocate moral reasoning now everyone's seen what you're really like? We have our school's reputation to think of. We can't possibly have you on the team this year."

My cheeks burned with humiliation. "You're dropping me from the team? But I'm vice-captain."

"Not any more," he said. "Mr Hall said I can't stop you from coming to the club. But as I'm captain, the team is up to me. And I've made the decision to replace you with Flora, so now Aakesh is vice-captain, William is sub and you will sit out the rest of the competition."

"Sit out?" I repeated.

"So, if you don't mind, Amelia," Miles said. "Your badge."

Miles pointed to the vice-captain badge on my lapel. I closed my hand around it, unwilling to give it up.

I turned to Flora. "You've taken my place?" Tears started in my eyes that I tried to blink away.

"I'm sorry, Amelia," Flora said. "Miles didn't give me any choice. It was that or we forfeit the competition. The first round's being held here, so we can't not enter a team."

"But I won that place fair and square."

"Your photo's gone all round other schools," Miles said, his nostrils flaring wider than ever. "This year's topic is *Our Lives Online*. What if one of the opposing teams brings it up? Do you really want to risk that happening in front of the whole school? Are you honestly prepared to embarrass our entire team because you decided to photograph your...*chesticles*?"

I literally shuddered.

"I'm really sorry, Amelia," Flora said. "I wish there was something I could do."

I couldn't believe what I was hearing. I'd been dropped from the team because of the photo? I tried to stop myself from crying in front of Miles but I couldn't. I ran to the nearest toilets and locked myself in a cubicle.

I squeezed my eyes shut but all I could see was that photograph. And my mum's face when I told her about it. I was thirteen years old and my life was over. I hadn't just lost the vice-captaincy, or my place on the team, I'd lost everything. My reputation, my chances of being popular. Even Evan. And I could never post any TikToks as long as I lived. Just then the door went and a group of girls walked in. I held my breath as I heard one of them say my name.

"I mean, was Amelia actually seeing Evan?"

"I doubt it. She was begging him to go out with her apparently."

"Is that why she sent it? Talk about desperate."

"Well, I feel sorry for her. Literally everyone in the school has seen it."

"She's probably glad. She's the one who was always posting those weird cello TikToks, right?"

I stayed there in the toilet cubicle until they left. I planned on staying there for the rest of the afternoon. But when the bell went, something in me couldn't skip lessons, no matter how badly I wanted to. I dumped my Debate Club notebook in the bin on my way out.

For the rest of the day I felt numb. Half-awake inside a nightmare. One where your entire school has seen you virtually naked. And nothing can make them unsee it.

On the way to French, there were wolf whistles in the corridor. I put my head down and ignored them as I walked up the stairs. But then I heard a revolting name hurled at me. I looked up and there was a group of Year Tens heading down the stairs towards me. I couldn't help but spot him right away. Evan. My stomach dropped the entire flight of stairs.

"There she is, mate," one of them said, followed by a word that meant what Miss Chabra called a "lady of the night" when we were reading *Oliver Twist*. He laughed at me and put up his hand to high-five Evan. I only looked at him for a split second. But I missed the next step and almost tripped over. "Don't leave me hanging!" said the boy with his arm up. I watched out of the corner of my eye as Evan slowly tapped his hand. I ran up the rest of the stairs and into my French room, ignoring the Year Seven I nearly sent flying.

In the lesson, DJ kept googling French swear words. Then he and Lachlan took it in turns to whisper them at me. I couldn't bring myself to tell on them. The thought of explaining what they were saying to Mr LaRue was too humiliating. Even in French.

I didn't wait for Hannah by the gates. I just ran all the way home and shut myself in my bedroom.

The next day, at lunchtime, it felt stuffy in Mrs Weaver's office. I could feel little sweat patches forming in my armpits. I hoped I didn't smell. There was condensation on the windows so the outside world looked like an impressionist painting. I kept thinking about Selina sitting outside in the corridor and wondering if she'd tell Dad I said her new perfume was toxic. I tried to focus on what she'd told me. That it wasn't my fault. That I had nothing to be ashamed about. But if that was true, why did my heart feel like it had the weight of the entire ocean inside it?

"And that's when you were first called those names," Mrs Weaver asked, "on the way to school with Hannah, is that right, Amelia?" She cleared her throat a few times but it still sounded gruff, like there was phlegm caught in it. "Amelia, are you listening?" I nodded. "But you don't know the names of the people who were shouting things at you?"

I shook my head. Mrs Weaver sighed like I'd given a wrong answer.

"And this photograph," Mr Harding said, shifting his weight around in his seat like he was the one who felt uncomfortable. I've never wanted the floor to swallow me up so bad. "That's the only one you sent to Evan Palmer?" I nodded again.

"Speak for God's sake, Amelia," my dad said. "You got yourself into this mess; you can get yourself out. Answer him. Is that the only photo you sent Evan?"

I hated Dad then. More than I did when he was yelling

at our baseball team from the dugout. Probably more than I did when he packed up his stuff and left.

"Yes," I said, keeping my eyes on my hands that were clenched on my lap. "That was the only one."

"Thank you," Mr Harding said. "And you only sent it to Evan? Nobody else?"

"I only sent it to him. And I deleted it right away." I turned to my dad. "It was supposed to disappear. After a few seconds it disappears."

Dad sighed, but it came out more like a growl. He put his head in his hands. I wondered if he would ever forgive me. Maybe I was as stupid as he thought I was.

"Thank you, Amelia," Mrs Weaver said. "Unfortunately, with the volume of sharing, and with some of the messages disappearing or being deleted, it does rather complicate things. We're talking hundreds and hundreds of shares. It's simply impossible to trace it back."

"You mean you don't believe me?" I asked, dumbfounded. "You think I *wanted* everyone to see me like that?"

Mrs Weaver closed her eyes and put her hands together like she was praying. A long sigh came out of her mouth. "Amelia, you are one of our most promising students. You're somewhat of a prodigy on the cello. And the emails I have had from your teachers over the past forty-eight hours are testament to your hard work and integrity. But, I have to take an objective view of this. Sharing photographs of young people..." She hesitated. I wondered for a moment if she was about to say "in see-through bras" but she said, "semi-nude is not only indecent, it's a crime. Even if you take the photograph of yourself."

As she said the word "crime" my dad sat bolt upright. "You're not telling me my daughter is a criminal in all this, Mrs Weaver, surely! I mean, yes, she's been completely stupid. That much is obvious," he said, which felt like a brick to the head. "But a criminal?"

"Please, Mr Bright," said Mr Harding firmly. "I'm afraid what Amelia has done is a crime. It's creating and sharing an indecent image of a minor. That's the law, I'm afraid. Even though it was of herself. I realize this is an isolated incident but—"

"And what about the people who have *shared* her image? Aren't they the real criminals here?"

"Yes, absolutely," Mrs Weaver said, her eyes remaining on me. "And we will certainly be speaking to as many as we can. I assure you, we will do everything we can to get Amelia's photograph deleted from their devices. But of course, we have no real way of knowing how far it's been shared. We are, of course, dealing with minors here. As a school, we prefer to take a restorative approach." My dad looked puzzled. "Educate them, Mr Bright. Make sure they understand the law. Anyone with Amelia's photograph stored on their phone is breaking the law, Mr Bright. We'll do as much as we can." She turned to me and smiled. "Amelia, I assume you didn't realize you were committing a crime when you sent Evan that photograph. But you were, technically, breaking the law."

I shook my head as hard as it would go. It felt like the floor was collapsing under my feet. I was a criminal now?

"It's our policy to contact the police on these matters, I'm afraid. As a school, we do have a duty of care." Mrs Weaver carried on, "Now I have the impossible task of tracking down the people responsible for sharing the image. You do understand, we're dealing with hundreds of students here, Mr Bright."

Dad snorted. "I think it's pretty obvious who the guilty party is, Mrs Weaver, considering Amelia only sent the picture to Evan Palmer."

"Yes, and I'll be speaking to Evan and his parents shortly," Mrs Weaver said. "But still, I have to remain impartial and wait until I have heard from both parties. The fact is, the image originated with Amelia. She has to take some of the blame."

"Amelia?" Dad said. "Tell her Evan made you send that picture."

I swallowed. "I…"

"Is that what happened, Amelia?" Mr Harding said, leaning forward. "Did Evan pressure you into sending the photograph?"

I thought for a moment. Did he pressure me into it? Didn't I think it was a good idea? Wasn't I supposed to be his girlfriend? I felt so confused, like my brain was filling with fog. All I could do was shrug.

Dad rubbed his face and turned to Mum. "Penny – are you just going to sit there?"

Mum took my hand. "No, I'm not just going to sit here, Mike. I'm giving our daughter the support she needs right now. Which is not an argument. Thank you, Mrs Weaver, for being so fair and understanding. None of us had any idea Amelia had committed a crime. It makes my skin crawl to think about it."

Mrs Weaver smiled and stood up. "Amelia, there's a little time left of your lunch break. If you haven't eaten yet, do get something. If you're late for your lesson, please explain you were with me." As if I felt like eating anything at that point.

"But what about the picture, Mrs Weaver?" Mum said. "How can we, I mean, how do we get it back?" Mum did an embarrassed laugh. "Not get it back, you know what I mean. Permanently delete it. Take it offline."

"Oh, Mrs Bright, I assumed…"

"We can't get it back, Penny," Dad said. "That's it. It's out there for ever."

And those words "for ever" sounded so permanent. Like the picture was carved in stone or tattooed on my skin. There was no deleting it. I'd thought it would exist for a few seconds. But it would exist for my entire life, maybe longer. People on the other side of the world might have seen it by now. The career I'd imagined as somebody important – a famous cellist, perhaps travelling the world, a YouTube sensation, appearing with the Royal Philharmonic Orchestra just like my mum had all those years ago – disappeared in front of my eyes like smoke. Because when anybody Googled my name now, that image would probably come up. It would haunt me for the rest of my life, like the monster in *Frankenstein*.

And when your dreams disappear like that, you're so empty you feel nothing. You can't even cry, because there aren't any tears left.

Mrs Weaver opened the door so we could leave, and sitting right outside her office were Evan and his parents.

"Oh, Evan. Mr and Mrs Palmer," Mrs Weaver said. "You're early. I'm so sorry, this wasn't supposed to overlap."

I can't express exactly how much I hated Evan Palmer

right then. The only person who hated him more was my dad.

"Proud of yourself, are you?" Dad said. I'd never seen Evan blush before. "Humiliating my daughter?"

"Mr Bright, please," Mrs Weaver said, "he's also a child. Come on in. I do apologize."

"We're so terribly sorry about all of this," Evan's mum said. She had the same melodic accent and dark brown curls as her son.

I stared right at Evan as he walked past me. But he only met my eyes for a second. And I'm not sure what I saw. But it wasn't hatred or fear or even guilt. It looked like sadness.

43

Mum let me go straight home after the meeting. I think she was so shocked about the crime thing she couldn't think about anything else. After dinner, I had to get out of the house so I went round to Nisha's. Only, when she answered the door she came outside and closed it behind her.

"Oh my God, I've had the worst day," I said. "Can't I come in?" But her face dropped. "Is something wrong?"

"This is so bad and you're going to hate me," she said. "But you know my dad's on the Parent-Teacher Committee, well, he found out about the photo. I didn't tell him, I swear. But he's overreacted a bit."

"What do you mean?"

"He's checked my phone, looked at all my social media. All my photos. Made me show him our messages and well, he says I can't hang around with you any more. He says you're a bad influence."

"What?" I could not believe what she was saying. "Nisha! We've been best friends since Year Three! We can't just stop hanging out together."

"I know. I've tried talking to him but he doesn't want to hear it." Her eyes pooled with tears. "I told him you're my best friend but…" Just then, her dad appeared at the window and he knocked on it. "I'm sorry," she whispered. I nodded and tried my best to avoid looking at her dad. I could practically feel his steely glare freezing me out through the glass. I barely dared blink in case my tears spilled over; I didn't want Nisha to feel any worse. "It's just outside school, that's all. I promise," Nisha said quickly, calling something in Gujarati into the house. "I'll speak to him again later. I have to go."

Before I could say anything she'd closed the door and I was left on the doorstep alone.

The last place I should have gone was the beach. I didn't even have my gloves. But I shoved my hands in my pockets and decided that if I was numb inside I may as well get numb on the outside too.

It was coming up to high tide, so most of the beach was covered by the sea. But the rock pools were still visible in the twilight. I headed towards them, forgetting Mum had taken my phone off me so I didn't have a torch. I was halfway across the rocks when I heard his voice.

"AMELIA!"

It was ridiculous. It was almost high tide. It would be dark soon. And Evan Palmer was at the beach. *My* beach. I turned around with such hatred that I almost slipped on some seaweed. It made me hate him even more.

"Leave me alone!" I shouted.

"Please," he said, coming towards me. "I need to explain. It's not what you think."

"You promised!" I shouted. "PROMISED! And now the whole school has seen it!"

"I didn't mean for any of this to happen," Evan said. He stepped towards the rock I was standing on, so I took a big step back, straight into a rock pool. I felt the icy water soak into my shoe. Evan held out his hand, but I refused to take it. I pushed past him and skidded and slipped my way over to the steps. I could hear he was following me. "Amelia, I know you don't believe me. But I'm telling you, I never shared that photo." I stopped on the bottom step. "I swear. Please listen to me."

I didn't turn around, but kept my frozen hands on the metal railings. "I suppose I deserve an explanation."

"I'm sorry," he said. "But I promise this is the truth. The first time I saw you, I knew you were someone special."

"Urgh," I said. "I'm leaving." I started up the steps but he carried on following me.

"It's true! I was getting out of the car for that first match of the season and there you were – standing in the sunlight looking like your hair was on fire. Then pitching to you? That was unreal. You smacked my fastball out of the park like it was nothing. I've never seen a girl play baseball like that. A swing like a tornado but you also rescue crabs from rock pools before they become seagull food. It was a fluke we even met as my dad wanted me to play cricket. But once I've made my mind up, I usually stick to it. I suppose that's what happened with you. I got stuck on you."

I'm not saying it wasn't a good speech. But when you've been in Debate Club for two years, it takes more than a good speech to win you over. "So stuck you decided to ignore me again and again? Then share my photo with the entire school?" I asked. "Ruin my life?" My teeth were chattering as I spoke. Evan took off his cagoule and offered it to me but I shook my head.

"That was the last thing I wanted. I was trying to do the opposite. When I started at St Clement's and I saw you that day, I couldn't believe my luck. It was like – what do you call it? – serendipity! I joked to my mum that we were 'star-crossed lovers'. Mum said I could get that idea out of my head. But I couldn't. We're doing *Romeo and Juliet* in English for a start. But that was the problem. At school I'm Evan Palmer and you're, well…Maggot."

"Are you honestly trying to apologize here? Because this is the worst apology I have ever heard."

"Just hear me out, okay? There was this list that had gone round before I even started. The Fit List they were calling it. Something like that. And they said you were ugly."

"Thanks for reminding me."

"Sorry," he said. "But you're not – you're something else. Hair like flames and you're into baseball!"

"I am not into baseball," I replied. "My dad makes me play."

"I mean, you're cute and interesting." I admit I blushed at this point. I'm not proud of myself. "But they said you were bottom of the list. Jayden said you were created by an infestation of maggots. I didn't know how to react. It's not exactly easy being the new boy. I liked you. But how could I tell anyone at school? That day at the beach, I panicked. I knew they would rip into me for liking you. I can't tell those guys half the stuff I'm into."

"So you kept us a secret until you got a photo of me half-naked?"

"I didn't plan on showing them. It's just that I wanted my mates to see you differently. I hated it when they called you Maggot. I showed them your TikToks playing cello. You're like someone off *Britain's Got Talent* or something. But they said it was sad. Nothing worked, you see. Nothing made a difference. And then when you came to the picnic benches…"

"That was when you did it? That's why they were laughing at me?"

"No. They called me Maggot Boy. That's what they were laughing at. They were laughing at me."

"Let me get this straight," I shouted into the wind. "Your *friends* laughed at you for *one lunchtime* and that's the reason you shared my picture?" I could feel fury warming my bones. "I've been teased relentlessly for two YEARS, Evan. I've had a bucket of maggots thrown at me! But I would never use that as an excuse to betray you."

"I know." Evan looked down. "I'm sorry. I just thought if they saw you the way I do they would leave you alone."

"Leave me alone? I can't even hang around with my best friend because of you. I've been dropped from the debate team! There's a picture of me in my dad's girlfriend's bra probably online for ever. The school are telling the police! This is going to haunt me *for ever*."

"I know, I get it. I'm in trouble over it as well. I just felt stupid, I suppose. Embarrassed. I usually don't care what

348

people say. But I was new. I wanted them to like me. Everyone was laughing and calling me Maggot Boy. Then I remembered I had your photo on my phone. I figured if my mates could just see you're not this mega geek they make you out to be then they'd stop. They were saying 'Maggot Boy' over and over again and I was sick of it. So, I told them about the photo. I wish I could pause time. I'd go back to that moment and stop it there. I'd suck up their name-calling and keep my stupid phone in my pocket. But I didn't. And I've regretted that every second since."

"That's your explanation," I said, turning to leave. "You were ashamed of liking me. So you shared the photo to prove you're not Maggot Boy. How noble. You got a cape under that cagoule?"

"I didn't share it, Amelia. Jayden grabbed my phone off me and it ended up getting passed round. Someone must have airdropped the photo to their phone. I knew you'd probably have taken a baseball bat to my phone if you knew the photo was even on there. But I thought it was okay, because they were my mates. If anything, I thought they couldn't say you're a maggot now, could they?"

"No, because what they're calling me instead is so much worse."

"I'm sorry. I had no idea the picture would leave that picnic bench. I just wanted them to see what you're really like."

I almost screamed. "Evan Palmer, you must be some kind of idiot! That photo is not what I'm really like. It wasn't even my bra! I only sent it because I was desperate to impress you. I would never in a million years have done that if you hadn't asked me so many times. People are shouting names at me in the corridor. My own parents are ashamed of me. I'm ashamed of myself! I'd never even kissed anyone until I met you."

"I'm sorry. I swear I did everything I could to get them to delete it. But I don't even know half the people sharing it. It was going all round school. I mean, what could I do? It's like trying to stop a tsunami with an umbrella. And all that was running through my head was that I should have told you, Amelia. But I couldn't. I felt so guilty. It all got out of my control."

Just as he said that, a giant wave crashed onto the beach. Like a full stop on our conversation.

"I have to go," I said.

"So, are we okay? The thought of losing you as a friend—"

"What you did is *irreparable*, Evan. You can't take the photo back. You should never have saved it in the first place. Please just leave me alone."

Evan wiped his eyes. I'm not sure if it was from the same drizzle that was blurring my glasses or if he was actually crying. But I'd cried too much the past few days to even care.

I couldn't forgive Evan. Not while people were still posting nasty things on my TikToks, like Ju Long had told me. They were the one thing I was proud of and even they had been ruined. Evan was getting high-fives in the corridor while I was being dropped by everyone like I had the plague. The unfairness of it all was what stung the most. And the fact it had gone round other schools meant I couldn't even change schools to escape it. It would never disappear, ever. My skin felt dirty every time I thought of it.

I left Evan standing there at the bottom of the concrete steps and went home. I put my soaked trainers on the radiator and went into the lounge. Mum was sorting through some boxes of gift wrap for the shop, so I sat on the floor next to Gramps's armchair. He smelled so strongly of mints my eyes started watering. Gramps reached out and held my hand.

"Amelia, you're freezing, love. Come here." He wrapped the blanket he had on his lap around my shoulders and gave me the biggest hug. There was the faint smell of cigarillos in his stubble. "Now, have I ever told you about your great-grandmother Joy?"

Mum gave him a look and said, "I'm not sure now is the right time, Dad." Which told me that, unlike most of Gramps's stories, this one would definitely be interesting. He winked at me and I followed him into the annexe.

"You've probably never heard of the Bluebell Dancers," Gramps said as he settled into the armchair with an old tin on his knee. "But they were an international sensation. Here. This one was taken in Brussels in 1946." He handed me a photograph of a woman wearing a feathery headdress doing the splits against a wall. She only had on a leotard, fishnet tights and long white gloves.

"*That's* my great-grandma?" I asked. "Your mum?"

"Oh yes, that's her. And here's one from Paris," he said, handing me another. "That's Joy, second from the right."

I looked at the photograph. There was a line of dancers all dressed in corsets and knickers with what looked like birdcages strapped to their heads. And another one. But this time they were only wearing knickers. And nothing else. Gramps was showing me a whole procession of topless women from the 1940s.

"Gramps!" I said, barely believing my eyes. "These women are—"

"Oh, I know," he said, winking. "Not one of them under five foot ten!"

"I didn't mean tall." I turned the photograph around. Handwritten on the back was *Le Lido, Paris, 1948*.

Gramps and I looked through the entire tin of photographs of my great-grandmother: a girl from Bristol who was too tall to be a ballerina, but toured Europe and the US as one of the world-renowned Bluebell Dancers.

"They look amazing!" I said, turning over another photo. *US Tour, 1950*.

"That was just before I was born," Gramps said. "See, you can just make out her wedding ring, look." He passed me the magnifying glass he used for crosswords and I could just about see. It was grainy, but it was there. A wedding band, and a small bump in the tummy of her costume.

I must have looked through hundreds of photographs and newspaper clippings that night. Gramps said I could take the tin to my room. There were photos of Joy performing. Some of her hanging out in dressing rooms backstage. Some having her hair done. And a lot of them performing semi-nude.

INTERNATIONAL SENSATION "THE BLUEBELL DANCERS" COME TO LONDON one of the headlines read. *INCOMPARABLE BLUEBELL GIRLS DANCE IN*

EDINBURGH said another. The caption underneath one of the photos said, *Bluebell Girl Joy Carpenter makes her way onstage.* She had the biggest smile on her face. My great-grandmother: an international dancing sensation. Wearing nothing but velvet knickers and ostrich feathers. It was like I'd discovered this whole secret life. My only memories of my great-grandma were of her owning a budgie called Jacques and baking fresh bread. And here she was living the most glamorous-looking life in Paris and Brussels and New York. *Half-naked!*

I lay in bed, thinking about why Gramps had chosen now to show me that tin. Mum had said now wasn't the right time, but she was wrong about that. Now was the perfect time to find out that my great-grandmother, all five foot eleven of her, had stood onstage half-naked, not feeling ashamed of her body at all. In fact, she flaunted it, and she was celebrated. And that was over seventy years ago! On the front page of newspapers! And here I was, feeling ashamed that people had seen one photo of me that was always supposed to be private.

It was the first night I didn't cry myself to sleep since the photo came out. Maybe I had needed to hear the apology from Evan, as annoying as it was. Somehow knowing he hadn't meant the photo to be shared made a difference. It meant everything between us wasn't a total lie. I could never forgive him, not really. But when I looked up at the moonlight, for some reason I felt less alone.

44

The next afternoon in PE we were playing volleyball indoors. It was chucking it down with rain, which usually didn't stop Miss Bevan from making us play outside, but I guess even she draws the line at thunder and lightning. Girls were at one end of the sports hall and boys were at the other. But I kept hearing names being hurled through the nets at me like spears. Then someone shouted for me to show them what was under my PE kit. My face burned red and I ran to the changing rooms, ignoring Miss Bevan's orders to come back.

She found me crying in the corner. I thought she would blow her whistle at me and tell me to get back on the court. But she didn't. She sat on the bench opposite and said, "Bright." She always calls us by our surnames. "It's tough for you right now, I get it." She leaned towards me and I saw she had tiny specks of mud on her face. Maybe she'd made the Year Sevens do cross-country earlier. "But what are you going to do? Run away and hide in here every time someone brings it up?"

"I was thinking about it," I said, my cheeks burning with shame that my teachers knew about the photo.

"You know some of the kids call me Bevan the Witch, right?" I wasn't sure if owning up to that would be helpful, so I pretended to be shocked. "It's fine," she said. "I've heard it a million times. You think I let it put me off my game? No way. See this?" She took out her phone and scrolled through it for a minute. Then she showed me a picture of a wooden shelving unit thing. We had something similar at home but with books on it. Hers was full of trophies and medals.

"Hockey, trampolining, triathlon, the London Marathon. And they're just the ones I've won for myself. You think anyone on the school hockey team who won the country championships last year calls me a witch?"

I doubted they would dare. "No."

"Exactly. You play rounders, right?"

"Baseball," I corrected her, then wished I'd just nodded because she sighed like I wasn't getting it.

"Right. Each time you hear one of those names, imagine the people shouting at you are on the opposing team, okay. They're just trying to put you off your game. Are you going to let them put you off your game, Bright?

357

Or are you going to send back another of those aggressive cut-shots with back spin that are impossible to return, like I just saw you deliver to poor Tally in there?"

I smiled. *Miss Bevan saw that hit?*

"Now get up. You've got a game to play."

And I didn't intend to disagree.

On the way home from school that day with the afternoon sunshine on my face, I somehow felt less ashamed of myself. Ever since my photo had been shared, I'd felt like my body wasn't my own. But here, with the sun's warmth bathing my skin, I didn't feel so bad. And my brain started ticking over. I wasn't going to frazzle away into nothing. I wasn't going to let one stupid photo dictate my entire life. I needed to take back control of this situation. My phone flashed up with a reminder: **Debate competition in one week.** Slowly a smile spread over my face. I didn't have long to prepare.

I was supposed to be going to Dad's that weekend, but he was still angry with me about the photo. So instead, I stayed at home and spent most of that weekend writing my speech. I practised until I could recite it word for word, then I emailed Flora from Debate Club. **Can you help me with something?**

On Monday, I waited for Nisha in the library at lunchtime. Mum still wouldn't give my phone back, and Nisha's dad wasn't budging about us not hanging around together. So we hung out by the non-fiction section, hoping that one day everything would go back to normal.

"What are you planning, Amelia?" Nisha asked as she sat down next to me.

"Nothing," I replied. But I couldn't stop my face from forming a grin.

"I know that look," Nisha said. "Please tell me this isn't Popularity Plan 2.0."

"Considering how badly the last one backfired? I don't think so."

"You're definitely planning something," she said. "Your eyes have got their shine back."

I smiled. "Just make sure you get a front-row seat at the debate competition. I don't think you'll be disappointed. Not this time."

Nisha squeezed my hand. "Is it a bucket of slime landing on Miles? Because I'm so here for that."

"Better than that," I said. "I might even render him speechless."

* * *

I had not intended to do my hair and make-up. That was Hannah's idea. She said if you're going to make a big speech then you may as well look big doing it. She insisted on doing a fishtail braid that curled over my head and finished by my right shoulder. It was almost the same as the way she'd worn hers for *The Little Mermaid*. But I didn't feel in the least bit like Ariel. I had my legs firmly on the ground and a voice in my throat. I was ready.

"What are *you* doing here?" Miles said as I walked into the hall at break with Hannah. "You're sitting this one out. And no offence, but even having you here might jeopardize our chances. I assumed you'd take a seat near the back."

I knew Miles was full of garbage, but suddenly I felt stupid being there and started to doubt my plan. I wondered if I should turn around and leave but Hannah grabbed my hand. It was like a shield of protection, reminding me I wasn't on my own.

"Listen, whatever-your-name-is," Hannah said. "Unless you want me to report you to Mrs Weaver for bullying my sister, I suggest you make her feel welcome."

"Right," Miles said quickly. "Sorry, Hannah. I didn't know Amelia was your sister."

"It's Amelia you need to apologize to, twerp."

"Right," Miles said again. "Sorry, Amelia. You are

welcome, obviously. You're technically still a member of the debate team. We've almost finished setting up. William's around here somewhere. He's got some snacks."

Hannah and I headed backstage and watched the rest of Debate Club setting up the stage. The IT person was checking the video camera and the microphones, and suddenly people started pouring into the hall and taking their seats. My stomach started doing backflips. I grabbed Hannah's hand. "Are you sure I can do this?"

"Absolutely. Although you should know that if you don't do it, I will."

"Oh God," I said, peering out into the audience. "Evan's here." I knew he would be. They make everyone watch the competitions held in school. But I didn't think he'd be sitting so near the front.

"Evan's here?" Hannah peered round the edge of the curtain. "Reckon I could fire a pretzel at him from here?"

"Don't! Please!" I said, thinking she was being serious. Actually, knowing Hannah she probably was. But she told me to stop worrying and focus on my speech.

The hall was filling up and both teams were taking their seats. Flora turned to wink at me. I watched as she switched Miles's microphone off while he wasn't looking.

"Good afternoon, everyone!" Mr Hall said from the front of the stage. "Welcome to St Clement's Academy!

We are delighted to be hosting the first and very important round of this year's debating competition. Please welcome our teams…"

I listened, my stomach churning with nerves, as Mr Hall introduced the teams. And for the first time I felt glad I was standing here, with this speech in my hands, instead of sitting out there beside Miles. A wave of applause filled the room once Mr Hall finished talking. I rubbed my diaphragm, trying to force out my nerves.

"You still got something to say?" Hannah whispered. I had butterflies in my stomach, but I nodded. I was ready. I was a Bright after all. And Brights don't quit. "Then go." And Hannah gently pushed me out onstage.

I stood there for a moment, not moving. My skin went cold as I looked out at the audience. Could I really do this? I tried to imagine Amelia Earhart on her final flight. Knowing there was a chance she may never return but getting into that cockpit anyway. Because sometimes you have to do the impossible. I looked down and saw Nisha's smiling face in the crowd. Right in the front row. And then I knew. I had to do this.

I stepped forward, took the microphone from Mr Hall's hand and walked to the middle of the stage. Half the audience gasped. Mr Hall looked completely confused, but Flora stood and led him down the steps as though this was something we'd rehearsed. One of the judges looked around nervously. Miles looked like he was about to explode. He stood up and said something into his microphone, but no sound came out. I heard the word *maggot* come from somewhere in the crowd. But I didn't care. My heart was beating like a tambourine. I stood tall and said the first word of my speech.

"Listen."

45

"Good morning, everybody. I'm Amelia Bright. You probably weren't expecting to hear from me today. After all, you know what people are saying about me. You've seen things written about me online. In fact, maybe you wrote some of them. I've seen those things too. Only when I saw them, they were printed out in front of me in Mrs Weaver's office.

"None of the things you wrote were very nice. Maybe you didn't expect me to read them. But, you know what, I bet some of you did. Some of you wanted me to see all of that nastiness and believe it. But I don't. None of those words were the truth about me. So how about you listen to the truth about Amelia Bright?"

The room was in absolute silence. Mr Hall started making his way over to me, but Miss Bevan ran up behind him and took his arm. *Let her speak*, was what she seemed to be saying.

"I came second in the spelling bee last year. My baseball team came third in the English Junior League. I've passed Grade 5 cello, which makes me something of a prodigy, actually. But none of you care about those things. You just see my pale skin and freckles and ginger hair – the ginger hair I got from my mum, by the way, who once toured the world playing harp in orchestras; the ginger hair that landed my sister the part of Ariel in the school play—" I heard Hannah cough behind me. "I mean, obviously it was mainly her singing talent. But she didn't have to wear a wig or anything. My point is…" I'd deviated from my cue cards and now I couldn't find my place. "My point is," I repeated, "that none of you saw any of my achievements. Or maybe you did see them and just decided they were worthless. *I* was worthless. Worthless enough to call me Maggot.

"And that name – the name you all use so casually like it doesn't even matter, like I don't even matter; a name I've had shouted at me in virtually every part of this school – even that is ironic. Because none of you have the first idea how amazing maggots are." I'd written *Pause for effect* in my notes so I waited for a moment. Until every single person was gazing at me, waiting for my next words. "Maggots are actually a medical phenomenon. They can save lives by munching on rotting flesh, leaving healthy tissue intact. Yes, those creepy, slimy maggots that some of you hurled at me in disgust – I know who it was, by the way – are incredible creatures with healing powers that are worthy of more respect than being thrown from a bucket as some kind of joke. But funnily enough, a bunch of grubs that feast on flesh is kind of an appropriate metaphor for what's happened to me," I carried on, building on the encouraging looks I was getting from Miss Bevan and some of the girls in the crowd.

"Because however revolting some people find me, however worthless they decided I was, they also decided it was okay to reduce me to a piece of flesh. That photo – you all know the one I'm talking about – was a photo I was persuaded to take. On the understanding that it was private and would disappear in a matter of seconds. But it didn't." I hadn't planned this next bit, but I had to address the Evan in the room. I turned to face him. "You told me it would be deleted. You told me I could trust you. But I couldn't." Evan looked down at the floor, his cheeks reddening, and I addressed the rest of the room again. Looking straight back at the eyes staring at me. "I believed him. Believed what he told me. That was my only mistake. Evan Palmer saved that photo without my consent. Without my knowledge. He betrayed me and yet I'm the one being shamed. And he didn't even have the courage to tell me when he had shared it. I found that out when someone hurled a name at me in the street." I scanned the crowd for the great crested grebe hairstyle. It wasn't hard to spot. And spoke to him directly. "That felt worse than that entire bucket of maggots, by the way." Arran Parsons met my eyes, but when I stared back without flinching, he looked down at his hands, embarrassed. I took a deep breath. My lips were quivering with nerves. I looked back at Hannah and she nodded at me, her eyes shining.

"Maybe you're one of the people who shared it. Maybe you're somebody in a group chat who forwarded it on. Maybe you're just someone who laughed about it. But that picture was only ever meant to be private. Every single one of you must have known that. That picture has ended up costing me friendship, my parents' trust, my place on this debating team. I'm supposed to be sitting over there! On the team! I'm supposed to be vice-captain. But I'm not. And yes, I should never have taken that stupid photo. But I was so desperate to be accepted." I sighed. "I was so desperate to not be me, because apparently being me was gross. And because of that, I had to sit in Mrs Weaver's office thinking I might get excluded! Arrested! But beyond all that, worse than the rules I didn't even know I was breaking, is knowing I betrayed my own heart.

"I've spent the last two years of my life trying everything to fit in. I would have done anything to be accepted by all of you. I would have changed every single atom of my being just to be liked. I would have scraped off these freckles if it were possible. I thought if I could just reshape myself to fit this magical mould, then my life would be perfect. Those TikToks some of you laugh at me for took hours! Hours of practising again and again because I thought I could impress everyone by being perfect. Hoping, praying you would stop calling me that name. Hearing it every single day of my life, and seeing myself – loads of us actually – rated in that disgusting list. With so many people laughing along, is it any wonder I had started to believe what you thought of me? That I wanted to make you all see me differently? That I wanted to *be* different?

"But if anyone here thinks that photo – that photo that was only supposed to exist for a few seconds – tells any kind of truth about me, then think again. A picture is one tiny piece of time captured for ever, but it never tells you the whole story. Some people choose to share their bodies with the entire world. That's their choice. This wasn't mine. So that stupid photo is not going to be my legacy, no matter how many people have seen it.

"I do not intend to shrink into corners any more when I hear the word *maggot* or any other words you want to throw at me. I do not intend to shrink in general. I refuse to live my life feeling ashamed of one mistake. That mistake is one grain of sand in a whole beach of mistakes I'll probably make in my life. But I'll never make the mistake of betraying myself again. Nothing anyone can say will put me off my game any more." I paused and smiled at Miss Bevan. "I plan to achieve big things. Great things! And I know you will all remember me. Not for that nickname or that photo, which are just tiny footnotes in the anthology of my life. One day, I think you'll be hearing the name Amelia Bright a lot. Because I have oceans to fly."

I could feel my cheeks were flushed, and my heart felt like it had suspended beating for the entirety of my speech. I swallowed, and let my cue cards drop to the floor. I closed my eyes. It felt as though a kite was lifting me high above the stage, into the clouds, and I was sailing above them all. I'd done it. A chair squeaked. Someone coughed. Then slowly, one pair of hands by one pair of hands, an applause sailed up from the audience and all around me. And it drowned out the background noise.

EPILOGUE

The day after I gave my speech, DJ, his cousin Jayden and his friend Louis got suspended for five days for throwing the maggots at me. Some people said it was harsh. But I thought it was *befitting*. Which was my new word that day. Mrs Weaver and Mr Harding contacted the police shortly after our meeting. Walking into a room with my parents and facing two police officers was one of the scariest things I've ever had to do. I do not recommend committing crimes. Even accidentally. It's way too frightening. But actually, the police officers were really kind. They referred to me as the victim, and I'm trying my best to see myself that way. To believe that what happened wasn't my fault. Not to blame myself too much.

Evan had to see them too. And some other people the Student Services team had investigated. I don't know what the police said to them. Hopefully that they were a bunch of *skunk cabbages* for sharing my photo. But I wouldn't know, since I haven't spoken to Evan or any of them. Nor do I intend to. I said everything I had to say in the assembly hall. They're not getting any more of me than that. If this whole thing has taught me anything, it's that I shouldn't waste my time on people who don't see that I am *splendiferous*. That was the last word on my poster. I'll have to enter the Year Nine Spelling Bee to have a chance at winning another one. Mum said I'll have to hoover up the gold bits myself if I do. But actually, I think I've got all the words I need right now.

Nisha's dad came round eventually. He said he was tired of seeing Nisha's sad face every evening. And he watched the speech I made too. Flora recorded the whole thing and sent it to me. Nisha made her dad watch it. We weren't sure it would do any good. But I guess it did the trick because she invited me to a sleepover a few days later. And they've invited me to the Diwali festival in Leicester with them in a couple of weeks. There will be lights and fireworks and dancing and parades and even a big wheel. Nisha's trying to teach me this special dance called Odissi in preparation. I'm kind of hopeless. Nisha says she doesn't understand how I can play the cello so gracefully yet be so awkward on my feet. If she saw my mum dancing, she'd probably understand.

Mr Hall made Miles give me the vice-captaincy back. He said anyone who can stand up and make a speech like that ought to be captain. But everyone knows I'd have to prise the captain badge out of Miles's dead hands to get that. And I really do not want to touch him. Or any boy. For a very long time.

Evan's apologized about a thousand times. He even wrote me a letter. I think his parents made him do it. They're also making him clear out their back garden, which is full of junk apparently. I wouldn't know since I never went over to his house. I can't forgive him. Not really. I know in *The Chronicles of Narnia* everyone gets forgiven. But in *The Wizard of Oz* one evil witch gets flattened by a house then Dorothy steals her shoes. And the other gets dissolved into nothing. So I think forgiveness is kind of a grey area. But I'm not angry with him anymore. I've accepted it. And I've moved on. There are still some days when I could happily throw a fastball at his head. But I've quit baseball now. And so has he. Which was a smart move because my dad would probably annihilate him if he ever saw him again.

Since getting suspended and everything, DJ has actually tried to be nice to me. He said, "Respect, Amelia," when he came back to school. It was the first time he'd called me Amelia in over two years. He even said please when he asked to borrow a pen in English the other day. It was so satisfying to smile sweetly and say no.

Like Mum said, it could have been worse. And that's saying something when a photo of you in your step-mum's see-through bra has been shared with the entire population. Well, kind of step-mum. I don't think Selina has plans to marry my dad any time soon. I can't blame her really. But still, she feels like a step-mum. Hannah still says stuff about her being fake. But she's only a bit fake on the outside. Inside she's real. And surely that's the best way round to be.

Dad still hasn't quite got over The Photo. But now both his daughters have quit baseball he has something more important to complain about.

"It's an insult to the Bright name!" he said when I told him I wasn't going to be on the team. "Your grandpa will be turning in his grave!" I feel bad for him, I really do. Grandpa Bright, that is. But Dad? I'm trying not to worry so much about what he thinks. I mean, I still put my name in the hat to be Class Representative this year. But this time, I did it for me. Because I think I would do a good job. Just before the ballot, DJ announced that he'd pound the meat out of anyone who didn't vote for me, so who knows? I might get lucky.

After my speech, Mr Malcolmson said I ought to go

into politics. I'm still undecided. But whatever I want to do seems less impossible now, for some reason. But less important too. Like maybe the entire world won't collapse if I don't try my best at everything. If I stop trying to be someone else. Stop playing catch up with Hannah. Because actually, I'm okay as I am. After all, baseball's a competition. But life isn't. And if it's not a competition, you can't win or lose. You can just play the game and be happy you're taking part. Weirdly I don't feel that way about volleyball though. There's something strangely satisfying about smashing a 250 gram ball into Madison Hart's face.

Since making my speech, I've joined a few more clubs at school. Creative Writing Club, Latin Club, Chess Club and Choir. I'm not exactly the best at them, but it keeps me away from the basketball courts. My blazer lapel is getting so full of badges it shines when it hits the sunlight. Every time one of them flashes I get reminded of the good stuff I've done. And who I really am.

THE END

THE END

LETTER FROM THE AUTHOR

Thank you for reading Amelia's story. Whilst this book is entirely fictional, the events are based on things that have happened and are happening right now to young people. The ubiquitousness of mobile phones has opened up our world to infinite virtual voices, experiences and wonders. It's enabled us to share, connect and record our lives in ways people never could have imagined when I was a teenager. However, it has come at a price: cyberbullying, predatory behaviour and – something I explore in *Bad Influence* – the sharing of nude and semi-nude photographs of minors.

Creating and sharing these sorts of images amongst teens is not usually intended to be criminal. In many cases, pictures are captured and shared with consent (although some, like Amelia, feel under an extraordinary amount of pressure to do so). Amelia longs for the bullying she's experiencing to end. She wants Evan to see her as more grown up. She hopes he will make her his girlfriend. She genuinely believes he won't share it with anyone. And Amelia is not alone. Research indicates that around 4% of thirteen year olds have sent a nude or semi-nude photograph, but this figure rises to almost 1 in 5 amongst teens aged 15 and older. The same research also found that 19% of those who shared nudes or semi-nudes were pressured or blackmailed into it, 14% were bullied or harassed as a result of the image, and 17% had their image shared without their consent. These figures are growing all the time.

Like Amelia says, a photograph is just a moment, one tiny piece of time captured for ever. But once a private moment is shared, it can cause an enormous amount of distress. Whether it's done thoughtlessly or deliberately, with the intent to bully, humiliate, or to help them fit in with the crowd, it is not an exaggeration to say that sharing these kinds of pictures, sent with the understanding that they would remain private, can cause lasting harm, sometimes even with fatal consequences.

I am eternally thankful that I grew up before the explosion of this digital age we find ourselves in. Adolescence can be incredibly tough, and the added pressure on young people today, exposed to an online world that doesn't quite match with their beliefs and values, constantly pinging away in their pockets, is perhaps one of the saddest things I witness as a teacher. When we encourage young people to embrace the online world, it is often without accompaniment, without guidance, without conversations, and without any real protection. Sadly, it is the most vulnerable in the real world who are most at risk online.

Amelia doesn't see herself as vulnerable. She doesn't even see herself as a victim at first. Neither do many of the people around her. But I hope you, as the reader, can see how vulnerable she is. She's a character, like so many of us, who doesn't believe she's good enough. She attaches a value to herself that others have prescribed – through the name-calling to The List, to the horrific bullying she is put through. Amelia believes that if only she was better, she would be worthy of their kindness and respect.

There is no doubt that young people like Amelia have the right to explore their burgeoning sexuality without fear or shame. It's natural that teens reach an age where they are curious and open to romantic relationships. But it's important too that they understand the risks of sending intimate pictures, even to people they trust. Someone who promises they won't keep it, they won't share it, they won't tell anyone. Because, in many cases, that's exactly what they intend to do. Whether it's deliberate or just plain insensitive, once your image is taken, stored or shared, you no longer have control over where it ends up. Amelia didn't mean to break the law by taking an "indecent" image of herself. Evan didn't realize he was breaking the law by saving it or sharing it. The many people who shared the photograph of Amelia were breaking the law too. It's a law designed to protect young people, but so many of them are unaware it even exists.

I wonder how many parents would react like Amelia's father. Firing questions and comments that make Amelia feel even worse than she does already. I wonder how many schools offer a nurturing, judgement-free, education-based approach to these kinds of issues instead of a punitive one. Or, even better, include high quality, engaging lessons on consent, and the sharing and receiving of intimate photographs, so that young people are better informed.

I also wonder how many young people who find themselves in a situation like Amelia's have no one to turn to. I hope this story reaches those readers and makes them feel less alone. Less afraid of speaking out. I also hope this story makes people think twice about sharing images without consent. I hope it opens up conversations between parents and teens. Amelia is able to pick herself up. She has people she can talk to and trust. She's still able to imagine a wonderful future for herself. I hope anyone who has experienced this scenario is able to see that they still have oceans to fly.

Virtual or physical, our world is far from perfect. And neither are we. All of us are bound to make mistakes, take risks, trust the wrong person, act in a way that doesn't make us feel very proud. But if we can navigate those missteps, learn, grow, apologize, use our voices in a positive way, and speak out about our experiences, then, in the words of Loretta Lynn's classic tune (I had to end on a musical note!), we've come a long way, baby.

Tamsin Winter

Statistics taken from the Cybersurvey from October 2020, Aiman el Asam & Adrienne Katz, for Internet Matters and Youthworks.

ACKNOWLEDGEMENTS

It's my name on the front of this book, but this was not like Amelia Earhart's solo flight across the Atlantic Ocean – there are so many incredibly talented people who contributed to making *Bad Influence* happen. Firstly, an enormous thank you to the incredible Luigi and Alison Bonomi at LBA for being THE most supportive, enthusiastic and positive agents a writer could wish for. You've believed in me and my writing from day one and I'm so grateful to be on your team. You always make me feel like I'm Big League, so thank you.

Sarah Stewart – this book would not have been possible, or ever finished, without your knock-it-out-of-the-park editorial skills. You deliver each note with pitch-perfect warmth, insight and energy, and this book would never have gone beyond the dugout without you. You respond to all of my OMGs and exclamatory emails with good humour, patience and you understood Amelia's heart and mind from the very beginning, so thank you. And just for posterity: BOOK 4 OMG!!!!!!

Rebecca Hill – this book would not have even crept into my mind without your amazing support for my debut, *Being Miss Nobody*, and you've been cheering me on ever since. Thank you for your enthusiasm and dedication to my writing; your unwavering passion for bringing empowering books to teenagers is an inspiration.

A huge shout-out to super ace hitters Anne Finnis and Alice Moloney for your insightful and valuable editorial feedback. You helped bring out Amelia's gutsy character and helped shut Evan's mouth when needed!! I am enormously grateful for the time and care you have given my story.

For an epic all-star sensitivity read, a huge thank you to Leila Rasheed. Your notes were on-point, thoughtful and enormously important to me and my readers. You helped Nisha's character shine her own light, so thank you. Hannah Featherstone, copy-editor of dreams, sending you a massive high five for catching all my many errors and oversights with grace and poise. And to the amazing proof-readers, Beth and Gareth, thank you for your eagle-eyed attention to detail, making sure nothing slipped through the net, and for your super lovely comments about this story.

A GIGANTIC thank you to the amazingly talented Amy Blackwell for your super awesome cover illustrations and the incredible Kath Millichope for your super striking and gorgeous cover design. Hannah Reardon Steward and Fritha Lindqvist – thank you for an out-of-the-park marketing and publicity campaign that will help this book reach the readers that need it.

I also want to say a gargantuan thank you to Laura Ryder, Youth Justice Worker (Crime and Prevention), for your enormous help with my research for this book. Your knowledge and insight on the topic of minors sharing images was invaluable, and the brilliant work you do to support and educate young people and their families is inspiring.

In many ways, *Bad Influence* is about the importance of sisterhood. Amelia Bright has a ferocious teammate in her big sister, Hannah. I would be nowhere without my own fierce and awesome big sister, Kirsty. You're not only a super intelligent and inspiring engineer, you've also got a fierce and gigantic heart (not to mention a mean singing voice). Thank you for being my big sister and loudest supporter (apart from Mum).

As I've thanked my sister, I had better dedicate a moment to thanking my equally awesome brother. Andrew, you've always got my back. Even though you hate my coffee, I hope you love this book. Mum and Dad – thank you for the endless enthusiasm for my books and the enormous amount of support you give me while I write them. My incredible son, Felix – you are human sunlight. Thank you for making me: cups of tea, breakfast in bed, the most beautiful cards and drawings, laugh every single day, and your sixth favourite author. Mummy is very proud.

Laura, Emily-Jane and Emmaline (The HCWKs), we've been friends for over thirty years and I am so grateful to have a supersonic sisterhood of my own. Thank you for all the support, hilarity and love over the years. Here's to many decades more.

Finally, I want to send a special shout-out to two awesome young girls I met back in 2019 at Cranleigh School's Awesome Book Awards. These two particular young ladies told me that they loved my name and hated their own. How surprised they were to learn that when I was younger I too, hated my name, but that I grew to love it. When I asked to hear the names they hated so much I was frankly shocked to hear that they were "Amelia" and "Bright". Properly awesome names! I promised you then and there that one day I would write a book with a main character called Amelia Bright, and here she is. I hope you like her.